Sign up for our newsletter to hear
about new and upcoming releases.

www.ylva-publishing.com

Other Books by Cheyenne Blue

Not for a Moment
For the Long Run
The Number 94 Project
All at Sea
A Heart This Big
Code of Conduct
Party Wall

Girl Meets Girl Series:
Never-Tied Nora
Not-So-Straight Sue
Fenced-In Felix
The Girl Meets Girl Collection (box set)

I Do

Cheyenne Blue

Acknowledgements

This book—my twelfth romance—is dedicated to all the readers of sapphic books. Thank you to everyone who has bought, borrowed, read, or listened to one of my books. Knowing you're out there enjoying my stories is a wonderful and humbling thing. I'm so very happy my writing finds a home on your bookshelf or e-reader.

To those of you who have left a review, recommended my books on social media or to a friend, talked about one of my books around the water cooler at work, discussed it in a book club, or emailed me directly—thank you, all you special people, thank you. I wish everyone joy in your reading, particularly when you read the many, many amazing authors of sapphic fiction who are out there.

As always, huge thanks go to Ylva Publishing for all they do in getting quality stories out into the world. A particular shout-out goes to my editor, Genni Gunn, for her insight and work on my story, cutting through my waffle to find the words that matter, and to Michelle Aguilar for the fantastic copy edit.

I'm lucky to have wonderful beta readers who all bring particular reading skills to the process. Sophie, Erin, Not-Happy-Jan, and Marg are all amazing and lovely to work with.

Happy reading, everyone. May there always be a comfy chair, a shady nook, or a soft bed in your life, and a great book to read.

Cheyenne Blue
Queensland, Australia

Chapter 1

"I may be desperate for work, but I'm applying for jobs I actually know how to do." Allie stared at her identical twin sister in disbelief. Why on earth did Sophie think Allie's accountancy skills made her the ideal person to stand in for her as an event planner? Maybe the strong painkillers were messing with her mind. "I can't do your job. You might as well ask me to split the atom. I've got as much chance of pulling that off." She puffed out her cheeks. "More, maybe."

"No chance—you failed physics at school." Sophie plucked the bedclothes away from her injured leg. "Please, Allie. There is literally no one else I can ask. My business is on the line."

"Literally anyone would do a better job than me. Aren't there agencies where you can hire people short term? Someone who knows event planning or at least the difference between an airwall and an AirPod."

"At least you've heard of an airwall. You're already in front." Sophie shuffled in bed, struggling to reach behind for her pillow. "I wouldn't ask if I weren't desperate, Al."

Allie stood and held out an arm, bracing herself as Sophie grabbed it and hauled herself forward with a grimace. Allie plumped up the pillow behind her. "You want another one behind your back?"

"No. Thanks." With a sigh, Sophie settled back. "It's not difficult. You just have to schmooze with people, show some tact and social skills—"

"Accountants aren't known for their social aptitude."

Sophie rolled her eyes. "Please. That's bollocks. People like you. You can make small talk with a gatepost. And accountants need to be organised and detail oriented. Essential skills for event planners."

Allie sat on the edge of the bed and twisted her hands together in her lap. Sympathy for Sophie fluttered its wings in her chest. The last thing she wanted to do was go to Quandong—a tiny town somewhere off the beaten path in New South Wales. She wasn't even sure where it was. And to go as the event planner for their festival? It was a disaster waiting to happen.

"Soph, I don't think I can do this. Even as your stand-in. If people see me on the phone to you every other minute, they'll realise I know less than an office junior on her first day. At least a junior can be sent out for coffee and sticky buns. They'll be stuck with me. Honestly, I think you'd be better off going to an agency."

Sophie pushed a hand through her floppy blue hair. Her blonde roots were starting to show. "The thing is, this job was going to make my business. The first big event of many. I can't afford to hire anyone else. I quoted on a shoestring to get it, and if I bail, not only will I leave Quandong in the lurch, but I can kiss my business goodbye." She took Allie's hands in her own. "I trust you like no one else, Allie. I know how efficient and competent you are. Kirkland & Partners shafted you in the worst way possible—no wonder you've lost confidence in yourself. Maybe this will help you regain it." She fixed her gaze on Allie. "I know I'm asking a lot of you—"

Allie managed a wobbly smile. "Thanks for the support. But I think you're asking too much of me. It's nearly as big an ask as when you got me to pretend to be you in high school and go on a date with Wallis Simpson, because you'd agreed and then changed your mind."

"Ellis Simpson, not Wallis. Wallis was something to do with a royal scandal back in the day. And I'd only agreed to go out with him because he asked me in the ten minutes when I figured I better at least try to be straight."

"Ellis, Wallis. Both forgettable." Allie shrugged. "My point remains. Going out with Wall— Ellis was torture. He talked non-stop about his Gangnam Style video."

"To be fair, everyone was doing that in 2012."

"Still. It wasn't his finest moment."

Sophie laughed, which ended with a gasp. She crushed her lower lip between her teeth.

Allie picked up her hand and squeezed it. "Breathe. The doctors said you'll get through this. You'll get better. The swelling will go down and the nerves will heal. It could have been so much worse." She closed her eyes momentarily, willing away the memory of waking in the night with her right leg aflame with pain. She hadn't needed the call from the hospital to know something was seriously wrong with Sophie.

Sophie's grey eyes, identical to her own, clung to hers as she panted her way through the spasm. When it ended, she seemed to deflate in the bed, her blue hair sweaty on her forehead. "If this is what labour is like, I'm never pushing a kid out my vag."

Allie laughed. "Any mother would tell you it's worse."

"Yeah, what do they know?" She fell silent.

Allie gripped her sister's hand, her thumb stroking over the back of it. Not for the first time, she cursed the driver of a stolen car who mounted the pavement and crashed into the front of the restaurant Sophie and her friend were leaving. No one was hurt—except for Sophie, her right leg crushed between the vehicle and brickwork. Initially, doctors had thought they'd have to amputate the leg to save her. Sophie would recover, but it would take many more months of rehab.

Allie hitched a breath. It was the worst time for her to go to Quandong—not only did she not want to leave Sophie right now, but there was her own career to consider. She had to keep her feelers out, keep applying for jobs, and not let the lack of response get her down.

But then…she couldn't not go to Quandong. She was being selfish. What was a couple of weeks from her life if it helped her sister keep her business? Love and sympathy for Sophie twined in her chest. So what if it interrupted her own job hunt? It wasn't as if job offers were falling out the sky, despite the shortage of qualified accountants in Sydney. The old boys' network at Kirkland & Partners had seen to that. She pressed her lips together as the familiar knot of anger twisted in her guts. And maybe Sophie was right. She was a good accountant. And skills were transferrable. She straightened her back. She could do this.

"I'll go to Quandong in your place."

Sophie closed her eyes for a second, and when she opened them, they were damp. "Thank you. You're the greatest sister on the planet." Her breath whooshed out. "When all this is over, we'll go to Laredo's and drink a cauldron of margaritas and stuff ourselves with smoky beef fajitas until we explode."

"As long as it's your treat." Allie pulled her lips into a smile even as her stomach plunged at the thought of time away from Sophie.

"It will be. We'll swagger in there, arm-in-arm, and raise the roof." Sophie glanced at the frame keeping the quilt away from her useless leg.

"So tell me what this festival is about. Should I take notes?"

"No need. You can take my file. It has everything you need to know."

"Tell me the bones now, so I don't go home and start panicking you've sent me to a doomsday preppers convention."

"Way more interesting and upbeat." The lines of pain around Sophie's eyes eased for a moment as her lips curved into a small smile. "Quandong is a cute and characterful small town forty-five minutes inland from Byron Bay. It's gorgeous—think rainforest, sparkling creeks, and a historic town centre. But few tourists make the drive out there. They stay on the beach in Byron because it's trendy and Instaworthy."

"Hey, I like Byron. It can't help its celebrity town status! I bumped into Chris Hemsworth at Hip Coast Coffee once."

"You know I don't share your lust for the Hemsworth hunks." Sophie's lips twitched. "Moving right along before you melt; Quandong wants its share of the tourist dollar, and they've come up with a great idea: they're going to bill themselves as the gay wedding capital of Australia. The town has the infrastructure already—there's a heap of accommodation, three wedding celebrants, indoor and outdoor venues, and a gorgeous location."

"So what's the festival?" Allie leaned forward. If she were honest, the town sounded appealing. Small and cute, like her friend Leila's Pomeranian.

"Gay Bells Festival. It's two days of events with a same-sex marriage theme culminating in a parade, a fake wedding ceremony and afterparty. Most of the arrangements are in place—there are teams of volunteers assigned to each event. Your job is to oversee them all, defuse any tension over differences of opinion, arrange, delegate, and then be on hand during the festival to sort out the last-minute snafus. Simple."

"I'm glad you think so." Allie pinched the bridge of her nose where a headache threatened. "I don't know how to do any of that stuff. You should implant a communication chip in my brain—it will save on the endless phone calls to you."

"Not constantly." Her twin's gaze shifted away toward the window that looked out over the street. "Only when there's no one around."

"Why? You'll have told them I'm standing in for you, right?"

"Not exactly." Sophie's fingers twitched on the quilt. "I'm asking you to pretend to be me. Go there and be Sophie Lane. My contract says I can't delegate my duties unless I have approval in advance."

The headache was now a reality. "Me pretending to be you must be in breach of that contract. Not to mention deceitful. There's no way I could pull that off—surely you've met some of the organisers already? What if they ask a question that you would know and I don't?"

"It's not ideal, I know that. But I can't think of any other way other than to pull out all together. You're right; they probably wouldn't knowingly accept you as a substitute, even though I have good reason." She heaved a shuddering breath. "I trust you, Allie. You're an *accountant*; sensible and practical is part of the job description—"

"Unemployed accountant," Allie muttered.

"Through no fault of your own. And this gets you out of Sydney. Gives you a break in a cute town with nice people. Everyone I've met there has been lovely."

"So you've met them. They'll know I'm not you." She pointed at her own natural blonde hair. "No blue hair. And it's longer than yours."

"Tell them you dyed it back to natural and that you're growing it out. Honestly, I've only met a couple of people—I doubt they'll remember me that well. Other than that, we're identical. We even sound the same."

"You've got a fleck in your left eye," Allie started, "and I'm half a centimetre taller, and—"

"You really think anyone will notice those things?"

"Probably not," she admitted. "But I'm not comfortable with this. The whole pretending-to-be-you part. What if I don't answer to Sophie? What if they realise I'm not you? Your business will be completely down the gurgler then." She shook her head. "I'm very afraid I'll stuff it up for you, Soph. It seems...wrong."

Sophie's body rattled with a dry cough, and she clutched her ribs. "Fucking cough. Fucking bruised lungs. Fucking body. Look, if you're not okay doing this, then don't worry about it. I'll go to the agency as you said."

Allie bit her lip. Would it really be so bad pretending to be her twin? If Sophie was on the other end of the phone, then she was, effectively, doing the job. Allie would just be her mouthpiece. And it wasn't as if they hadn't pretended to be each other in the past. Exhibit A: Wallis Simpson. Or Ellis. She hung her head for a moment. "You don't need to call the agency—I'll go to Quandong. Just make sure you answer the phone if I call."

"Of course I will. I've got nothing else to do, after all, except lie here and heal. Thank you. I'd hug you if I could move and my lungs weren't pulped."

Allie leaned in for a careful hug. Her sister smelled stale, as if she'd aged a few decades. She pressed her nose to the side of Sophie's neck. "I love you. Of course I'll do this for you. I'm sorry I didn't agree immediately." She released her. "When would I have to go?"

"Ten days' time, for four days over the weekend. Then the festival is six weeks after that, and you'll need to be there for two weeks."

"I can do that." She hoped. She swallowed away the nerves that threatened even now, and the curl of worry that the idea of deceit brought. "So that's it? You'll give me your file to read?"

"You can take it now. It's on the desk in my office." Sophie jerked her head toward the sunroom she'd made her home office.

Allie tilted her head. "There's one thing still bothering me. Who's going to look after you if I'm not here? You still need help getting to the bathroom and making food, and someone to drive you to doctors and rehab."

"The insurance company has finally agreed to pay for around-the-clock care. I'll take them up on it. I'll be all right." Her grin was a faint approximation of her smile from before the accident. "It'll be okay."

"Then that's settled. I'll read the file later. Is Bettina still coming to stay with you tonight?"

"Mm. She'll be here in a couple of hours, so you can go home." Sophie glanced at her fingers twisted on the quilt. "There's just one other thing I haven't told you about the festival."

The hesitancy in her voice jolted Allie in the chest. *What else can there be?* Was she to be Lady Godiva, naked on a white horse at the head of the parade? Was she to source a full gay choir and orchestra? Or simply arrange a sit-down meal for three hundred people? Sophie's voice alerted her a big ask was about to come her way.

"You better tell me."

"Part of the reason I got the job is because I'm part of the queer community. As you're pretending to be me, you'll have to pretend to be a lesbian."

Allie slumped. *Pretend to be gay?* Her stomach gave an uncomfortable lurch. "How do I do that? It seems…wrong. Pretending to be something I'm not."

"There's no magic to it. You've been around gay people ever since I came out at fifteen. Before then. There isn't a homophobic bone in your body. You march in the Pride parades—"

"As an ally."

"But you do it. You come with me and my friends to queer clubs and bars. You've been hit on by women. And I know you've kissed at least one."

Allie looked down at her hands. Her skin itched as if it were a tight fit around her body. "She was lovely. And, well, I wanted to know if…because you were…and she understood…and we kissed."

Sophie's cough rattled her body. "Al, you don't have to explain—again. We talked about this at the time. You kissed a girl, you liked it, but you've never done it again. But you're a part of the queer community all the same. Not because you kissed a girl necessarily but because you support us, enjoy being with us. You're an ally in the truest sense. So you don't have to do anything different in Quandong; just be yourself. And if anyone asks questions just deflect them. You don't have to explain to anyone."

"You're right. It just seems like the deceptions are piling up. I hope I keep it together in my head."

"You will. And thank you. I love you."

"I love you too."

She went through to Sophie's office to find the Quandong file. It lay on the desk, thick and bursting with papers stuffed into the folder with Sophie's usual haphazard lack of organisation. How she managed to be such a meticulous event planner was beyond her. She put the file on the hall table next to her car keys. Despite Sophie's assurances, nerves jumped in her belly. Could she pull this off? Maybe. Hopefully. For Sophie's sake she would have to try.

Allie went into the kitchen for a glass of water. She'd agreed, and that was all there was to it. She just hoped she could do it.

Chapter 2

Tarryn adjusted her safety goggles, put on her earmuffs, and picked up her welder. The steel plating she'd salvaged from the local tip, once cut to shape, would be perfect to create the rounded body of the metal emu she was crafting. She paused to visualise it in her mind's eye, then pulled her gloves higher and turned on the welder.

"Is that a piglet?"

The voice reached her over the sizzle and pop of the welder, and she looked up. Will stood in the doorway of her workshop, hands on hips as he studied her creation.

Pleasure warmed her at the sight of her best friend despite the chill of her workshop. She turned off the welder, removed her earmuffs, and tugged off her heat-resistant gloves. "It's an emu. Or it will be once I find something for the legs and the neck."

"And if you don't, you could put chubby little legs underneath, a slot in its bum, and I'd have the mailbox you keep promising me."

She laughed. "Not this one. Soon." She removed her visor and set it on the bench.

"You keep saying that."

"Is that why you're here? To harass me for freebies?" She ran a hand over her close-cropped iron-grey curls.

"No. I'm on a mission from on high."

"What sort of on high? The Happy High Herb Shop, or have you finally found religion and want to convert me?"

"Neither. Phyllis-on-high." Will grimaced. "She wants to make sure you'll be at tomorrow's planning meeting for the festival." He side-eyed her.

Tarryn snorted. "I wonder why that is?"

"Is that a serious question?" Will leaned against her workbench, then bounced away once he saw the dust. "Who in the entire town of Quandong is the person least likely to embrace a wedding? Who has made her views perfectly clear about the ridiculousness of spending the equivalent of a house deposit on what is essentially a big party? Who states—often—that while it's great that Australia has same-sex marriage, it's ridiculous for the queer community to embrace such a rigid heterosexual institution. Who—"

"Yeah, yeah." Tarryn grinned at Will's drama and rested her butt against the bench.

"However, who, in this entire town of fifteen hundred people, has got the job of assistant to the event planner and therefore should be at tomorrow's planning meeting, if only to meet her boss and make a good impression." He pointed with both hands. "Tarryn Harris should."

Tarryn scrunched her lips. "I'll meet her soon enough. I'm only her glorified gofer—I won't be doing anything important. I don't need to ooh and aah over frills, balloons, and wedding favours any sooner than I have to." She guessed the planner would be prissy and insist that every tiny detail be exactly just-so: the perfect shade of lavender, the stalls lined up to the centimetre, the music the exact volume allowed by the council. Event planning didn't seem like a job where you could wing it. And that meant she and this perfect event planner were polar opposites.

"If Garrett and I ever get married, we won't be having frills. The Gay Bells Festival isn't just for the girls."

"I don't want to coo over matching bow ties and poodle ringbearers any more than I do over floral bouquets and white dresses. What an impractical colour!"

"I went to a wedding once where the couple's spaniel was the ringbearer. The dog jumped into the lilypond and emerged to shake itself over all the nearby guests. At least the rings were still on its back. You look good in white, by the way, with your gorgeous olive skin. Not all clothing has to be practical."

"You're the perfect person to be on the planning committee."

"Which is why I am. And you need to show your face tomorrow afternoon." Will made puppy-dog eyes. "Please say you will. It's such a pretty face." He laughed at Tarryn's horrified expression. "So, are you coming?"

"I really can't. I have to go to Kyogle to weld a truck tray for one of my regular customers. I'll call Phyll and let her know, and I can call in to the planner later to say hi. I might not agree with the purpose of the festival, but I hope it brings business into the town. I'll do a good job, just as long as I don't have to embrace the ideals of the festival."

"I know you will, hon. You always do your brilliant best. And this might not be as bad as you think—Kirra's met Sophie and says she's okay. And of course, she's community." He edged closer and fingered the high-vis jacket she wore. "Fluorescent yellow really isn't your colour—it's too harsh for you. Does this come in purple?"

She rolled her eyes. "Purple is not a high-vis colour. And it's good the event planner's queer. Some things need to be kept close."

"I'll drop you a text if there's anything you need to know that comes out of the meeting before you go see Sophie." He lifted his gaze to the ceiling. "Pray for me. With Phyll in the chair, this could go on all night."

"If it goes on too long, pull out your phone and stare at it, make a horrified face, then hurry out the room looking anxious. They'll assume it's a family emergency." She shrugged. "It's worked for me."

"Sometimes, you have the best ideas." Will winked.

"That's not what you said when I asked you to come bungee jumping."

"That's not a good idea; that's an ambulance ride to the hospital to have your eyeballs put back in their sockets."

She pointed at her face. "Eyeballs. Two of them. Still in place."

"For you maybe. I think mine would have ended up drifting down the river." Will pulled his jacket tighter around himself. "Now that I've fulfilled my committee duty by asking you, I'll see you around."

"I'm sure you will." Tarryn kissed his cheek and screwed up her face. "Ew, stubble."

"I'm embracing my masculine side." He stroked his pale cheeks. "Bye."

Tarryn replaced her safety gear and turned the welder back on. The assistant's job had sounded like an easy few weeks' work when Phyll had suggested it. Now she wasn't so sure.

It all depended on how this Sophie was.

Chapter 3

THE COMMUNITY HALL WAS BUZZING with people when Allie climbed the wooden steps to the entrance at one minute to four. Butterflies twirled in her stomach. She stopped at the top of the steps and smoothed a hand over her hair, pushing the wayward strands back from her face. Her stomach lurched uncomfortably. She cursed the roadworks that meant the journey from Sydney had taken longer than expected. She was always punctual, and worry she might be late had her on edge. At least she'd arrived on time—just. She took a deep breath. *Oh, Sophie, I hope I don't mess up.*

She stood in the doorway and looked around. A knot of people chatted in a corner, and an older white woman with precision-cut grey hair directed a skinny guy in the tightest jeans Allie had ever seen to set chairs out in rows. The older woman must be Phyllis—or Phyll as she preferred to be called—the chairwoman of the festival committee and overall busybody.

A tall, brown-skinned person with wildly frizzy hair and dressed in a black shirt with white dragonflies printed on it was talking with a petite woman with a long auburn plait. The brown-skinned woman matched Sophie's description of Kirra—the owner of the Airbnb where she was staying. Sophie's email jumped into Allie's head: *I've met Kirra—she's a proud Bundjalung sistergirl, pronouns she/her. She's one of the organisers. The town is on Bundjalung country.*

Allie licked her lips. Who to approach first? Walking into a roomful of people feeling unprepared was so not her thing. She owned the room when she talked about accountancy, but this? Impostor syndrome. This time she warranted it.

She took a steadying breath, pasted on a smile, and entered the hall. The woman talking to Kirra moved away, so Sophie went across. Her first test. "Hi, Kirra." Her palms were instantly clammy, and she wiped them surreptitiously down the sides of her pants. What if Kirra took one look and asked who she was? What if she proclaimed, "You're not Sophie!" to the entire hall?

Kirra flashed a wide grin showing crooked, white teeth. "Sophie, how lovely to see you again." She frowned. "What happened to your hair?"

Allie put a self-conscious hand to her new ear-length bob, which feathered and curled around her head. She and Sophie had agreed there was no way anyone would believe Sophie's hair had grown six centimetres in as many weeks, so Allie had agreed to the cut. She was still trying to get used to the lightness of it. "I dyed it back to my natural colour."

Kirra studied her with pursed lips. "It suits you. But I did like the blue."

"And I like your shirt." She hoped it wasn't Kirra's everyday wear.

"Thank you, possum. It's one of my favourites."

Up close, her skinny body towered over Allie. Her legs were bare under a short skirt, despite the cool day, and her large feet were covered by canvas tennis shoes with no laces.

"I brought the key to the Airbnb," Kirra said. "I can take you there after the meeting's over. Assuming it finishes before midnight." She cast a meaningful glance in Phyll's direction.

Surely, she was joking.

Kirra nudged her. "Not really—it's never later than ten. Maybe you can keep them in order tonight."

Ten was bad enough after the eight-hour drive from Sydney. Allie supressed an internal sigh. "I better catch Phyll before we start. See you later."

Kirra nodded, and Allie stepped away.

Phyll swung around as she approached the table. "Will, once you've put the chairs out, can you make sure the urn is heating up for tea?"

The skinny man nodded and, abandoning the chairs, headed for the kitchen off the hall. Escaping Phyll? Maybe.

Allie moved closer. "How are you, Phyll? It looks like a lot is happening here."

"Sophie, welcome. Glad you got here." Phyll nodded, her grey hair moving stiffly with her head as if welded there. "Yes, everything is under control—so far." She stared at Allie. "Glad you've got rid of the blue hair.

It undermined your authority." She glanced at the solid watch on her wrist. "You cut it a bit fine—wondered if you were going to make the meeting."

Uh oh. Exactly what Sophie warned me about. As for the comment on her hair, well, she wouldn't go there. She inclined her head. "Roadworks. But I'm here now. It was important I come up this weekend so I can patch any holes and keep things moving along."

"Well, that's good." Phyll swung away and clapped her hands. "If we could all take our seats now, we're ready to begin." She moved behind the table facing the room and took the seat in the centre.

Allie dithered. Was Phyll expecting her to sit at the table? Well, she *was* the event planner. Sort of. She set her shoulders back and moved to sit next to Phyll, who gave her a brief nod. The other seat remained vacant.

When people had sat and more or less fallen into silence, Phyll stood. "Welcome everyone. Now, before we all give our reports, I'd like to introduce Sophie Lane from Events Done Right in Sydney. Sophie is here to keep us on track and help with the festival."

Allie smiled and nodded at the faces. Most looked interested, a few scrolled on their phones. Should she say something? Panic gripped her chest—she had no idea what.

Phyll kept talking, obviously not expecting her to speak.

Allie heaved a deep breath and concentrated on keeping a calm, interested look on her face. She pulled her pad and pen from her bag ready to take notes.

Phyll consulted her own pad. "First, an update on the wedding fair in Silver Creek Park. This is my baby. So far, we have almost seventy registered exhibitors, eighteen of which are local. We have a marquee for the wedding attire parade and the singer."

"Then the marquee will be sitting empty for a lot of the time." The woman with the auburn plait popped up from her seat. "We'd like to use it for our celebrity chef talk on Saturday. It's at ten; you should have enough time to set up for the frocks and jocks parade at two."

Phyll pushed her tortoiseshell-rimmed glasses up her nose. "We'll need that time to arrange the wedding attire parade."

"Three hours?" the original speaker asked. "We'll be out by eleven, and it will save us hiring a second marquee."

Allie swallowed her nerves and tapped her pen on the pad. Did Sophie know this woman? "I'm sorry, I've forgotten your name?"

"Ziggy," the woman replied. "We haven't met. Myself and Will are organising the local food showcase."

Of course. That had been in Sophie's notes. "What would you need for your speaker?"

"Just what's already available: the podium and sound set-up. We're happy to use the chairs around the catwalk."

"That sounds reasonable," Allie said. "Does that work for you, Phyll?"

"It should do." Phyll's lips thinned. "As long as they don't overrun."

"I'm sure that won't be the case. Ziggy, can you make sure whoever introduces your celebrity chef also wraps them up in good time at the end?"

"No worries." Ziggy bobbed back into her seat.

Relief made her limp for a moment. One tiny test passed—at least she hoped so. She listened to Phyll droning on about the wedding attire parade. It all sounded terribly formal. White dresses and tuxes. The same-sex weddings she'd attended had been more about fun than frills. At the last one, the brides had worn rainbow sneakers, and their person of honour had been their gay friend who wore a mismatched multicoloured suit that was anything but formal.

"What about the fun element?" she asked when Phyll ground to a halt. "The less formal approach many people like. Do we have anything to showcase that?"

Phyll shot her a look from under lowered brows. "We discussed this the last time you were here—I'm surprised you don't remember."

Oh shit. Allie searched her memory. They'd been nothing in Sophie's file about that. She opened her mouth, but her mind blanked and she had no reply.

Phyll gave her a strange look. "We've had a few more stallholder applications since then, but my reservations are the same as I discussed with you then." She pursed her lips. "I haven't made any decisions. I'm concerned they may lower the tone."

Sophie wouldn't have gone along with that, surely. She squared her shoulders and offered Phyll a smile. "I think it best that we go through the applications together. How about we do that tomorrow?" She didn't wait for Phyll's acknowledgment but instead looked out across the seated people. "Who's next to report?"

Ziggy jumped to her feet again. "Now we've got the celebrity chef venue sorted"—she flashed Allie a smile—"the local food showcase is under control. We've got a good mix of produce and products and a few wineries. A couple of caterers have asked if they can be part of it. I'm not sure if they wouldn't be better off in the wedding fair. What do you think?"

Yikes! What would Sophie do? Maybe she should have that slogan put on a T-shirt. The nerves that had settled when she'd been able to deal with the first issues leaped anew. She swallowed hard. "Phyll? What do you think?"

"In the wedding fair, definitely. Unless they're selling food on the day, they're promoting a service."

Of course. Allie let out a quiet breath. It was so obvious when Phyll put it like that. Sophie would have picked it immediately.

"Thanks," Ziggy said. She looked at a pad in her hand. "Sophie, we could do with help dealing with the council—they're being difficult with a couple of permits. Is that the sort of thing you can do?"

"Absolutely." Allie nodded. *Oh fuck.* "Anything else?"

"Sometime this weekend, I'd like if we could walk through the stall area and discuss the best layout for flow of foot traffic."

"Great idea." Her armpits were clammy. It seemed Ziggy knew far more than she did. Flow of foot traffic? Surely people just wandered around as they pleased.

Ziggy sat, and immediately Kirra sprang to her feet. "Saturday's parade," she announced. "Starting at four on the dot, or as soon as we can herd everyone into line. We've got just over forty floats and marchers so far. The usual community groups, local politicians, and businesses, plus the fun stuff. We've got reptile handlers, drag queen cheerleaders, and the boys from the Gay Pride of Lions—the local rugby team."

"I hope there won't be any inappropriate clothing," Phyll said with a sniff. "It's a family day, after all."

"I'm sure there will be," Kirra said. "It's a Pride parade, after all. Don't worry, Phyll, we'll keep it legal. We've still got to sort out the best running order—Sophie, your input would be great. The Bundjalung Nation float will be first with our sistergirls, brotherboys, and queer mob on board, and dancers following. I've lined up an elder to give the Welcome to Country. Then the next float will be the brides or grooms who will get 'married' in the fake wedding ceremony which takes place at the end of the parade. We have their float, and we've got a couple of businesses willing to supply the dresses or tuxes. We just need our couple."

Allie frowned. "Isn't this leaving it somewhat late?"

Kirra pouted and gave Allie a "you're telling me" look. "We can't decide. There are a few volunteers—some more serious than others."

"Who's volunteered?"

"Two sistergirls, the drag queens from Sydney who are performing at the afterparty, two high school teens, and one or two real-life local couples."

"We shouldn't play this for laughs," Allie said slowly. "We want people to be caught up in the romance of a wedding, to get that fuzzy loving feeling inside, the ooh and ahh moments. If we treat it as a joke, that's how people will see weddings in Quandong. A real couple, or people prepared to play it seriously, might be best."

"I agree," someone shouted from the back of the room. "This is about love."

"Fun too," said Kirra, "but yeah. It's mainly the love." She made a heart shape with her fingers and thumbs. "Will, are you and Garrett adding yourself to the volunteers?"

"I didn't say that," Will said from the back of the room.

"Maybe you should." Kirra fluttered her lashes at him.

"Why don't we get everyone involved?" Allie said. "Everyone gets to vote for the two people they'd like to see do it. The winners get first option to be our couple." Was there a word for non-binary wedding participants? Her mind buzzed, but she couldn't think. She'd have to look it up later. So many small traps for the unwary. "How long is needed to organise the wedding clothes?"

"They all can do it in a week. Off the shelf only, of course," Kirra said.

"We'll set up a couple of ballot boxes and count the votes the week before the festival." Allie gripped her thumbs in clenched fists. Was this a brilliant idea or an absolutely crap one that was destined to flop? She wished Sophie was there to whisper in her ear. No, that was selfish. She wished Sophie was there, full stop. Healthy and pain-free, with a body healed and back to how she was before the accident. *Oh, Sophie.* Tears pricked behind her eyes, and she blinked fast, trying to clear them.

"That will work," Kirra said. Others nodded as well.

Only Phyll appeared uncertain. "What if a totally unsuitable couple wins?"

Kirra folded her arms across her flat chest. "Define 'totally unsuitable.'"

Phyll flapped her hand. "Comedians. Underage children. People who don't reflect the values of our town."

Values? Phyll sounded dangerously close to an extreme right-wing politician on a mission to purify Australia. *Ha! Good luck with that.* "If we let people know our reasons, hopefully everyone will consider them when they vote. You have to trust people." Allie gave Phyll a soft smile. Getting on Phyll's wrong side would be a shortcut to failure.

Phyll gave a soft harrumph and settled lower in her seat.

Allie scribbled more notes on her pad.

Phyll leaned across. "You know we hired you an assistant? She can take notes in future. She's not here today, though. Had a prior commitment with her other work."

"No, I didn't know." She dropped the pen on the pad. This was *great* news. Hopefully the assistant was a whiz at event planning. "Is she local?"

Phyll nodded. "Yes. Her name's Tarryn Harris and she's very efficient. She runs her own metal-work business, but she also picks up many of the short-term jobs around town."

"I hope to meet her soon." She tapped the pad. "There's already a lot she can be doing."

Phyll's eyebrows lowered until they closed in on her nose. "I'll tell her to get in contact with you."

Allie pressed her lips together. It was a pity Tarryn wasn't at the meeting, but hopefully, she would make life a lot easier.

Despite Kirra's dire prediction, the meeting wound up by six. Allie arranged to meet one-on-one with the various organisers the next day.

Her car was a mess. Guiltily, she threw the clutter that littered the passenger seat into the back so Kirra could ride with her.

Kirra fastened her seat belt. "The apartment where you're staying is above my café."

Allie's eyelid twitched. She'd driven along Quandong's main street on her way to the meeting but hadn't noticed the café. And what if there was more than one? Sophie had mentioned Kirra owned a café, so she had probably been there. What if she went to the wrong one? She fumbled the key in the ignition of the Pajero and pulled out of the car park and headed into the centre of town. The wide street had cars parked in the middle, and the shops on either side of the street were a mishmash of architectural styles. The only common denominator were the brightly painted doors. She drove underneath the large banner that spanned the street announcing the Gay Bells Festival. Large silver bells—wedding bells, she presumed—adorned each end. She looked around, trying to see a café.

"You're in luck." Kirra pointed. "There's a park right outside the door."

Thank goodness. The brightly painted sign proclaiming *Kirra's Kafé* was decorated with pictures of the vivid blue rainforest fruit that gave the town its name. A rainbow flag fluttered from a pole next to an Australian Aboriginal flag.

Allie parked and grabbed her case.

"This way." Kirra used the key to unlock a lime-green door sandwiched between the café and the health food store next door.

The door swung open, and Kirra led the way up a steep set of stairs which opened into a large room with high ceilings. Light streamed in through tall windows, illuminating a large, dark wooden table, a couch with a coffee table in front of a TV, and a compact kitchen.

Allie caught her breath. The apartment was gorgeous, perfect. Nicer—and bigger—than her low-ceilinged apartment on the twentieth floor of a huge complex in Sydney. She turned a circle, humming in appreciation.

Kirra led the way to the rear and flung open the door to the bedroom. The small room was dominated by a queen bed covered by a quilt with an aboriginal design. "Bathroom's through there." She indicated another door.

"The apartment's gorgeous." Allie smoothed the soft cotton quilt, tracing the blue and green patterns. "I love this design."

"It's Bundjalung. There's an artists' collective up the street. They do beautiful things. This design is a representation of the clans."

"I'll go and take a look at what else they have."

"You do that. Is there anything else you need?"

"I'm good, thanks.

Kirra flashed her white grin again. "We're glad you're here, Sophie. We need your skills."

Allie pasted on a smile. She just hoped Kirra still thought that after the next couple of days.

Chapter 4

THE WEAK COFFEE ALLIE HAD at the meeting had done nothing to stop the hunger pangs. She made a couple of slices of toast and Vegemite and sat on the couch to eat it while she read over her notes. Her to-do list was huge. She suppressed a sigh; most of it were things her assistant could handle—if she showed her face.

She picked up her phone. The balcony beckoned, but she didn't want to be overheard. Sophie answered on the second ring. "Please tell me you're in Quandong and you didn't meet a sinfully handsome American who whisked you away on his private jet."

"I wish," Allie replied. "How are you doing?"

Sophie's sigh wafted down the line. "Same old. I had a shower today, slipped and almost fell. Today's carer must have been half my height and a quarter of my weight and wasn't able to catch me. It nearly ended badly, but I managed to grab the towel rail."

"So your carer is six years old? Half your height would be under a metre tall, and a quarter—"

"Don't be so bloody literal." Sophie huffed a laugh.

"Didn't you have rehab today?"

"I did. She got me walking holding onto two rails. Dragging my right foot, but at least I can now swing my leg. I'll get there. Eventually." Sophie's snort was audible over the phone. "It's painful. But it's supposed to be."

Oh, Sophie. Allie closed her eyes and clutched the phone. What was this disruption in her life compared to what her twin was going through?

"Enough about me, though," Sophie continued. "I've been on tenterhooks waiting to hear from you. How did the meeting go? I'm so relieved you're in Quandong taking control."

"That's putting it a bit strongly. I'm blundering along." Allie fingered the ends of her choppy bob. It still felt strange and light on her head.

"I'm sure you're doing great."

"'Great' might be a bit optimistic."

"What happened?" Sophie's voice held a brittle gaiety.

"A couple of minor personality clashes, both involving Phyll. But it's okay—I think. I made a couple of suggestions, and I hope they're all right." She related her ideas for the fake wedding couple.

"Good idea, Al." Sophie's approval hummed down the line. "There was a bit of wrangling about that when I was there, but I thought they'd sort it out among themselves. Obviously, it hasn't happened."

"Apparently, I have an assistant, but I've yet to meet her."

"That's fantastic. If she's any good, you can give her all the routine stuff to do."

"Right now, nothing about this is routine." Allie sighed. "I miss you."

"I miss your tales of woeful Tinder dates and endless snacking."

"And I miss your stories of lesbian pirates and derring-do."

"I might have invented the pirates." Sophie sighed. "I'd kill for a good swashbuckling adventure right now. I'm stuck with bad TV and Silent Kev the Carer."

"I'll be home soon, and after a few days of my care, you'll be begging Kev to return."

"Don't bet the farm. I better go. A rerun of *Days of Our Lives* is starting. Vivian's about to bury Carly alive."

"You don't want to skip that." Allie blew a kiss into the phone. "Miss you, sissy. Now, wish me luck."

"Good luck. Don't fuck up."

Allie laughed. "Succinct as ever." She ended the call and brought up the job ads on her laptop, and armed with her research, started drafting application letters. Two positions were a step above her previous job—and she was well-qualified to apply for them—but the other was a junior accountant's role. She could do that with one arm tied behind her back. Surely, even if

Kirkland & Partners gave her a poor reference, with her experience, surely, someone would give her a go.

Hopefully.

Maybe.

Allie closed her eyes briefly, and taking a deep breath, resumed the application letter. *I have five years' experience in a similar role managing small to medium sized clients with minimal supervision.*

Surely, her experience would be enough to at least get her an interview.

Chapter 5

TARRYN FLUNG HERSELF ONTO THE battered old couch. Her shouse—a liveable shed/house that occupied the other half of her workshop—was comfortable, but still cool at this time of year, despite the pot-belly stove radiating a cosy warmth.

The truck repair had gone well, and the delighted owner had asked her to do some extra work around the farm. The money would be welcome. If only her metal art paid as well as the welding jobs, but at least she had that work—as well as various odd jobs from time to time, like cleaning Kirra's Airbnb, and helping out in businesses when someone called in sick or needed a breathing body to stand at the photocopier for a few mind-numbing hours. It wasn't how she'd seen her life when she started her metal art business, but it paid the bills.

Her empty stomach prodded her to move. She needed to chop more wood for the stove and put away her tools from the day. But instead, she was lying on the couch frowning at a text from Will.

Don't "forget" to introduce yourself to Sophie soon, or I will be grumpy. See my grumpy face? :(We need this festival to work!

She eyed the family bag of cheese-and-onion chips sitting on the kitchen bench. Those, plus an apple, a huge glass of water, and a square of actual cheese were the perfect meal right now. It covered all the major food groups—except chocolate. The last thing she wanted was to drag her butt three kilometres into Quandong to hunt down the event coordinator. She couldn't even call as she didn't have her number—her own fault.

Chips or work. Work or dinner?

She rose and went to the small window at the front of the shouse. Her truck was parked haphazardly in the driveway. If she made the effort to meet Sophie, she could pick up a block of chocolate on the way home and totally nail all the food groups. Despite her gut recoil at the idea of weddings—well, marriage in general—this was a paid job she'd agreed to do. Damn her work ethic that even now was pointing to her truck keys and prodding her toward the door. It was just gone seven—that wasn't too late, was it? Surely Sophie would be pleased Tarryn was keen enough to introduce herself even after a day's work.

Tarryn looked down at herself. She was grimy from the day and—she sniffed her armpit—definitely sweaty. That wasn't the vibe she wanted to give to Sophie, who no doubt wore a pink business suit, tittered rather than laughed, and thought a mammoth wedding was the pinnacle of existence. Although she was gay, so maybe she was a bit more enlightened than a fifties housewife.

With a resigned sigh, Tarryn headed for the shower, shedding her dirty clothes along the way.

Fifteen minutes later, dressed in her usual straight-leg jeans and a T-shirt covered by a maroon fleece jacket, her close-cropped curls towelled dry, she looked at herself in the mirror as she put on lip balm. If Sophie was expecting an office girl in a skirt and heels, she had another think coming. Tarryn ran a hand over her iron-grey hair. One advantage of going grey in her twenties was it gave her an air of maturity which had done her well over the years. At thirty, she still had a youthful face with only a few fine lines—thanks to her Mediterranean skin—but the grey hair had earned her the trust of many people. She'd have to do.

She scooped the truck keys from the counter and headed out the door.

Kirra's Kafé was closed for the day, but a light burned in the apartment above. Tarryn rang the bell and hunched further into her fleece against the chill wind that twirled down the street.

After a minute, footsteps came down the inside stairs, then the door swung open and a lightly built white woman stood there. Her choppy blonde hair hung to just below her ears and looked like she'd repeatedly run her fingers through it. She wore a simple cream T-shirt and a pair of faded jeans. Her only concession to the cool evening was a pair of slouchy sheepskin boots. Tarryn's jaw locked for a second. Sophie was definitely not what she'd expected. For starters, she appeared younger than her own thirty years, for second, she was already smiling a greeting that looked genuine.

"Hi, can I help you?"

"Sophie? I'm Tarryn Harris, your assistant for the Gay Bells festival. I'm sorry I couldn't make the meeting today—I have another job, and they clashed. I came to introduce myself, but if this isn't a good time…"

Sophie's smile dimmed. "Hello, Tarryn. I'm sorry, I wasn't expecting you—did I miss a call from you?"

Tarryn shuffled from foot to foot. "Uh, no. I don't have your number. And I was coming to town now anyway, so I thought I'd drop in and introduce myself."

Sophie shot her a cool look from clear, grey eyes. "That's good of you—if a little unconventional. I'm in the middle of dinner, but, seeing as you made a special effort, if you don't mind that, come on up." She turned and headed up the stairs without waiting for an answer.

Tarryn shrugged and followed. It wasn't unconventional in Quandong. Most people were happy when she turned up to work, whatever the hour. Even during dinner. Her stomach gave a soft growl of hunger.

Sophie might only have been in town a few hours, but her belongings were already scattered over the apartment. A thick file sat open on the dining table, papers spilling out over the wooden surface. A half-eaten plate was abandoned on the other side next to a glass of red wine. Tarryn side-eyed it. Salad, coleslaw, and—she surreptitiously sniffed the air—yup, sausages. Her mouth watered.

Sophie moved to the table and gathered up some sheets of paper, turning them face down. "Can I get you anything? A glass of wine, tea, coffee, water?" Sophie stood with both hands tucked into the front pocket of her jeans. It showed off her taut abdomen and made her small breasts jut forward. Not that Tarryn was looking or anything.

Tarryn averted her gaze. "Do you have any beer?"

"Sorry. I'm more of a wine person."

Of course she was. "Wine's fine."

Sophie went to the kitchenette and grabbed a glass from the cupboard, then poured from the open bottle on the counter. "Here you go. I hope you don't mind if I keep eating?"

"Go for it." She accepted the wine and followed Sophie back to the table.

"I'm glad to meet you," Sophie said. "I only heard about you from Phyll this afternoon. It's a pity you couldn't make the meeting." She cut a piece of sausage and put it in her mouth.

"I had an emergency repair to do some kilometres away. I knew about the meeting, of course, but I didn't have your number."

Sophie's grey eyes sliced right through her. "You could have got it from Kirra or Phyll. It would have saved you a trip."

Tarryn shifted from foot to foot. Sophie hadn't suggested she sit, but she'd be damned if she would stand like a pupil in the principal's office. She pushed the file aside and sat opposite. "I'll put your number in my phone now." She pulled it out, opened the contacts, and stared at Sophie with one eyebrow arched.

Sophie recited her number, then took a sip of wine. "So, have you done anything like this before?"

Tarryn sent a text and heard the ping of a mobile as it was received. "I've never done anything like this before, but I know my way around an office and have local contacts. Something you'll need. I was told you just wanted someone to run around and do the grunt work."

"Mm, yes. Is that what you're good at?"

Was that a smothered grin? Her stomach jumped in irritation—or was it hunger? Was Sophie implying she was some knuckle-dragging gorilla with muscles and not much else? "I'm a qualified welder, but most of my business is metal art. If you count that as grunt work, then the answer's yes. If you want me to fold napkins into the shape of swans and ice cupcakes to look like vaginas, then you better find someone else."

Sophie shot her a startled look. "Hey, I'm not trying to put you down. I'm just trying to get to know you better. You were highly recommended, you know."

Maybe she'd been a bit too quick on the draw. She lifted a shoulder. "That's okay. I'm sorry if I came across as cranky. I've had a long day but thought I better come and see you before finishing up." On cue, her stomach gave a loud gurgle. "Or having dinner."

Sophie's eyes widened. "That sounded like a drain. I didn't realise you hadn't eaten." She hesitated. "There's a couple more snags on the pan, salad and coleslaw in the fridge. You're welcome to them."

Tarryn considered. It was a kind gesture, but would this Sydneysider think it too informal for what was basically a meeting with her boss? Screw it. She was hungry, and her chances of getting that bag of cheese-and-onion chips anytime in the next hour were remote. "I was going to forage in my pantry for junk food."

"Plates are over there," Sophie gestured with her head. "Help yourself."

"Thanks." She went to do that, watching Sophie out the corner of her eye. She ate heartily, as if she, too, was hungry, rather than because it was dinnertime.

For a few minutes, there was only the sound of scraping cutlery and food being devoured. The simple meal warmed and filled her. Tarryn put down her cutlery with a sigh. "Thank you. I needed that."

Sophie took the plates over to the counter then gestured to the couch. "Take a seat, I'd like to hear your thoughts on the festival. You must be very enthusiastic about it, to have taken this job."

Enthusiastic? Yeah, right. As excited as a vegetarian at a meat-tray raffle.

Tarryn sat at one end of the couch and waited for Sophie to join her.

"So?" Sophie cocked her head. "What do you see this festival achieving?"

Achieving? This was starting to sound like the job interviews she'd bailed from when she was a teenager. *Tell me where you see yourself in ten years. What is your greatest flaw?*

She shrugged. "It's a money-making exercise to bring business to the town. Nothing more, nothing less."

Sophie blinked. "That's it? No heart-tugging speeches about love is love, or giving couples the wedding of their dreams?"

"No. If people want to marry, they'll find a way to do it. It's irrelevant to me."

"Oh…kay." Sophie drew the syllables out as if giving herself time to think. "I didn't expect that. Everyone else is caught up in the love and romance of it all. So you're not a fan of marriage. What about marriage equality? If you're someone who thinks marriage is between a man and a woman, then we could have a problem."

Tarryn's laugh came from her belly and bubbled up her throat. "Really? Do you have no gaydar at all? I know you're queer—it was part of the reason we went with you. Look at me." She indicated her haircut, the leather cord around her neck holding the metal spiral against her throat, the gender-neutral clothing. "People can marry whomever they want. Why would I not want my friends to do what makes them happy? Even though I think it's a waste of time and money, I'm still happy for them."

A pink flush coloured the pale skin on Sophie's cheeks. "Yeah, okay, I'm sorry. That was a stupid comment." Her mouth turned down. "And my gaydar's always been a bit iffy."

"It's not iffy if you didn't ping me, it's outright broken." She tilted her head and considered Sophie, her gaze sweeping from the top of her messy hair down to her fleecy boots. *Nice.* She pushed that thought aside as quickly as it had arrived and tapped a finger against her lips. "You, though… There's nothing wrong with my gaydar. You're queer as a coot."

The flush deepened, and Sophie fiddled with the hem of her T-shirt, not meeting Tarryn's eyes. "You already knew that. No gaydar needed."

"Still. It's relevant. The more gay people involved in this the better." Tarryn waved a hand. She caught the flash in Sophie's eyes. Maybe Sophie thought she was being overly familiar. She gave a mental shrug. That wasn't her problem; she was hired to do a job alongside people who were mostly volunteers. Sophie would have to get used to informality and plain speaking. Quandong was no Sydney boardroom, or whatever she was used to.

"So you're not a fan of weddings, and you think this festival is purely a business proposition. Tell me: if you were to get married, what would you, personally, want?" The flush had receded from Sophie's cheeks, and she was back to cool and collected.

"It's a hypothetical question I can't answer because it won't happen."

"Humour me." The grey eyes drilled into her, dissecting her brain into neat slices.

"Okay. Something simple. I'd be dressed pretty much as I am now, my partner would be in something equally comfortable to her. We'd be outdoors. The bare legal minimum from the celebrant: No flowery speeches about love eternal, no personalised vows, certainly no poems. Whoever of our friends wanted to come would come, no formal invitation necessary. No flower-decked arches, no earnest folk singers, no processional music, and certainly no flower kids."

"And the reception?" Sophie's eyes lit with curiosity.

Tarryn shrugged. "A few bottles of wine, an ice chest of beers. Snacks. No presents."

"You've given this some thought. Despite saying you don't want any-thing to do with the tizz, you've actually planned your wedding." Her lips twitched. "You're a fraud!"

"You asked me! I answered. Honestly, why would I willingly take on an outdated heterosexual institution?"

"For love?"

"Love doesn't need a certificate."

Sophie rose and went over to the table. She pushed the facedown papers further to the side and shuffled through the open file. "We're getting away from the point." She returned with a couple of pages and handed them to Tarryn. "These are the minutes from the meeting earlier. I've highlighted some things that need follow up. Can you work through these? I'm only here for another three days this time, but you've now got my contact details so you can call with questions. My email's on the minutes."

Tarryn scrolled through the list. Council permits. *Two hours of my life I won't get back.* Check the suppliers for the wedding attire for the fake mar-riage. She rolled her eyes. Who would want to go through with a real wed-ding, let alone a fake one? "Sure."

"And Phyll's organising models for the wedding attire parade. She thought you'd know young people who fit a standard size."

Young people? "What about older folk and differently sized people? Not everyone doing the wedding thing is twenty years old with a waist like a twig. Given Australia only legalised same-sex marriage a few years ago, there are plenty of older people who want to marry because they couldn't before." She frowned. Why didn't Sophie think of that? Phyll, she could understand, but Sophie?

"Of course. Good thinking." A tiny blush crept up Sophie's cheeks once more. "And that will give us a great pool of potential models. Real people. This isn't a pro-model catwalk parade. We want smiles and wrinkles as well as teenagers."

The praise felt good. Let no one say Tarryn Harris couldn't be profes-sional when needed, despite the lack of smart clothes.

"And finally," Sophie said, "we need ballot boxes for people to vote for their favourite couple for the fake wedding. I'm thinking three: outside the community hall, in Kirra's Kafé, and…somewhere else. Any ideas?"

"Outside the library maybe?"

"Can you organise them too?"

"Sure." A puff of air escaped Tarryn's lips. This gofer role was already a lot more time-consuming than she'd first thought.

"You don't sound very enthusiastic." Sophie folded her arms.

Tarryn averted her eyes from Sophie's chest, thrust into prominence by her posture. "I'm not. This may be your dream job, but it's not mine."

Sophie tilted her head. "Then maybe you should step away in favour of someone more enthusiastic. I need someone committed here, not a half-hearted sort of help."

The dollars that would tumble into her bank account when the festival was over flashed through Tarryn's mind. Sure, Gay Bells wasn't anything to get excited about, but it was easy work. Well, apart from dealing with the council. That was never a happy time. "Don't worry. I'll never attend a hen party, but that doesn't mean I'm not professional. I'll do a good job—you'll get your money's worth." She dredged up a small smile.

Sophie assessed her for a couple of seconds, then gave a quick nod. "No worries, then. We're good. No doubt I'll need to contact you when I'm back in Sydney."

"To organise cake boxes and a wedding playlist?"

"No to the cake boxes. But we'll need a playlist for the fake wedding."

"Sure. Everyone likes heavy metal and punk rock, don't they?"

"Is that your taste?"

"Some of it. If you're wanting Barry Manilow, you're out of luck."

"I'm starting to wonder if you've ever been to a wedding." Sophie picked up the bottle of red and topped up her glass. Quirking an eyebrow, she offered the bottle to Tarryn. At her nod, she topped up her glass as well. "While this isn't a real wedding, at the least, we'll need background music while the couple are introduced. Then something for the first dance. Maybe a dance number to finish and get people in the mood for the afterparty. But nothing too obscure. People like to shout along to the lyrics and proclaim everlasting friendship after the first two bottles of wine."

"Now who's sounding cynical."

"Well, that's how the last couple of weddings I went to played out."

"I'll see if I can do better. No Barry Manilow, plenty of ABBA. It'll give the drag queens something to work with."

"Perfect." When she smiled, Sophie looked a lot more relaxed. The pinch of worry that creased between her eyes disappeared. If she quit being so… stuffy at times, she'd be a lot more likeable. Was Sophie single? If she was, there'd be a couple of women in town who'd start the chase. She supressed a smile. They were welcome to her.

She sipped her wine. "Anything else?"

"Can you review the stallholder applications for the wedding fair with me?" Sophie asked. "Phyll is going for traditional and staid. I think we need to include fun things and informal wear. Maybe what you'd wear to your casual outdoor wedding." A quick smile. "I need someone with me to persuade Phyll."

"Right. Phyllis, by royal invitation. At least, that's what she tells everyone. She was invited to the garden party at Buckingham Palace once, and she never lets anyone forget it. I can help you persuade her."

"How about tomorrow morning? We could meet at Kirra's Kafé at nine if that works for you."

"I can do that. Anything for a piece of Kirra's ginger slice."

"Is nine too early?"

"That's fine. I can do a couple of hours of metalwork first. See you then."

Sophie scribbled a note on a pad. "I'll let Phyll know. I'll see you tomorrow, Tarryn. Thanks for dropping by."

"No worries. Thanks for feeding me and for the wine."

"Lucky you caught me on a shareable dinner kind of evening. Another night it might be a takeaway."

"Thai Dreams is best," Tarryn said. "Great green curry. They understand the true meaning of spicy."

"Sounds like my sort of place."

She finished the last mouthful of wine and set the glass down. "I'll see you then."

At Sophie's nod, she clattered down the stairs to her truck. At least it hadn't been chips and an apple for dinner.

Chapter 6

Tarryn was late, damn her.

Allie surreptitiously glanced at her phone under the café table as Phyll droned on. It was now 9:10 a.m., and, of course, she and Phyll had both been ten minutes early.

"White dresses and dark tuxes reflect the traditional aspect of marriage and the serious nature of the commitment," Phyll said. She'd also managed to put away two scones with plum jam and cream and half a pot of English breakfast tea, all without interruption to her speech.

Allie clenched her teeth against the festering irritation which was fast reaching boiling point. She needed to stop Phyll while she could still be civil about it. How someone as behind the times as Phyll had got herself in charge of the planning committee for a modern festival was beyond her.

"That's just it though, Phyll. People are moving away from rigid traditional weddings and want to include their own personalities and flair in their ceremonies. And same-sex weddings are embracing this more fully than heterosexual couples—maybe because they don't have the weight of tradition behind them." Was that even true? Allie had no clue, but it sounded as if it could be, and that was the main thing. She pushed her uneaten scone to one side and forged on before Phyll could draw breath. "Now, these clothing companies here"—she lined up two brochures on the table—"their look is bright, happy, and exuberant. Just like Gay Bells. I think we should include them."

Where the hell was Tarryn? She'd have Phyll wrapped up like a parcel before Tarryn showed up.

"It's irreverent." Phyll chomped her final mouthful of scone and eyed the one on Allie's plate.

Allie nudged it closer. "There are already enough vendors who embrace the traditional look. We need more sass and sparkle."

The bells on the front door jangled, and a waft of cool air followed. Allie glanced over her shoulder and blew out a relieved breath. Tarryn sauntered to the counter, her cheeks ruddy from the cold, her curls almost hidden under a striped beanie.

"Hi, Kirra." Tarryn perused the display cabinet. "Can I get a flat white and one of your ginger slices, please."

"Sure thing. I'll bring them over."

Tarryn nodded and changed the direction of her saunter to where Allie and Phyll sat by the window.

"Hi again, Sophie. Hi Aunt Phyll."

Aunt Phyll? Allie set her jaw. Tarryn had kept that under her beanie. Maybe that's how she got the job.

"Tarryn, dear." Phyll fluttered her fingers.

"I'm sorry I'm a few minutes late." Tarryn turned to Allie. "Ally escaped again, and I had to repair the fence."

Allie's hand stopped midway taking her coffee from the table to her mouth as a chill settled in her chest. Had Tarryn figured out the deception? But the part about the fence made no sense. She made her hand complete the motion. "Who's Allie?" she asked after she'd swallowed her coffee.

"Ally is the most beautiful girl in the world." Tarryn's eyes crinkled. "She has big, soulful eyes, the longest lashes in history, a smile to make you melt, and soft touchable hair. She can also beat anyone in a spitting contest, including her sister, Elly."

Oh per-lease. Tarryn was obviously messing with her. "She sounds quite the girl. Is she a dog or a donkey?" She kept her voice cool.

Phyll tapped Tarryn's hand. "It's an old joke, Tarryn. To most of us anyway."

Tarryn's mouth quirked up at one corner. "Ally's and Elly's full names are Ally-Paca and Elly-Paca. They're alpacas I found wandering in the state forest a couple of years ago, and although I tried to find their owner, no one ever claimed them. I think they were unwanted and simply turned loose. They're the most adorable girls."

Relief made her limp. "They sound sweet."

"Come and meet them sometime. They'll make you melt."

"Maybe they could join the festival parade?"

"I don't think they'd do well in a crowd. They're like a girlfriend who never wants to go out in the evening, preferring to curl up with a hot chocolate and a good book."

Phyll tapped her fingers on the table. "As wholesome as this alpaca chat is, we need to get back to the matter in hand." She pushed the brochures across to Tarryn.

"Two Boys Tuxes have applied?" Tarryn raised an eyebrow. "We absolutely have to accept them. They're the in-demand attire for the it-crowd. I'm surprised they need to get their name out, to be honest." When Phyll's gaze dropped to study the brochure again, Tarryn shot an exaggerated wink at Allie.

Allie stifled a smile. Most likely, Tarryn had no idea who Two Boys Tuxes were. She would bet her entire snack cupboard they were another struggling small business with great ideas fighting to get their name out there.

"Well, in that case, we should take them," Phyll said.

"And this lot," Allie pulled the second brochure over. "They're flirty and bright and are a great option for nearly-weds who want dresses. I love this one." She pointed to a mid-length turquoise layered dress worn with Doc Martens. "We'll include them as well. Who else is on your 'maybe' list, Phyll?"

Phyll pulled out a sheaf of other brochures and dropped them on the table.

Kirra came up with Tarryn's coffee and cake and set them down. "Ooh, that's gorgeous!" She picked up a flyer depicting a woman, arms spread to show her rainbow cape over a lacy white dress. "I could so marry in this."

"That's a yes for them, then." Tarryn added it to the acceptance pile.

Kirra sat. "This and this and this... Oh my God, my sweet gay heart is melting at all this gorgeousness. Take them all."

Allie flicked through the pile. "I agree. They all depict same-sex weddings in their advertising. They belong in the fair."

"Can we look at the ones for acceptance, Phyll?" Tarryn asked.

A customer approached the counter, and Kirra went to help them.

Phyll pulled a folder from the enormous tote bag at her feet.

Allie shuffled through the glossy brochures with their romantic curly script and posed models. All very fine, all beautiful and traditional, with misty photos of brides in white and pearls, and handsome men in dark tuxes. Phyll was a widow; she'd probably got married wearing something like this.

Tarryn flipped through the brochures. "We can't accept this one." She frowned as she read aloud, "*We believe marriage is the God-given seal of the love between a man and a woman.* We can't allow language like that."

"We've accepted their deposit," Phyll said.

"Unaccept it," Allie said. "Tarryn's right. It's totally the wrong message for Gay Bells. Are there any more like that? Can you check them all, Tarryn."

Phyll's chin jutted like a prize fighter. "This business is a leading light in the social wedding set."

"And they're a bunch of homophobes and smug enough not to care who they piss off." Allie stared back at Phyll, not breaking eye contact until she dropped her gaze.

"You're right," Phyll said with a sigh. "I admit I went on their glowing reputation and didn't read the brochure. I'll return their deposit."

"Thank you. You've a lot on your plate. That's where I come in—and Tarryn. We'll manage this between us all."

Phyll nodded slowly.

"The rest seem okay," Tarryn said. "While they don't necessarily show same-sex couples, they don't have exclusionary language." She took a bite of cake and chased it with a mouthful of coffee.

"That's good. Thank you both for being here this morning." Allie nodded at Tarryn and Phyll. "Anything else you want to discuss, Phyll?" Allie said.

"No." Phyll's mouth pursed. "I'll deal with these." She scooped the leaflets from the table. "I'll see you later." She left, the door closing firmly behind her.

Allie checked Kirra was still busy and then looked at Tarryn. "That was quick thinking on Two Boys Tuxes. Do you actually know the business?"

Tarryn's mouth formed an impish grin. "Never heard of them. But they had some spark and colour in their brochure, unlike those formal clothes Phyll likes."

"We have a good mix now. Thank you for your input. But"—she kept her voice steady— "I realise you had something to attend to this morning, but we need to talk about your timekeeping. You were ten minutes late for this meeting."

Tarryn lifted a shoulder. "I apologised and explained why. My animals are important to me—I couldn't let them escape to wander the roads. Besides, you must have been here early to get through all you did."

Allie squirmed inside. As a fairly junior accountant, she'd never needed people-management skills. She'd just plugged away in her office and socialised with her colleagues around the coffee machine. Timekeeping, under-performance, verbal warnings—those had all been someone else's responsibility. Was she being unreasonable now? Yes, she probably was. "I understand your reason for this morning. I simply want to stress the importance of timekeeping in the future."

Tarryn's face was a blank slate. "I'll leave earlier next time to allow for the unexpected. But anytime I am late—which is seldom—it's always for a good reason." She took a slurp of coffee.

"Thank you," Allie managed.

"Girlfriend, your auntie needs a firm hand." Kirra bustled back and flopped into Phyll's vacated seat. She quirked an eyebrow at Tarryn.

"I don't think Phyll deliberately included those suppliers," Tarryn said. "She's just an old-fashioned straight woman who resists change—whether it's Kirra's orange cake recipe or same-sex marriage. She's not homophobic; just a bit…unthinking." She bit into the ginger slice with even, white teeth.

"She was a lot tougher on the orange cake," Kirra said. "She's refused to buy it since I changed the recipe nearly a year ago."

"She doesn't seem like the ideal choice to lead the committee." Allie stared at the door where Phyll had departed. "How did she get the job?"

"How does anyone get a job like that?" Kirra said. "Because she volunteered and everyone else sighed in relief they didn't get pressganged into it. That's how she ended up organising the school fete, the weekly chook raffle for the RSL, the Gardens of Quandong open day, and the petition to get bus service to Byron Bay. She's very good at getting things done."

"Is that how you got this job?" Allie asked Tarryn. "Because Phyll volunteered you?"

"She asked, yes," Tarryn said through a mouthful of cake. "Good ginger slice, Kirra. But I would have offered anyway. It's a paid position, and one of the solar panels on my shouse is broken. That's an expensive repair, and I need the money. And I have a reputation as a reliable worker."

"So no other reason. Of course not." Kirra leaned back in her chair. "We all know how much you love the flounces and frills of weddings. If I ever get married, I'm going to ask you to be my person of honour."

Tarryn's horrified expression had them both laughing.

Chapter 7

ALLIE HURRIED ACROSS MARTIN PLACE. Sydney's CBD teemed with people, and she dodged between them. It was her first day back, and the city felt comfortingly familiar after the peace of Quandong, although her small, dark apartment came a poor second to Kirra's airy Airbnb. All she'd done when she arrived home late the day before was call Sophie and fall into bed.

She picked up her pace to make sure she arrived first for lunch with Leila. Kirkland & Partners were pedantic about lunch breaks, and overrunning meant a salty email from HR about the importance of timekeeping. Unless it was unpaid overtime. Then timekeeping was an ethereal concept and anyone who logged off on the dot of five was likely to get a lecture from their boss about not being a team player.

Leila had suggested the café, one far enough from the usual staff beat they were unlikely to run into anyone they knew, close enough she could get there and back in her break. Allie sat at a table by the wall where she could see Leila arrive. She hustled in at five past one and straight over to Allie, her arms held wide.

Allie rose for the hug. The wisps of hair escaping Leila's hijab tickled her nose, and her floral perfume and the brief press of her soft lips on Allie's cheek brought a wave of warmth. She'd missed Leila and their quick coffee breaks, hurried lunches, and shared stories of trench warfare at work.

"Work wife," Leila put her hands on Allie's shoulders and took a good look at her, "I've missed you so much. I now sit next to Justin, who eats tuna-and-onion sandwiches at his desk and uses too much hair oil. Hair oil? Who uses that if they're under thirty? Now, can we order lunch? I can't be late back, because—"

Allie held up a hand. "Don't apologise. I *know* how it is, remember?"

Leila's lips twisted. "Of course you do."

They went to the counter to order then returned to their table.

"You're looking well." Leila scanned Allie's upper body and lingered on her face. "The new haircut suits you. And you've got a bit more of a tan. Guess now there's sunlight in your life." She tugged at her own long sleeves, settling them more firmly down to her wrists.

"You're right. Did you know sunlight is warm and lifts your mood? I'd forgotten that until I…" Until she what? "Resigned" was the official word, and that was the agreement she left with—one that would avoid the ignominy of being escorted off the premises. That's what she'd told Leila: that she'd had it and she was resigning to clear her head. But now, it seemed wrong to continue the fabrication.

"Until you what?" Leila leaned forward. "There's something you haven't told me, isn't there?"

"You're right, and I'm sorry." Allie heaved a deep breath. "I didn't exactly resign from Kirkland. I was given an ultimation: resign or be fired."

Leila's eyebrows rose up her forehead as if on strings. "What could you have possibly done to merit that? Whatever it was, I don't believe it. Even if you committed the cardinal sin and stole a pack of Post-It notes."

Allie glanced around. Nobody she recognised in the café. "According to my boss, I falsified the Business Activity Statements for a major client to reduce their tax debt. The tax office investigated and recovered the debt. The client said they believed them to be accurate and is blaming Kirkland & Partners."

Leila's eyes widened. "No! But you've *never* done anything like that. You're straight down the line. I remember you telling me you lost a couple of clients when you wouldn't help them fudge their returns."

Allie sat back as the server brought their lunch. She smiled her thanks and picked up her fork to toy with her salad. The way her guts were churning made eating impossible.

Leila took a huge bite of her chicken wrap. "There's more to this, isn't there?"

There was no way she'd be able to eat a bite. She put her fork down. "I didn't do it. While I'd worked on the client's file, it was very minor fill-in stuff and nothing to do with their BAS returns."

"Then who?"

The name sat heavy in her chest. But she had no proof, only a gut certainty of who it was. Who had mainly worked on that file, who had signed off on it…and who was a senior partner, the biggest ol' boy in the big ol' boys' network. She turned the fork over in her hands. "I'm not sure I can tell you. I have no proof."

"But you are fairly sure, aren't you?"

She nodded.

"Don't say it. I can guess. The person who signed off on your work." Leila set down her wrap. "Did they give you a reference?"

"I didn't ask. They implied they would, as after all, I'd 'resigned'. But I had an interview a couple of weeks later, and they all but offered me the job at the time, said they just had to check references. They gave the job to someone else." The hopelessness of the situation swelled again, sitting heavy in her chest. She'd worked her guts out at Kirkland since qualifying, and this was her reward. Taking the fall for someone simply because she was the expendable one. What was one junior accountant more or less? It fucking sucked, but social media told her it was the way of the working world. The amount of clickbait she'd read since about the world's worst bosses. Slightly less than the number of best revenge stories she'd consumed.

"My mate's an employment lawyer. You could talk with him. Or the industrial relations tribunal. Or the newspapers. You can't just let it go, Allie."

"I'll take his number, but I think I need to work out what's best for me first. I lost a lot of sleep obsessing over it, running through the big denouement scenario in my head, plotting their downfall where I crashed the directors' meeting and threw proof of my innocence down on the boardroom table." She snorted. "It was fantastic in my head, but the reality would likely end with me being removed by security, followed by assault charges. It might be best to let it go and move on."

"I'll look around. Keep my ears open. I can—"

Allie touched her hand. "I appreciate that more than you know. But please don't. It would likely end with you being fired as well. You have a family to support. I'm just me."

For long moments, Leila stared at her, her long-lashed dark eyes damp. "It feels wrong to do nothing."

"I'm getting over it," Allie lied. "Please. Just drop it." She bent her head and stared at the wooden table until she was sure she wouldn't cry. "Now, tell me what's new and great in your life?"

"Hammie started school. Big boy school, as he likes to call it, although there are as many girls as boys. But he's conveniently ignoring that for the moment."

"You'll have to stop calling your son Hammie now he's at school. Muhammad or nothing."

"Yeah. I give it a week. But right now, that's still what he calls himself. He's learning to play soccer. It's super cute. The kids don't have actual matches as no one is allowed to lose when you're five years old." She snorted. "They save that pleasure for later."

"How's work going for you?"

Leila waved a hand around. "Same old. I've got a new assistant—she's really good. Makes my life a lot easier. I even got away at 5.45 p.m. the other day."

"Whoa, girl. You'll be gunning for the leaving-on-time record at this rate."

"Let's not get too carried away."

The chit-chat continued until, with an exclamation, Leila checked the time and stood, gathering purse and phone and stuffing them in her bag. "I have to fly. Don't be a stranger, okay?" She kissed Allie on both cheeks and fled out the door, the ends of her hijab fluttering behind her.

Allie pushed aside her barely touched salad. She may be an unemployed accountant, but it was still better than being an employed one at Kirkland & Partners. Maybe she'd even forge a new career as an event planner.

"Your personal food delivery is here." Allie closed Sophie's front door, stuck her head into the bedroom to say hi, then continued to the kitchen to set the takeaway containers on the counter. She returned to the bedroom.

Sophie clicked off the TV and straightened herself in bed. "I hope it's sushi. Please tell me it's sushi."

"It's sushi." Allie lowered herself to lie on the bed and hug her twin. "And yes, I included seared salmon nigiri."

"Best sister ever."

"I've definitely earned that title—I also bought your favourite wine."

"Ohh." Sophie closed her eyes. "I've died and gone to heaven. Well, apart from the whole fucked leg and nerve pain thing."

"Shall I open the wine?" Allie carefully rose from the bed.

"How about you help me to the living area? Then we can sit at the window and stare out at the yard while we drink our wine, just like normal people."

"We are normal people. Well, I am." Allie stuck her tongue out at Sophie.

"Says the person who wears odd socks and dates men. Weirdo."

"It saves time. Both the men and the socks. I'm never stuck looking for long."

Sophie laughed. "Except you haven't dated anyone since Liam, what, four months ago?"

Allie blew air out her mouth. "I've been busy. And broke. And the only men I've met lately still live at home, and their mothers do their laundry. I don't match my own socks, let along anyone else's." She positioned the wheelchair at the side of the bed and waited while Sophie manoeuvred into it.

Once in the living area, she parked Sophie so she could look out the window and poured two glasses of wine.

"Cheers." She tapped her glass against Sophie's.

"This is a treat." Sophie took a sip. "First wine I've had in most of two weeks."

"The sushi should be good too. I went to the new place on Stanley Street."

"It'll be wonderful. Anything that's not lying in bed watching TV is heaven these days. At least I have visitors." Sophie stared into her glass. "Bree came this morning."

"Oh?" Allie set down her glass carefully. "Was that unexpected? The last time you mentioned her, 'fucking bitch' was in the same sentence."

"She heard about the accident. She came to see if I needed anything. We had a pleasant chat. She loaned me her e-reader and went out to get milk."

A five-alarm warning went off in Allie's head. "Are we talking about the same Bree? Bree, your ex who cheated on you, then moved out while you were at work and sent you a text to let you know?"

"We are." Sophie's lips curved up. "But the Bree who came around this morning was the kind, friendly Bree from the old days, before the corporate ladder pulled her up and she had no time for me anymore. Before she cheated with her boss."

Allie compressed her lips. Hopefully, the 'nice chat' with Bree had included an apology.

"She's going to drop around again soon. She's not dating anyone." The small smile curved once more.

She put out a hand and squeezed Sophie's. "Guard your heart this time. Please. Don't forget there were bad times as well as good. Please think hard before you go there again."

"I will."

If only it were as simple as putting up a Perspex shield. Sophie didn't need any more hurt or heartbreak in her life. Not now. Not ever.

Together they stared out at the yard. The wisteria needed trimming, and as many weeds as flowers sprouted from the planters. Allie blinked against moisture in her eyes. The yard had been Sophie's pride and source of relaxation. She'd make time to tidy it up for her.

"I had a call from Tarryn today," Sophie said. "She must have looked the number up on the website as she came through via the landline—apparently the mobile didn't answer. Obviously, she thought she was talking to you."

"The mobile you gave me is turned off. What did Tarryn want? Another lecture about the pointlessness of marriage?"

Sophie gave her a startled look. "Is she that bad?"

"Not really, but she's hardly the poster child for the festival."

"She updated me on the council permits for the wineries. They should arrive tomorrow. And the ballot boxes are in place. She seems very competent. However, apparently Phyll is trying to take over the organisation of the parade. Kirra's at her wit's end. Phyll got a couple of local church groups involved. That's no problem, apparently; they're the welcoming ones. But she's also got the local kindergarten signed up to march dressed as little brides and grooms—all in traditional white dresses and mini tuxes, although she has specified two brides or two grooms per pair."

"Oh no," Allie murmured. "I thought we'd steered her away from her fixation on white lace and gendered clothing."

"Exactly. Apparently, some parents are happy for their kids to march, but don't want the expense of hiring that sort of costume. And other kids just want to run in a group. Phyll's sticking her nose in the other committees too. Tarryn asked if there was any chance I could come back three weeks before the festival, instead of two. I'm also to call Phyll and tell her to back off."

"Surely, Kirra would be best to do that. Or Tarryn. Phyll's her bloody aunt."

"Is she? Wouldn't have picked it." Sophie sighed. "Please don't hate me, Al, but I said I'd call Phyll tomorrow and would arrive back a week earlier. And of course that means you, not me."

Allie's insides plummeted. It had been hard enough pretending to be Sophie for four days. She'd already been worried about the upcoming two weeks—and now it was three. Three weeks of not stuffing up, of pretending to be Sophie, acting like she knew what she was doing rather than winging it more than a crackle of cockatoos.

But then what else did she have to do? And even if her diary was stuffed fuller than a politician's on election day, she'd drop everything to help Sophie. Concern for her sister pushed into her throat. What if Sophie's leg didn't get better? What if her nerve pain continued and she couldn't bear it any longer? Her sister was suffering through her days, and Allie was only slightly put out by having to spend an extra week in Quandong. She was the fucking bitch, not Bree. "That's okay." She reached out to clasp Sophie's hand. "Kirra's apartment is gorgeous. A lot nicer than mine. It would be a free holiday if it weren't for all the work."

"Thanks." Sophie squeezed back. "At least there's one less thing I have to worry about."

Allie crossed her fingers. Hopefully, that was true.

Chapter 8

THE TWISTY ROAD TO QUANDONG ran alongside Silver Creek into town. Allie wound down the car window and took a lungful of cool air. She could almost taste the freshness, so very different from the smog that hung over Sydney on warm days. The back of her car was jammed with various things Sophie had deemed essential items for the well-organised event planner.

She pulled up outside Kirra's Kafé and swept the scrunched sausage roll wrapper and empty chip bag into the footwell where they cosied up to the apple cores already there. Despite those, her stomach had a Kirra's lemon-slice-sized hole in it. Entering the cafe, she looked around. A muted mid-afternoon buzz of noise reached her ears from a couple of women chatting over their drinks. Kirra stood behind the counter with an irritated look on her face as she punched a calculator.

"Girlfriend!" Kirra hustled around to kiss Allie on the cheek. "You've timed this perfectly." She thrust the calculator at her. "I'll read out the numbers, you enter them in. So far, I've done it six times and got six different results."

"Sure." This was the easiest thing for an ex-accountant to do. Her fingers flew over the keys as Kirra rattled off the list. "$3,185.27."

"Hm. That's the seventh different result. One more time for luck?"

The total was again $3,185.27. Kirra high-fived. "I should have called you earlier." She set down the paper and put a piece of lemon slice on a plate. "Your reward. It's good to see you back. You've been missed."

"Oh? What fires do I have to fight on your behalf?"

"You have to rein in Phyll and remind your gorgeous assistant of the jail time if she murders her aunt."

"I called Phyll. I thought she was backing down." Allie blew out a breath.

"She did. For a couple of days. She's agreed the kindergarten kids can march in whatever costumes they like, either in same-sex pairs or in a big happy group. It's going to be so cute. But Phyll's gone away and rattled her brain and what fell out was a flower-arranging competition and wedding handicrafts. Best crocheted wedding dress. Even if someone could crochet something in the three weeks left, I don't think the result would be what she's expecting. All those holes."

"Phyll will have to be tomorrow's project. Today, I just want to grab some takeaway and sit in the sun on your balcony with a glass of wine."

"Sounds like a plan." Kirra handed her the key. "Do you want your lemon slice to go?"

"If you don't mind." Allie eyed Kirra's angular shape, funky and somehow graceful in her polka dot dress and woolly cardigan. "I'm sure I'll see you tomorrow." She'd already met some of the other sistergirls and brotherboys who would be on the Bundjalung float. It would be colourful and joyful—exactly the thing to lead the parade.

Kirra fluttered her fingers in reply.

The apartment was neat, clean, and welcoming. Allie set her bag on the bed and returned to the car for her box of snacks and wine. Was it too early for wine? She smiled. She was in charge here, and she'd just made an executive decision it definitely was not. She poured a glass of dry rosé and took it to the balcony with a bag of chicken-flavoured chips.

She was contemplating a second glass when someone standing in the middle of the street waving their arms caught her eye. She stood for a better look. A chubby Asian man with tufty dark hair sticking up like a toilet brush was staring in her direction.

"Sophie," he shouted in an exasperated tone. "I've been ringing the bell and shouting for the last five minutes."

Oh! Sophie. Of course. Her sister's name was now hers again. "Sorry, I was dreaming. One moment." She ran down the stairs and opened the door.

Up close, his exasperation was replaced by a beaming smile. "I thought you were ignoring me. I'm Garrett, Will's partner."

Better not explain she just wasn't used to the name. "Come in."

"I'm part of the committee for the fake wedding and the afterparty."

"How's that going?" One part of her mind registered Garrett's presence here meant the answer wasn't going to be "fine."

"Call off Phyllis, and it will be going well." Garrett flung himself onto the couch and immediately bounced up again. "Ooh, pink wine. My favourite."

Allie took the hint and fetched him a glass.

"I'm pretty good at corralling Phyll, but it's a full-time job. But that's not why I'm here. Would you like to come to dinner with me and Will tomorrow night? No festival talk, just good food, excellent wine, and a short walk home. Please say yes." He made puppy dog eyes.

Allie laughed. "That would be wonderful. I haven't had a purely social evening here. What can I bring?"

Garrett took a gulp of wine. "Just your beautiful self and a bottle of this beautiful wine."

"I can do that."

Garrett wrote their address on a piece of paper and handed it to her. "Seven?"

"Perfect. Thanks, Garrett."

He tipped the rest of the wine into his mouth and left, bounding down the stairs.

Tarryn parked her truck outside Will and Garrett's place. Although they often invited her for dinner, tonight's invitation had been oddly specific: *Seven. Don't be late. Bring pie—something lemon.* She picked up the six-pack of craft beer, and the lemon meringue pie she'd bought from Kirra and walked through the front yard to their door.

Will answered, an apron wrapped around his lanky frame. "Pie." He swooped in to kiss her cheek. "You are my best girl."

She laughed and handed it over before following him into the living area. The table was set for four.

Tarryn swung around and glared at Will. "You promised you'd never set me up with anyone again."

He raised his hands and backed away. "I promised. Garrett didn't."

"I plead the fifth. Or is it eighth?" Garrett said.

Tarryn set down the beer. "Who is it? A lonely waif-like student of Garrett's, who's in town for a few days and needs a tour guide? Or a woman abruptly dropped from her motorcycle gang when she traded the Harley for a Subaru?"

"Neither. And you're jumping to conclusions. This isn't a set-up. Well, not exactly."

Tarryn thrust her jaw forward. "Who?"

"Sophie," Will said. "Garrett invited her, and then I invited you. And Jason is dropping in to borrow the food dehydrator. He needs a huge amount of dried citrus slices for the pub before the festival. All those cocktails he's going to sell. But he can't stay for dinner."

"It's not a working dinner," Garrett said. "Poor Sophie's had no social time in Quandong. And who is more social than us?"

"You two maybe. I'm not sure where I fit."

"Tar-ryn," Will scolded. "You're my best friend. Well, apart from this handsome hunk." He cooed at Garrett. "We often invite you over. You seldom invite us, but given how badly you cook, it's probably a good thing."

"I can takeaway with the best of them."

"You're the obvious person to invite as well."

"She's my boss. Sort of."

Garrett shrugged, and his belly popped out from under his T-shirt. "Since when have you cared about that?"

"Since never," Tarryn admitted. "That's why I mostly work for myself."

"So just be charming, drink beer, flirt a little. Who knows what will happen."

Flirt a little. Tarryn rolled her eyes. That had already crossed her mind the first time she set eyes on the rather cute Sophie, but the urge had receded in the face of Sophie's prickliness. "I'll be social. I'm not promising anything else. Hold off on the wedding invitations."

Will exchanged a glance with Garrett. "One step at a time."

The doorbell rang, and Garrett bustled off to answer it.

Tarryn lifted a beer from the six pack and twisted the top off to take a gulp. "Want one?"

Will shook his head. "I'm saving myself for the luscious bottle of red Garrett bought to go with the beef en croute." He frowned. "I hope she's not a vegetarian."

"I doubt it. She's a rubbishtarian, going by the junk food wrappers in her car."

"And here she is!" Will's loud exclamation cut over what Tarryn might have said next, something about Sophie having no taste.

She turned to see Sophie standing there, a bottle of rosé in her hand. A heat flush crept up to her throat and down into her belly. Sophie looked adorably cute. Gone were the business suits she'd worn around town and the T-shirt and jeans that had been her casual wear. Now she wore a muted pink dress in a soft-looking material that skimmed and clung in all the right places. The neckline rolled down in such a way as to hint at the tops of her breasts, and the dress continued to smooth over her narrow hips before ending above the knee. Silver-grey tights shimmered in the overhead light, and chunky flats finished off the outfit. It was the perfect blend of chic and funk.

Tarryn's mouth watered. Sophie was gorgeous. Her own jeans and loose sweatshirt seemed scruffy and overly casual, despite how Will and Garrett were dressed. "Hi." Her nonchalance didn't quite come off, and her voice rose to an embarrassing squeak. "I wasn't told you were coming. If I'd known, I'd have dressed up a bit."

Sophie's gaze ran a leisurely assessment from the top of Tarryn's grey curls down to her tennis shoes. "You look fine to me."

"Drinkies." Garrett announced. "The pink wine Sophie brought is delicious, or we have beer, gin and tonic, or white wine."

"I'm sorted." Tarryn lifted her beer.

The others opted for a gin and tonic and waited while Will fussed with sprigs of rosemary and dehydrated grapefruit slices. "It has to be *better* than what you get in Sydney." He squeezed a twist of lime in the top before handing it to Sophie.

She took a sip. "Delicious."

Will ushered them to a pair of couches facing a low coffee table, where an array of cheeses, olives, and dips awaited. "Sit, socialise. I just need to do a few last-minute things to the meal."

Sophie lowered herself to the couch. With Garrett blocking the way to the opposite one, Tarryn had to sit next to her. She reached for an olive at the same moment Sophie did. Their fingers brushed, and Tarryn stilled a tiny jolt that raced up her arm. *Wow.* Had Sophie felt it too? She withdrew the olive and glanced over. Sophie was staring at her fingers as if something very unexpected had happened.

I guess that's a yes.

"We thought it would be nice to get to you know you a bit better, Sophie. Do you get called Sophie at home? Or a shortened version?" Garrett rested his arm along the back of the couch.

Sophie blinked, as if floating back to earth. "Er, I get Soph sometimes from family and friends."

"Soph, then," Garrett said. "After all, once you've had dinner with us, you're a friend. Where do you live in Sydney? Let me guess." He tilted his face up and closed his eyes as if summoning the spirits. "Inner city terrace house in Paddington that you share with your cranky cat and… a girlfriend?" His voice rose at the end in question.

"Jeez, Garrett, why not go straight to the point and ask her if she's married, engaged, or 'it's complicated.'" Tarryn brushed a hand over her curls.

"You're wrong." Sophie's laugh had a breathy, nervous edge. "I have a small apartment in Darlinghurst. It's nothing special, just somewhere to be."

Garrett made a moue of sympathy. "That must be difficult, then, as you work from home."

A pink flush crept from the neckline of Sophie's dress. "Er, yes. Yes, it is. I manage." She glanced around the room. "This is a lovely space. Did you do it yourself?"

Tarryn stifled a smile. Sophie's obvious discomfort with the personal questions had inadvertently ensured Garrett wouldn't ask her another one. She'd hit on his passion.

"Oh, my dear, did we ever! Will and I spent weeks on this room, and it took us a long time to get it right. At first, we decided on cream for the walls, but no. It was so old-fashioned, like my granny's house. So we thought white. But everyone does white—it's so practical, after all, and never any paint-matching woes. Then we hit on this delicate colour. It's called Maiden's Blush—white, with a hint of pink. We just knew it was perfect from the first roller stroke."

Tarryn looked across at Sophie. She'd sunk back into the couch, following Garrett's conversation with a small smile and something else. Relief? It looked like it. Relief at her successful deflection of the conversation? Maybe Sophie was just an extremely private person and trying not to let the line between work and play blur, but the back of Tarryn's neck tingled. Maybe it was more.

When Garrett wound down in his enthusiastic recounting of the difficulties of deciding between curtains and blinds, Tarryn said, "You didn't answer the question about the cranky cat or cranky girlfriend." She tempered her words with a smile.

"No, I didn't, did I." A corner of Sophie's mouth lifted.

The doorbell rang, and Tarryn gave an inward sigh. Another reason for Sophie to avoid the question.

Garrett hurried to answer it and returned with Jason in tow.

Jason bent to press a kiss to Tarryn's cheek and offered a smile to Sophie. "Nice to see you again. I hope you'll find time to come down for a drink before the festival starts. Relax some."

Sophie's expression had frozen into a polite smile. "Nice to see you again too. Er, yes. I'll try and drop by."

"Good." Jason accepted a beer from Garrett, pulled the top and took a mouthful. "It will be good to continue our previous chat. It's not often someone shares my more unusual interest."

A flash of something crossed Sophie's face before she smoothed her expression. She set down her wine glass and her hands twisted in her lap. "Mm. Yes, we'll do that."

"I realise you're foot to the boards with the festival, but all the same, don't be a stranger."

Weird. Since Jason had walked in, Sophie seemed suddenly on edge. But Jason was one of the most relaxed people in Quandong despite his busy life as owner of The Hollowman—the only bar in town.

Will left the dinner prep and came over to clap Jason on the shoulder. "The dehydrator's on the counter. Don't cut the slices too thick. Seventy degrees for about twelve hours should do it. There's also a bag of lemons and limes on the porch to get you started."

"Thanks. I'll get on to it right away. If I start now, I hope I'll have enough by the time the festival starts. After all, I'm expecting great business from it. Isn't that right, Sophie?"

Sophie's face smoothed. "Absolutely. I hope all the shops in Quandong do."

"Not just the shops, I hope." Jason laughed. "Given my location, I hope to have my best couple of days ever."

The closed-in expression was back. "I hope you do too."

"Those trading cards won't buy themselves. Have you found any good ones since I last saw you?"

Sophie grabbed her glass and raised it to her face for a long moment, as if buying time for her reply. "No, nothing new. I've been too busy to look."

"Shame," Jason said. "Still, you can come over and see what I've scored. I grabbed a Seiya Suzuki rookie baseball card. It was in a batch of other, mainly worthless cards."

"Congrats."

Tarryn studied her. So she and Jason had bonded over trading cards. She suppressed a smile—good for Jason. No one in Quandong was interested. But the way Sophie was acting, maybe she wasn't as knowledgeable about them as she'd obviously made herself out to be.

Sophie's fingers tapped a pattern on her leg, and she set down her glass and rose. "Can someone point me toward the loo?"

"Through there, second door on the left." Will pointed.

"Thanks." Sophie slung her bag over her shoulder and disappeared.

Once the door had closed behind her, Jason asked, "She okay? She seems very quiet."

Tarryn shrugged. "I don't know her well enough to say." But Sophie had closed in on herself since Jason's arrival.

Sophie was gone for a few minutes, but when she returned, she gave them all a bright smile. "I know this evening isn't for talking about the festival, but I need to arrange a time to get together with you, Jason, to discuss the final details. The Hollowman is central to the parade, after all."

"Of course," Jason said. "We'll do that."

"And maybe I can finally see your famous card collection then. You promised to show me your 1920 Babe Ruth card."

"You betcha." Jason beamed. He finished his beer and set the empty tinnie on the coffee table. "But now, I better leave you to your dinner—and I need to get back to the pub. Thanks for the dehydrator, Will. There's a burger and beer with your name on it the next time you come in."

Garrett went to the door with him.

Tarryn shot a look at Sophie. Her earlier tension had evaporated, and she was back to being the friendly but slightly formal person of earlier. Was there something between her and Jason? She searched her memory. She'd heard Sophie was queer, so maybe she was bi or pan. She gave a mental shrug. *Not my circus. Not my monkeys.* Just because she appreciated the sight of Sophie in the pink dress didn't mean she was going to stomp into the ring to declare her interest.

An uneasy silence fell between them. Tarryn glanced at Sophie, only to find her looking right back.

Sophie's gaze skittered away, and they sat, each intent on sipping their drinks.

"Ladies and gentleman, please be seated. Dinner is served." Will indicated the table with a flourish. Bowls of soup were set at each place, and the mouth-watering smell of a crusty loaf filled the air.

"Garrett says you haven't been anywhere around Quandong," Will said as they ate their tomato and basil soup and sipped the rosé wine Sophie had brought. "So you haven't been to Silver Creek Falls—"

"That's only famous for skinny dipping," Garrett said, "and it's still too cool for that."

"And the leeches." Tarryn shot Sophie a grin. "The falls are in the middle of the rainforest, and it's almost impossible to avoid leech attack."

Sophie shuddered. "That's a definite no to the falls, then. And to the skinny dipping."

"Shame," Tarryn murmured. She thought she was too quiet for Sophie to hear, but her eyes widened, and that adorable pink blush stained her chest once more.

"No leeches, then," Will said. "There are some lovely beaches forty or so minutes' drive away. Not the ones at Byron Bay—they're jam-packed year-round—but there's a quiet cliff top walk, then down to a hidden cove where you can go—"

"Skinny dipping?" Sophie said with a lift of her brow.

"Why, yes. How did you know?" Will asked.

"Lucky guess." Sophie took another spoonful of soup. "This is delicious."

"I don't skinny dip," Garrett said. "I chunky dunk."

Sophie's snort of laughter as she sipped her wine made the others laugh.

"It's still too cold for skinny dipping," Tarryn said. "Not unless you want your nipples to drop off from frostbite."

"I'll pass," Sophie murmured.

Tarryn shook her head. That was a stupid thing to say. Not only because it was a totally inappropriate thing to say to a work colleague but also because now she had a visual in her mind of Sophie's breasts. Small, obviously, and going by her pale skin, she'd have nipples as subtly pink as Garrett and Will's living room walls.

"What sort of things do you like to see?" Will asked. "What would you do for fun in Sydney?"

Tarryn put down her spoon, not wanting to miss the answer. The enigmatic Sophie must have hobbies, interests, even if she was reluctant to disclose the existence of a cranky cat and hopefully less-than-cranky girlfriend.

"The usual city pursuits, I guess. I meet friends for coffee, brunch, go for a walk somewhere along Sydney Harbour. See galleries, live bands, a new cocktail bar."

Tarryn sucked her lower lip. Well, that showed Sophie had different social expectations to her. And more disposable income, if that list was anything to go by. "Brunch and coffee here happen at Kirra's. Walks go around the fitness circuit in town if you don't want to brave the leeches. There's one gallery, but the only live bands are at The Hollowman."

"Don't sell Quandong short." Will tapped her hand. "We have open mic nights, an occasional drag show, karaoke sessions, and there was a poetry slam once. Only once, though. I wonder why?"

"There were reasons. Mainly because everyone's awful at poetry." Garrett reached for another slice of bread.

"You don't have to entertain me," Sophie said. "I don't need a city experience."

"That's lucky," Tarryn said. "Because you won't get it. Where do you take a date in Sydney?"

Sophie shuffled in her seat. "A café for lunch, if it's a first date with someone I don't already know."

"So the two degrees of sapphic separation still holds good in Sydney." Will sighed. "Here in Quandong, it's less. Just ask our resident serial dater here."

"That's you?" Sophie asked Tarryn.

"It is," Garrett answered. "Our Tarry's a hot mess, but she attracts women like bees to a honeypot."

"I didn't realise there was such a dating pool here." Sophie finished her soup and set the spoon down.

"There's not." Tarryn glared across the table at Garrett. "Garrett, king of exaggeration, lives up to his title."

Will rose and collected the soup dishes. "Take a breather, pour more wine, and relax."

"Hot mess, eh?" Sophie raised an eyebrow. "So should I know who you've dated here? For potential issues. Difficulty working together, that sort of thing."

"I'm friends with all my exes." Tarryn backed up the bold-faced lie with a direct stare. "It's a lesbian thing, as you doubtless know."

Sophie's gaze slid away, and she took a sip of wine. "It must be different here. Sydney's not like that."

"Are you friends with your exes?"

"No. The last one threw her coffee at me."

"So the sweet and kind sort." Tarryn huffed a laugh.

Garrett leaned forward. "Sophie, do you have a girlfriend—or partner? Maybe they'll be visiting on the weekend?"

"No, I'm single."

Tarryn let that sink into her mind. Interesting. Not unexpected—Sophie had never mentioned anyone, but then again, why would she? This was a work contract, not really the place for social chit-chat. But here, at Will and Garrett's, well, it was different. A buzz started in her stomach. Sophie was free and available—if she wanted to go there. Maybe not. She seemed somewhat prissy. Restrained. The irritation of Sophie calling her out for being late rose in her mind.

Will bustled over and put a serving dish of roast potatoes and green veggies on the table. He returned with warm plates, a gravy boat, an opened bottle of red, and then finally a platter containing a magnificent—and massive—beef en croute.

"You can voice your admiration now," he said and clasped his hands. "I'll start. I think it looks like something from *Masterchef*."

"Better than *Masterchef*," Garrett said. "There was no smoke, minimal swearing, and you don't look as fake-worried as the contestants do."

"The pressure was intense. In here." Will thumped his chest. "What if the pastry's hard? What if I burned the decorative shape on the top?"

Sophie leaned forward. "The shape is very different. Imaginative."

Garrett hooted. "He had to use his imagination, love. Look closer."

Sophie tipped her head on one side. "I'm not entirely sure what it is? Some sort of flower?"

Tarryn looked as well. At first, she couldn't see it—the pastry had spread slightly in the cooking—but the golden-brown shape, a bit crusty on one side, suddenly became clear. She laughed, "Some may call it a flower. I may have, in my more poetic moments."

Sophie scrunched her nose. Surely, she could see what it was with that enormous clue? And then the ball must have dropped with a clang, and that adorable flush stole up her neck again. It was worth embarrassing Sophie just to see that again. "It's a vagina croute?"

Will cackled like a maniac. "Of course. In honour of you gorgeous sapphic women."

If anything, Sophie's flush became deeper. "Well, thank you." She glanced away, up at the wall.

Maybe she was uncomfortable at the blurring of the lines, at letting her professional image slip. Well, the sooner she learned that wasn't taken too seriously in Quandong the better. She just hoped Will wouldn't make a terrible beef en vagina joke.

Luckily, although she was making a good job of hiding it, he seemed to sense Sophie's discomfort and picked up the carving knife without further comment. "I hope you both like rare beef." The first two slices fell, softly pink in the centre, encased in golden-brown pastry.

Tarryn was really glad there were no vagina jokes.

"I love it," Sophie said. She accepted the plate Will passed, and when Garrett nudged the veggies in her direction, she took a generous portion.

When everyone had been served, Sophie lifted her glass. "Thank you for making me welcome. Here's to the Gay Bells festival being a huge success."

"We have the A-Team here. I'm sure it will be." Garrett went to get Will's luscious red wine and poured fresh glasses, then got a second beer for Tarryn.

"Make sure you do more than just work. There are plenty of people who'd be delighted to show you around." Will kicked Tarryn's ankle under the table, and when Sophie was looking the other way, he mouthed, "Like you!"

She glared at him, rubbed her ankle, then picked up her cutlery and began to eat.

"Honestly, you don't need to babysit me. I have a ton of work to get through for this festival. I won't have much time for socialising." Sophie flashed a smile. "This will probably be the social highlight of my time here."

Did she know what an appealing smile she had? Tarryn sliced a piece of the tender beef. Sophie was a mix of innocent ingenue and cool business-woman—and that was intriguing. It was almost as if she didn't know how to behave in either world.

"It can be work. After all, you need to know what to do around Quandong if you're to promote it successfully. Don't you have a term for ex-periencing something so you can promote it?" Tarryn turned to face Sophie. She told herself it was to see if she agreed with that, but a wiggle of delight suggested it was also to follow the graceful curve of Sophie's neck up to the choppy bob, and the plump earlobe that peeked out from underneath, decorated by a plain gold stud and just begging to be bitten.

"You're right; we do that sometimes. This beef is fantastic." She flashed a smile at Will. "Can you give me the recipe?"

"I could—if I thought you were actually going to cook it and weren't just being polite."

"Why do you assume I can't cook?" Sophie challenged.

"Because I have it on good authority the floor of your car is carpeted in junk food wrappers. And a friend works at Thai Dreams. Seems you're quite the regular customer, especially given you've only spent four nights total in town."

"Neither of those mean I can't cook. Just that I'm busy."

"True. If I give you the recipe, you'll have to cook it one night for us. You can use my kitchen."

"Okay, you've caught me out. I can cook, but I seldom have time. And beef en croute would be a stretch for me. But that doesn't mean I won't give something new a try." She turned her head and stared Tarryn full in the face.

Tarryn's breath stuttered in her throat. Was that an invitation? Surely not. There had been nothing from Sophie to indicate that so far. Yes, she was gay, yes, she didn't have a partner, but no, she wasn't flirting.

Not yet.

But maybe. Soon.

And once again, she'd deflected the conversation away from something personal to a neutral subject.

"What are you wanting to try?" she asked. For a heated second, possible sexual firsts flashed through her mind.

"I'd love to meet your alpacas. You said one of them was called Allie— the same as my sister."

"They are adorable," Will said. "But watch out for Ally. She can be a bit feisty. Has been known to nip as well as spit."

"Just like my sister." Sophie cut a potato into bite-sized pieces.

The mental picture of Sophie trying something new bloomed to a feature movie. "Remember that thought when she spits stomach contents on your shirt."

"Does she do that often?" Sophie asked.

"Slightly more often than Tarryn does," Garrett said. "More red wine, Soph?"

"Please." She held out her glass for Garrett to fill.

"Not for me, thanks," Tarryn said. "I'm driving."

"And I know pink and red are not your colours." Garrett winked.

"They're not yours either." She nodded to the ash-pink T-shirt he wore and laughed as he blew her a kiss. "But pink is yours, Sophie. That dress suits you."

"Thanks. It's one of my favourites."

"I'll make sure you meet my best girls, then," Tarryn said. "Ally and Elly, in case anyone's wondering."

Sophie's smile reached her eyes. "I'd like that. I'm a sucker for anything fluffy and cute with long eyelashes. Do you use their wool?"

"I trade it to the craft group in town in exchange for a sweater or a blanket."

"Maybe they would weave an alpaca wool wedding dress for Phyll's parade," Will said. "It would be a bit hot, though."

"Phyll." Tarryn huffed a sigh. "I know she's my aunt, but she's driving me nuts. If she doesn't back off soon, I'm going to chuck this job in."

"No festival talk, that's the deal for tonight." Garrett rested his chin on his hand. "But we can make an exception for gossip about the lovely Phyllis. I quite like the old bat."

"What's she doing to annoy you?" Sophie asked.

"I should have made a list. She's calling me day and night, asking that I chase up stallholders for payment, get them to sign things. I've done that—I'm only waiting on one more payment."

"Well done," murmured Sophie. "That's a huge achievement."

"Thanks." Tarryn nodded in Sophie's direction. "It's taking a lot of time, though—six or more hours each day. The agreement was it would be a maximum of four, apart from the week of the festival, when it's as many as you want me to work."

"I'll make sure you get paid," Sophie said. "I'll call Phyll—again—and remind her she can't monopolise you. Now I'm here, I'll be her first point of contact."

"She has heaps of ideas," Tarryn continued. "I'm not sure how she expects to make them happen at this late stage."

"What are they?" Will asked.

"They're all a bit old-fashioned. She wants to have a decorated dinner table competition at the fair. And a handicrafts stall. And a best wedding pet competition. She mentioned poodles in bridal gowns." Tarryn poured herself a glass of water. "It's bad enough all this wedding fever around at the moment, but I think Aunt Phyll's lost the plot. Who wants to see decorated dinner tables?"

Will exchanged a look with Garrett. "Me. I'd enter."

"And handicrafts?"

"Darling, your metal sculptures could be considered handicrafts. You could enter."

"Oh, per-lease. Handicrafts are knitted tea cosies and pressed flower cards. Not scrap metal bent into large shapes. I use a welder, not crochet hooks! Not that I've had time to do any welding right now, thanks to Phyll."

"Not everyone who comes will be a twenties hipster," Sophie said. "The Facebook page has seen quite a bit of interest across the generations. We should cater to a variety of interests. Like the dinner tables and the wedding pets, for example."

"If I ever mention getting married, I'm relying on you two"—Tarryn pointed from Will to Garrett— "to lock me in my shouse until I see sense. What's the point of marriage? No one here has tied the knot."

Garrett and Will exchanged a look.

"The point of marriage," Will mused. "Let's see. So you can fight without worrying it's break up time. To save on living expenses. Married people live longer."

"Because he can cook and you can't. It makes it less likely a relative will contest a will. More rewarding sex," Garrett added.

"There's always someone else to put the bins out and buy milk. Never having to go on another awkward first date," Sophie said.

"Never wondering if a date is a date or if the other person thinks it's just two friends having coffee." Will tapped the back of Garrett's hand. "Like someone I know."

"You looked straight!"

Will lifted a shoulder. "But you didn't. And I accepted your invitation."

"And love." Sophie twisted her wine glass. "Because you love someone so much and want to spend the rest of your lives together and want the world to know." Her voice held a wistful note.

"Yes, love," Garrett said. "Love that binds us together." He exchanged a tender look with Will.

The silence hung for a moment, heavy, anticipatory.

"But you can have all those without marriage," Tarryn said. "De facto partners have as many rights as married ones in Australia. Why spend all that money on something ostentatious just to prove to people you're in love? Surely the most important person to show your love to is your partner."

"People like to share in the love," Sophie said. "Have you never cried at a wedding or gone gooey inside at how the newlyweds looked at each other? As if the moon and stars were in the other person's eyes?"

Tarryn smiled. "It's cute. But I get that same happy feeling when I see them declaring undying love in a bar after two bottles of wine. Will, Garrett, you've been together four years now and aren't married. Why are you defending marriage?"

"We're not married yet. That doesn't mean we won't," Will said. "Sophie, what about you?"

"I'd like to get married one day. If I find someone I want to be with for the rest of my life."

"So no quickie divorce for you, then," Tarryn said.

"I'd hope not, but you can't ever really tell, can you?" Sophie said. "My parents are divorced. They're happier apart—they're both doing their own thing overseas."

"Do you have siblings?" Tarryn asked. Why was she asking this? It wasn't like she was particularly interested in the answer. Just being polite, that's what it was.

"One sister. We're very close."

"The Allie you mentioned?" Will asked.

"That's her. Allie, short for Allison."

Will jumped to his feet. "Let me cut the amazing pie Tarryn brought. I'd say 'Tarryn's amazing pie,' but we all know Kirra made it." He bustled off and returned bearing four large slices.

"Is this a quarter of the pie?" Tarryn asked. Her mouth watered. Will's food was incredible, but Kirra's pies were next-level.

"Pretty much. I saved a slice for brekkie tomorrow."

"Maybe Kirra will be voted as one of the people for the fake wedding," Sophie said. Her gaze hadn't left the pie since Will brought it to the table. "She'd be great."

"She would," Tarryn agreed. "But you might have a hard time persuading her to do it. It would depend who the other person was. My money's on you two winning." She waved her fork at Garrett and Will. "All these years together, and neither of you has asked the other yet."

The men exchanged glances. "We'll get there, Tarry," Garrett said. "And when we do, you'll be the last to know, being so opposed to marriage and all."

Sophie laughed. "He got you there."

Tarryn narrowed her eyes at Garrett. "Maybe I'll vote for you to get fake married."

"And maybe"—Sophie tapped her fingers on the table and flicked a glance at Tarryn—"I'll vote for you. Just to see your look of outrage when your name is announced."

Tarryn widened her eyes. "No outrage from me. Just a firm no." She picked up her fork and took a mouthful of pie simply to escape the intent look in Sophie's grey eyes. If she was plotting, she had another think coming.

"You couldn't say no. This is your town; you want the festival to succeed. Just as you want your emu sculpture to strut her stuff in Silver Creek Park," Will said.

"I do. And she'll get there one day. I have a hot line to the Silver Creek Beautification Project committee."

"Phyll again? Is there anything she doesn't do?" Sophie scooped some meringue off her pie and ate it.

"She doesn't leave me alone," Tarryn muttered. "Don't forget to get her to back off or you'll be looking for a new assistant."

"Better that then you have to find a new fake bride at the last minute," Sophie said. "I'm starting the Will and Garrett's Wedding campaign. It has a nice ring to it, don't you think?"

Will laughed. "But not a nice wedding ring."

A couple of hours later, after coffee, chocolate marzipan, and a luscious muscat that made Allie think of honey and raisins and sweet summer evenings, Tarryn stood to leave. Allie glanced at her phone—gone midnight. Not late by Sydney standards, but Quandong was different. She stood, too, and her head swam in a pleasant haze of tiredness and muscat.

Will glanced at her. "Tarry, love, drop Sophie off on your way; she'll fall asleep on Phyll's doorstep if she has to walk."

"It would save me calling her tomorrow," Allie said.

Tarryn shot her a glance. Probably assessing the chances of her falling asleep between here and her apartment. "No problem."

Allie kissed both Garrett and Will on the cheek. "Thank you for a wonderful evening. You can take your beef en croute recipe to the grave. It's safe from my attempt."

Will hugged her back. "You must come again before you leave. We still have to figure out some trips for you and places to go."

Tarryn, having said her goodbyes already, waited at the bottom of the steps, jingling the keys to her truck.

As she walked down the path behind Tarryn's tall shape, Allie glanced back at Will and Garrett, silhouetted by the light, arms around each other's waists. They would make a great couple for the fake wedding.

Tarryn moved the welding helmet and gloves from the passenger seat of her truck to the floor and shoved the box of copper pipe to the centre of the bench seat. She started the engine and pulled away.

"Thanks for this," Allie said. "Is it much out your way?"

"A little." Tarryn shrugged. Her profile was shadowy in the darkness. The moon coming in the side window turned her iron-grey curls to silver. "I'm a few minutes out of town. It's no trouble, though."

"So we're not going to pass Ally-paca and Elly-paca tonight?" It was as if Allie's eyes were welded to Tarryn's profile. A strong face, she thought hazily. Attractive. And when she smiled—Allie flicked her tongue over her suddenly dry lips—it made butterflies dance in her belly and heat curl its way into her chest.

"No." Tarryn's eyes crinkled. "They'll be asleep in the barn. You can come and see them, though."

"I'd love that. Cute, furry animals. What's nicer?"

"Cute, smooth-skinned women, since you asked. But Ally and Elly come a close second. So you don't have a cranky cat. Do you have any pets?"

"No. I live alone."

"Nothing warm to snuggle at night?" Tarryn flashed her a quick glance, her quirky half smile lifting the corner of her mouth.

"Just my fleecy quilt. Every girl should have one. Especially you—it's cold here!"

"I prefer my bed-warmers to be more active."

Allie wrapped her arms around her midriff. Was Tarryn flirting? No, surely not. For all the warmth and banter of the evening, Tarryn wouldn't do that. Not with her. This was a light-hearted comment, nothing more.

But what if she were the gay woman Tarryn believed her to be? What would Sophie do? A smile tickled her mouth at the thought of her twin. Sophie would laugh at that comment and tease right back. "Then curl up with the alpacas. I'm sure they snort and wiggle enough for you."

"They also stink. So not an option."

"The Hollowman might still be open. You might be able to find a less stinky bed companion there."

Tarryn laughed. "I doubt it. At this time of night, it's normally only Mike and Mal propping up the bar. They're both in their sixties and don't want to go home to their wives. See? That's what marriage does to you."

"I'm sure that's nothing to do with marriage and everything to do with Mike and Mal." Allie's head spun as Tarryn took a corner fast. Too much wine. She wasn't a big drinker, but it had been too easy to sip wine and laugh and enjoy the relaxed company. It was almost like being with her Sydney friends.

Jason's arrival had thrown her, though. Damn Sophie for forgetting to mention him. She hoped he hadn't noticed her vague answers. She thanked her lucky stars Sophie had immediately answered her frantic text from the loo. What were the odds of someone in Quandong sharing Sophie's, quite frankly, weird interest in baseball cards? Allie had always glazed over when Sophie mentioned them. Tonight was the only time in living history she'd wished she'd paid attention.

She snuck another look at Tarryn, at her hands confident on the wheel. Would Sophie find Tarryn attractive? She was nothing like Bree, Sophie's last girlfriend. But there was something very appealing about Tarryn's long, lean figure, the combination of her olive skin and iron-grey tight-cropped curls. A shudder ran through her. She must have drunk too much to be thinking like that.

She forced her thoughts back to the evening. Tarryn hadn't appeared totally relaxed. Her prickles had appeared a couple of times. Allie didn't think it was their working relationship; that didn't seem to faze her. More likely it was her antipathy to the whole marriage thing—and pressure from Phyll. Allie sighed. That was a job for tomorrow morning.

Tarryn pulled up outside Kirra's Kafé. "Here you are. Think you can manage the stairs alone?"

"Of course." Allie fumbled in her bag for the key and clutched it in her fist. "I'm not that smashed."

"I'm not saying you are, just that the stairs are steep."

"Thanks, I'll be fine." Allie turned to Tarryn in the dark truck. Her eyes were mysterious and dark, like coals. She reached out and touched her arm. Her sweatshirt was pushed up and her bare skin was surprisingly warm in the cool night. "Thanks for driving me home. We'll talk tomorrow."

"No worries. Night, Sophie."

The truck idled as Allie fitted her key into the lock, and only when she reached the living area and turned the light on did it drive away.

Chapter 9

IT HAD BEEN A COUPLE of days since dinner at Will and Garrett's, and Tarryn had had enough. Enough of wedding dresses, enough of canapés, and photographers' portfolios of staged cute pictures designed to look spontaneous. And certainly, she'd read enough wedding celebrant brochures to last her a lifetime.

Whose stupid idea was this festival anyway? She cast a longing glance to the end of her shed that housed her workshop. The tall gas cylinder and the blocky shape of the welding machine taunted her, as did the still legless metal emu she hoped would end up in Silver Creek Park. The Gay Bells festival was sucking her time and energy like the worst sort of clingy girlfriend.

But it was a job, and a well-paid one that benefitted her town. So she'd spent what seemed like hours on the phone to the Council sorting permits and emailing all the vendors of the slow food festival and wedding fair with the parking and access arrangements for the festival. She'd also arranged for the feedstore at the edge of town to provide truck parking. That would ease congestion around the main festival area.

She slid into the truck, threw her bag on the passenger seat, and started the engine. Ally and Elly stared at her over the fence as she drove toward the road. It had been a few days since she'd taken them for a walk. Yet another thing she'd had no time for this last week. But right now, she had to meet Sophie, Kirra, Garrett, Jason, and the ever-present Phyll for a run through of the requirements for the fake wedding and the afterparty.

Two and a half weeks until the festival. Right now, it seemed like two and a half years.

When she pulled into the car park for The Hollowman, the first vehicle she saw was Sophie's Mitsubishi emblazoned with signage promoting her business. The second was Phyll's microscopic Nissan. Tarryn checked the time on the dash. She was seven minutes early, but no doubt Sophie and Phyll had arrived twenty minutes ago and had already worked through most of the agenda with Jason.

She locked her truck and entered the pub via the back door. Sure enough, Sophie, Phyll, and Jason were sitting around one of the tall tables in the empty bar, steaming mugs in front of them.

"Hi, Tarryn." Jason jumped to his feet. "Coffee?"

She shot him a grateful smile. "That would be wonderful, thanks, Jase." She turned to the others. "You both are nice and early. Again. Maybe you should tell me to arrive twenty minutes earlier so I don't miss anything. Again."

Sophie blinked. "I guess we're both early birds. And you're not."

"Seven minutes early. Plenty of time to get settled for a *nine o'clock* meeting. If you don't need me here, I'd have appreciated knowing ahead."

"You're needed," Sophie said. "We haven't started yet. Just chatting. Besides, Garrett and Kirra haven't arrived yet."

Tarryn let her gaze drift from Sophie's mussed hair, down her slender neck, to narrow shoulders. She was wearing a lavender sweatshirt today that somehow enhanced the grey of her eyes. The baggy top skimmed rather than clung, but her slender forearms and delicate hands, exposed by the pushed-up sleeves, gave plenty for Tarryn to absorb. Graceful hands, with long fingers and short, buffed nails. For a second, she wondered how those hands would feel on her skin. She shook her head. Sophie still had a no-touch vibe about her.

"Glad to see you here on time," Phyll said.

Did Phyll have to niggle at her every time? She buried the surge of irritation in an artificial sweet smile.

Jason arrived back with a mug of coffee and set it down in front of Tarryn. "Here you go. Double shot. You look like you need it."

So much for being alert and ready to go, then. She cupped it in both hands and inhaled the smell.

The door crashed open, and Kirra sauntered in, followed by Garrett. Kirra hitched up her floral skirt above her knees and hoisted herself onto the barstool. "Jason, I smell coffee, and if someone who isn't me makes me one, I will kiss them."

Jason blushed pink. "No kisses necessary, but you still get your coffee. Garrett, you as well?"

"Please," Garrett said.

Kirra looked over at Jason as he fiddled with the coffee machine behind the bar. "Nothing is guaranteed to make a straight man blush more than a trans woman offering to kiss him."

"Jason's a good man," Phyll said. "It's wrong to embarrass him."

Kirra gave her a pensive look. "You're quite right, Phyll, darling. I was wrong." Her gaze tracked Jason as he moved back and forth making coffee.

Jason returned, setting coffees in front of Kirra and Garrett.

"So, how's afterparty central coming along?" Sophie smiled at Jason.

"Good. The stage for the fake wedding will be right outside the front door. The bar will be serving, and we'll have a wedding special of mimosas for people to cheer the happy couple."

"How big is the stage?" Sophie asked. Her forehead crinkled, and she flicked through some sheets in front of her.

"However big you ordered," Phyll said. "That's your department: stage, sound system, steps, and the backdrop for the wedding ceremony."

"Tarryn?" Sophie said. "Can you remember?"

She shrugged. "No—you were arranging it."

The colour leeched from Sophie's cheeks, and she scribbled a note on the top of her pad. "Right. I'll need to check." Her thumbs rubbed back and forth along her index fingers.

"Once the ceremony has finished and the happy couple has had their first dance, the afterparty starts," Jason said. "DJ Strokes is booked for the music. If we have a screen on the stage behind the celebrant, he can set up behind that ready to go."

"Screen. Right." Sophie looked at Tarryn. "And is this arranged?"

"This is the first I've heard of it." Tarryn bit back an acerbic remark about shaky organisation.

Jason shuffled in his seat. "I've only just thought of it."

"Sophie, this is your forte. I would have expected you to have this under control." Phyll's brows lowered, and she stared fixedly at Sophie.

Tarryn hid a small smirk. For once, Phyll's displeasure wasn't aimed at her.

"And it would be, Phyll," Sophie said coolly. "However, Jason has only just suggested the idea. I'll get onto it this afternoon."

Tarryn sipped her coffee. Surely an event planner should have thought this through. A screen was obvious. Sophie was making notes on her pad. Tarryn tried to read them, but her writing was too small.

"Jason, do you need anything else for the afterparty?" Sophie asked.

Jason scratched his balding head. "Where are we putting the portaloos? I'm hoping they'll be close enough to cope with any overflow—no pun intended—from the party."

"Tarryn, can you answer that?" Sophie inclined her head at Tarryn.

She wracked her brains, but "portaloo" was not to be found. "Sorry, that wasn't anything on my list."

Sophie frowned. "Arranging the portaloos was on your to-do list. Since well before my first visit."

It was? "That's the first I've heard of it. Although I always get the shit jobs."

Kirra laughed. "At least you won't have to empty them."

Sophie's face folded further into a frown. "So the portaloos haven't been ordered?"

"Looks like it. They weren't on my list."

"I wrote your list, Tarryn. They most definitely were. You need to check again." Sophie's pen tapped a staccato beat on her pad.

"I would have remembered." Anger coiled in her stomach. Who the hell was Sophie to treat her like a six-year-old? She pulled out her phone and scrolled through her emails to find the to-do list. Swiftly, she scanned it. Nope. Definitely no portaloos. She thrust the phone at Sophie. "See for yourself."

"And the second email? Sent a day after the first?"

"There was no second email." Tarryn shrugged. "This is my only list." She levelled an irritated stare at Sophie.

The pink flush that the other day Tarryn had found so adorable stained Sophie's cheeks. "It was sent."

"So, who's going to fix it?" Phyll placed her hands flat on the table. "Sophie, this sort of thing is why we hired you."

"I apologise, Phyll. We'll get it sorted. Tarryn, consider it now on your to-do list. I'll forward you the original request from my second email when I get back."

She resisted the urge to salute. "Yes, ma'am."

"There's no need to be sarcastic. There was a mistake, we're fixing it." The pink flush rose higher in Sophie's cheeks. "Jason, I'll check the plan for the portaloos and ensure they're close enough to here. Is there anything else?"

Jason shook his head. "I've arranged extra security and bar staff. I'm good."

"When are we going to count the votes for the couple to get married?" Kirra asked.

"This Friday," Sophie said. "That gives the hire shops time to come up with the clothing. I hope you've all voted."

"Not yet," Kirra said. Her gaze flicked from Sophie to Tarryn and back again. "Hmm."

"Hmm what?" Tarryn asked. At Kirra's wide grin, Tarryn pushed her stool back and held her hands out in front of her. "Oh no. Absolutely not. Don't even think of it!"

"But the two of you are so perfect," Kirra said. "Both so gorgeous, both so gay, such a perfect couple."

"You've just watched us fighting!"

"Every marriage needs a bit of spice. Even a fake one."

The others' heads were going back and forth as if at a tennis match.

"What are you suggesting, Kirra?" Garrett asked.

Kirra pointed first at Tarryn, then at Sophie. "Our fake couple. They're perfect."

"Not so perfect if one of them doesn't turn up." Tarryn stood and stuck her hands on her hips. "A total failure if one of them refuses to wear wedding clothes or say vows."

Garrett pursed his lips. "They are perfect. Think how glorious the photos will be. Every queer couple in eastern Australia will want to get married in Quandong after seeing our beautiful brides."

"Not to mention it gets you and Will off the hook." Kirra winked. "I wouldn't be surprised if you're the frontrunners at the moment."

Garrett smoothed his turquoise T-shirt. "Tall and skinny plus short and chubby makes for awkward photos. I think these two would be perfect. Both gorgeous, and lovely contrasting styles. Tarryn's androgynous butchiness and Sophie's girl-next-door charm."

"Uh-uh. I think you're forgetting Tarryn and I are the organisers here. We both need to be on hand to sort out any last-minute issues." Sophie folded her arms.

"It's a well-oiled machine, darlings," Kirra cooed. "I'm organising the parade, but I'm also on a float. Delegation matters."

"I can't delegate to Tarryn if she's marrying me!" Sophie hunched her shoulders.

"Trust me, I'm not marrying you—or anyone." Tarryn narrowed her eyes. "The idea's insane."

"It's a great idea." Phyll said. "I can cover any last-minute issues while you're getting married."

"Phyll, I know you're good, but it wouldn't be just for twenty minutes," Sophie said. "We'd need time to get ready, and the fake couple are then to be the centre of the afterparty. Photo opportunities, playing a loving couple. Dancing and socialising. We're talking at least a couple of hours here."

"No problem." Phyll waved a hand.

"No *way*," Tarryn said. "I'm not doing it."

Sophie flattened her hands on the table. "And I can't do it. Despite Phyll's offer, I'm being paid to organise, not to act as a bride."

"You're being paid to do what we want," Kirra said. "And if we want you to be a fake bride, then I consider that an essential part of the organisation."

"I'm not under contract," Tarryn said. "I would resign."

Garrett stood and wrapped an arm around her shoulders. "I wouldn't worry too much. We're all forgetting it's down to the popular vote. Whoever gets the most votes on Friday will be our couple."

"True," Kirra said. "It's likely to be Garrett and Will. After all, the whole town can vote, and not everyone knows Sophie. It could still be one of the couples who volunteered."

Tarryn allowed herself to relax a little. That was true. Why would anyone vote for a stranger? And her friends surely wouldn't vote for her as they knew her anti-marriage views. No, it would be Garrett and Will, or maybe Euli and Bernice, the sistergirls.

"So," Phyll said, "are we all agreed we let the popular vote stand?"

Tarryn nodded along with everyone else.

"And if, by chance, the popular vote picks Tarryn and Sophie, then you two agree to do it?"

Tarryn frowned. She could smell week-old fish here. Garrett and Kirra looked neutral, certainly not like they were plotting anything. But what could they do? They could hardly influence the whole town. "Who's counting the vote?"

"We haven't decided yet," Sophie said.

"I'll do it," Phyll said. "Will one of you volunteer to check it?"

"I will." If she checked it, she'd know there was no set up by her friends. No conniving, no shuffling of votes from pile to pile. "How hard can this be? It's hardly the US presidential election."

"As long as no one claims afterward the vote is stolen," Garrett said. "So, are we agreed? Phyll and Tarryn will count the vote, and if, by chance, Tarryn and Sophie are the winners, they'll do the dirty deed."

"It's the wedding we're talking about, not the wedding night," Jason said with a wink.

Sophie's horrified face jammed into Tarryn's vision. So, she was unappealing enough that Sophie looked like she'd rather eat worms than do any sort of deed—dirty or otherwise—with her? She pushed away the thought that she wouldn't turn down the chance to get Sophie underneath her and to taste those plump, pink lips. To see exactly how Miss Perfect was when she was naked. "I agree," she said coolly. "Sophie?"

Sophie's lips twisted. "I suppose so. Given it's unlikely we'd win."

"Great." Garrett rubbed his hands together. "Now, is there anything else? I have to go to Byron Bay once we're done. Will wants me to source squid ink for some gastronomic creation he wants to make for dinner."

"We're done." Jason stood. "Thank you for coming."

"Myself or Tarryn will let you know about the stage and the portaloos," Sophie said.

Tarryn mentally rolled her eyes. That job had her name written all over it. She sighed. Sometimes, Sophie seemed less than experienced at this event planning business.

Chapter 10

ALLIE CLOSED THE DOOR TO Kirra's apartment with a sigh and plod-ded up the stairs. What a morning. What a terrible morning. She threw herself on the couch. She'd been winging it in the past few days, but nothing as nail-biting as this morning. What stage? She couldn't remember anything about a stage in Sophie's folder…but there had to be one. She didn't think Sophie would have forgotten something that important. And the portaloos… she knew she'd seen them on Tarryn's to-do list. She definitely remembered a second email; she'd have to find it.

And then the whole fake-wedding thing. Damn Garrett and his inspired ideas. There was no way she could stand next to Tarryn and marry her. Fake-marry her, she amended. She was needed for her supposed event planning skills, not her negligible acting ones. Although maybe her acting ability would be better.

For a second, she imagined herself up on stage, her hand in Tarryn's, both of them dressed in…in what? Tarryn would probably pick a tux, and she would… Her mind went blank. She had no idea what she'd wear, but it wouldn't be a white dress and a veil. That would be for any real wedding she may have. She pictured turning to Tarryn, clasping hands and saying marriage vows.

"And you may kiss the bride." Her mind went white. Would she have to kiss Tarryn? Something long buried uncoiled in her stomach. The feel of a woman's lips on her own. Soft, smiling, tasting of white wine—the only time she'd kissed a woman. Yes, she'd told Sophie it had been an experiment, one she'd liked, but, really, she preferred kissing men. She'd acknowledged the other options, ones marked bisexual or pansexual, but the need to keep one thing for herself, separate from her sister, was strong.

She and Sophie were so alike in most things— in ways that went deeper than simply their preference for chicken salt over plain. They'd been each other's rock since their parents split, and she could confidently state how Sophie would react in most things. Sophie was a lesbian. Allie was straight. Men were her thing. Women were Sophie's.

And had been, from way back in school, when she'd gone on that date with Wallis—Ellis—Simpson in Sophie's place. Their friends used their sexualities to differentiate them: Sophie was the gay twin. Allie was the straight one. Ying and Yang. Separate, but strong together. Being straight was part of her identity.

Tarryn's handsome face swam into her mind: high cheekbones, her prematurely grey hair, her dark eyes that could dance with mischief as they had at dinner with Garrett and Will or could be cold like granite as they were earlier this morning. And her lips.

Would she kiss Tarryn if the playacting called for it? She'd have to; she'd agreed. And she already knew that like the long-ago kiss with a woman, she'd like it.

Enough. Allie pushed those thoughts from her mind. That would never happen. The popular vote would go to others, someone local and known in town. Not to her, and not to Tarryn. Right now, she had other problems to deal with.

She turned on her laptop and went to her email, clicking into the folder of emails Sophie had forwarded to her about Quandong. A quick search found the original to-do list that Tarryn remembered receiving, and then the second one, a day later. She opened it and looked at the email address. *Oh no.* There was a typo in the address. Tarryn wouldn't have received it. Sophie must have typed it in directly, maybe from her phone, and got it wrong. *Crap.* There was the request for Tarryn to hire the portaloos set out in black and white—and no doubt in some mail server's undeliverable pile. Why hadn't Sophie seen the bounce? The only other thing in the email was a request to source a florist to provide flowers for the fake wedding. Luckily, that was all. At least there hadn't been 'hire stage' written there.

Stage.

Another quick search found an email from the equipment hire place, detailing the different sizes of stage they had and asking Sophie to confirm which she wanted. Had Sophie confirmed it? Allie went cold, and her fingers shook on the keyboard. She looked at the date of the email and the reason why Sophie hadn't replied jumped out at her. It was the day after Sophie's accident.

Allie blew a shaky breath, and a chill ran through her. She should have double checked—she'd read through Sophie's emails, after all. What if now there wasn't one available? Maybe though, Sophie, had followed up.

She picked up her mobile. She'd have to call Sophie and hope she wouldn't think it was all going to hell in a handbasket. She pressed her number.

"Hey, big sis. How's life in New South Wales's gayest wedding town?"

"Gay. Friendly. Good food."

"That's good. The food part is especially important."

"How are you doing?" Allie drew her knees up and curled into the back of the couch.

"Okay. I've got new pain meds, and they actually do dull the pain. And the rehab is finally starting to do something. I have more mobility in my foot now."

A happy warmth spread through Allie's chest. "That's great news. Do you still have Silent Kev as your nurse?"

"Just in the evenings."

"So who's there in the day?" Allie frowned. "Surely the insurance company should have arranged someone?"

"They have. I'm now driven to a rehab place three days a week, and I spend the day there. It's more intensive, plus great care, and I get to talk to other people like me."

"You mean blue-haired, queer, sarcastic old cows?"

Sophie laughed. "I actually meant people in rehab with similar injuries. It's been good—I can now see a way out of this. A way to get my life back."

"That's fantastic." Guilt churned in Allie's stomach. "I wish I was there with you, taking you to this magical place, doing more to help you."

"You're the best, Allie. No one else could do what you're doing for me right now in Quandong. You'll be back soon enough. We can catch up then."

"Yeah." A pang of longing knifed her gut. Oh to be sitting in Sophie's yard with a glass of wine, and the comfort of talking to her twin and best friend.

"Soon, Allie. It won't be long. I miss you too."

She always knew. A wave of love swamped Allie so hard she couldn't breathe.

"What about the other days?" Allie tucked her feet under the cushion. "Who's with you then?"

There was a slight hesitation on the line, then Sophie said, "Bree's been working from my place a couple of days a week. She's been looking out for me."

"Bree? Bree the bi—"

"Don't say it. We've been talking. She was having a hard time when we split up. It doesn't excuse her—and Bree knows that—but, well, we're becoming friends again. And she's being very good to me."

Allie sucked her upper lip. There was an uplift at the end of Sophie's words, as if hope was being reborn. Bree had broken her heart. Now, it seemed she thought Bree would mend it again.

"And don't tell me to be careful," Sophie said. "Please, Allie. I know what you're thinking. But this time… Maybe… I can't help being a bit hopeful. After all, she's spending time with me now when I'm at my lowest."

Allie expelled her breath in a long sigh. "I won't say anything. Please… send her my best."

"I will. Thanks, Allie." A pause. "Now, did you call for a chat or do you need an event-planning consultation?"

"The latter. I wish I didn't have to dump this on you, but I have a couple of problems." Swiftly, she outlined the lack of portaloos and the reason, and the stage issue.

"I fucked up Tarryn's email address, didn't I?" Sophie said. "But I think we can fix this. I'll call the original companies for both the stage and the portaloos and see if they can help at short notice. If they can't, well there are a couple of others I can try, but it will mean arranging delivery from further away. I'll have to wear the extra costs. Cross your fingers for me."

"Do you want me to call them?"

"No." A small sigh. "I can do this. I want to do this. Not because they were my mistakes but because I need to believe I can get back to running my business."

"You will. I just hope I leave you enough of a business to run."

"You're doing great, Allie. I'll call you once I've got an update on the stage and toilets."

"Bye, little sis. I love you."

Allie ended the call and sent a quick text to Tarryn saying she'd sort the portaloos and not to worry about it. She uncurled herself from the couch and went over to the kitchenette and pulled a ready meal from the freezer for lunch and put it in the microwave. For a moment, her mouth watered in memory of Will's beef en croute with crispy potatoes and fresh vegetables. Real food, not this cardboard imitation spinning in the microwave. Now she didn't have Kirkland & Partners sucking her time and energy, maybe she could again start to cook real food. That would be her next project.

The microwave dinged and she removed her lunch. Homecooked food would have to wait. She pulled her laptop over to browse while she ate. A notification popped up in her email of matches for her job search. She huffed a breath. The jobs she'd applied for in Sydney had gone nowhere. Oh, she'd had a couple of interviews followed by polite rejections. Was Kirkland still badmouthing her? Her lips tightened. Probably.

She scrolled, eliminating positions too junior, too senior, or with salaries so far below the industry standard they were laughable.

One particular ad caught her eye, and her breath caught. An intermediate accountant's position in Byron Bay with a generous salary and benefits. Her hand stilled on the mouse. The advert stated it was suitable for remote working as long as the successful applicant was willing to visit regional towns in the Byron Bay area once per month. Allie scanned the list of towns. Quandong was the last one mentioned.

She could apply for this, travel up once per month. Maybe she could stay in Kirra's Airbnb each time, eat at Thai Dreams, visit The Hollowman, catch up with Will and Garrett. And Tarryn.

Her breath left her chest in a whoosh. She couldn't apply. Not now. While people in Quandong knew Sophie had a sister, they didn't know she had a twin. It was simply too close. What if she applied and then bumped into someone she knew while attending an interview? And if she got the job, how could she reappear in Quandong as someone different? It was hard enough, pretending to be Sophie. But the deceptions would pile up if she then reappeared as Sophie's sister, Allie. How could she double-deceive these people who were becoming her friends?

No. There were simply too many potential difficulties. Her fingers stilled on the keyboard for a moment, and she wished she could simply click the *Apply Now* button.

Instead, she clicked the back button and resumed searching the available jobs in Sydney.

Tarryn turned the mug of coffee one-eighty and watched Will as he bustled around his kitchen. "I probably shouldn't have been so snippy with Sophie, but I didn't appreciate being thrown to the wolves. She'll be swanning off back to Sydney soon, but I'll still be here, doing my metalwork and paying my bills with odd jobs. And if people think I mess up those jobs, then I won't get as many. Phyll glared at me. I think she thought it was my fault the bloody portaloos weren't ordered." She drummed a pattern on the counter with her free hand. "This festival seems to be in shaky hands all of a sudden."

"I'm sure it's fine," Will pulled a tray of almond biscuits out the oven, set them on the counter, and slapped Tarryn's hand away when she reached for one. "Let them cool first."

"Sometimes, Sophie looks unsure, as if she doesn't know what she's doing, and then she says she'll get back to us about whatever it is. She always does, but she's a bit vague for someone who's supposedly the expert."

"We checked out her business beforehand. Phyll and Kirra met her—they said she was genuine and pleasant." He squinted at her. "I thought you liked her? That the two of you were getting along."

"I do like her. Most of the time, anyway, when she's not sniping at me. But liking someone doesn't mean you don't question their suitability for the job." She reached for a biscuit again and this time Will just watched her with pursed lips. Tarryn took a bite then fanned her mouth. "Hot."

"I warned you." Will smirked. "Common sense should have told you. Should I question your suitability for working with red-hot metal if you don't know when something's going to burn?"

"You don't have to ram it home. Maybe I'm being a bit hard on Sophie. She's come up with some great ideas—"

"Like the vote for the fake-wedding couple."

"That's a fantastic idea, as long as I'm not part of the chosen couple. Then it's a terrible idea."

Will snorted. "Who better?"

"You and Garrett. I voted for you. You've probably got it sewn up."

Will's phone pinged with a text, and he picked it up to read it. "It's from Kirra." He grinned. "She says, *I've just voted for the fake couple. Who do you think I voted for?* Then there's a whole line of winking emojis."

"There you go. She voted for you and Garrett. Why else would she send you that?"

"Why else indeed," Will murmured.

Chapter 11

THE PAJERO JOUNCED OVER THE potholed dirt that passed for Tarryn's driveway, making the box of metal clips and pins clatter on the back seat. Allie studied the corrugated iron shed in front of her. Did Tarryn live there? One end of the barn-like structure was open sided, the rest closed in. Smoke coiled from a chimney, and a veranda shaded a low table and two chairs which looked out over a fenced paddock and a dam to the forest beyond.

She parked near the open end of the shed and got out. A magpie gargled its song, and a couple of willy wagtails twittered at her from the roof. A strange whooshing sound came from the shed.

Leaving the box of clips in the car, she followed the noise.

One side of the barn was sectioned off, and the floor was covered in straw. Two long-necked furry animals stood chewing in the enclosure. Their big, dark eyes, surrounded by the longest eyelashes Allie had ever seen, watched her enter. *Oh! The darlings!* One of the alpacas was dark brown, the other a pale grey. What had Tarryn said about them? She couldn't remember if they were friendly, but if Tarryn was going to let her meet them, she thought it would be okay. Cautiously, she approached their stall, crooning nonsense in a low voice. The grey one stood her ground, watching with a curious expression, but the brown one flattened her ears and moved away. *A bit like her owner.*

Allie stood by the bar forming the side of the stall and held out her hand. The grey alpaca—was that Ally or Elly?—came closer until she reached out and blew hot breath over Allie's hand. Apparently satisfied Allie was a friend, she took the final few steps and allowed Allie to stroke her fuzzy neck.

The whooshing noise stopped, and both alpacas swung their heads in that direction. Allie turned too. Tarryn had her back to them, peeling off heavy gauntlets and lifting away a protective face mask. The structure in front of her was of a great bird in mid stride. The neck, body, and long legs were complete, but there was no head. Allie caught her breath. Even headless, the sculpture was recognisable as an emu, and the metalwork contained a caught-in-motion exuberance. Allie imagined it, wreathed in early-morning mist in Silver Creek Park. It was beautiful—and perfect for the park.

She walked toward Tarryn, calling out a hello.

Tarryn swung around, and her face cracked a small smile. "So you found me. Good."

"Your directions were good. Interesting place you've got here." Allie subdued her reaction to that small smile, pushing down her own answering one. This was business. Nothing more. She waved at what she could now see was a workshop area filled with stacks of rusting iron and half-finished sculptures.

"Is 'interesting' a polite way of saying I live in a junk yard?" Tarryn's smile widened.

"Maybe." Allie returned her smile as a feeling of relief thrummed through her. Only now did she let herself admit she'd been worried about the visit. But Tarryn didn't seem to hold a grudge from their last meeting. "This is amazing." She walked around to the other side of the emu and bent to see how the "feathers" were made with overlapping steel plate. "It must have taken a long time to do this."

"Longer than I'd like—but I've been busy with other things."

Of course. "Hopefully you'll have some more time soon."

"That's the idea. I won't take on any extra work for a while after Gay Bells." She put down her gloves on a bench. "You've brought the clips?"

"In the car. I'll get them."

"Thanks." Tarryn hesitated. "Would you like a coffee? I was about to stop for one."

An olive branch? Whatever it was, a coffee would be welcome. "I'd like that, thank you."

"When you've got the clips, come through there"—she pointed to a door half-hidden by a pile of rusty barbed wire—"and I'll put the kettle on."

Tarryn's living space was more spacious than it appeared from the outside and cosy from a pot-belly stove pumping heat into the room, A kitchen area took up one corner with long benches of polished steel and a metal "tree" holding all manner of pots and pans on its branches. The tree spread overlapping metal leaves over the ceiling above the stove—no doubt to reflect rising heat back into the room. The effect was both beautiful and practical.

Tarryn reached for coffee mugs. Freed of the heavy welding gloves, her bare arms were smooth and tan with a defined crease of muscle at her biceps. Her iron-grey hair was cropped even closer to her head—she must have found time to have a trim. Or maybe she did it herself—the tight curls had the even look of clippers. *Nice.* Allie let her gaze run back down from Tarryn's neat hair, along the strong ridge of nose, down to her surprisingly soft and sensual-looking lips. Strange how such a strong and angular woman as Tarryn had such pillowy lips.

A flash of Allie's one and only kiss with another woman leaped into her mind. What was the woman's name? Her mind drew a blank, but those lips had been as soft as clouds as she'd teased Allie's upper, then lower, lip with her own. There'd been a flick of tongue, a taste, a delicate sip, and Allie's hands had tightened convulsively on the woman's waist even as she'd pushed a hand into Allie's hair and her lips had coaxed Allie's apart and her tongue—

Allie jerked away from the memory. Yes, that kiss had been amazing. But Allie's motivation had been wrong. Unfair. She'd been purely looking for the experience of a same-sex kiss. It hadn't been fair to the woman, even though she'd given her reasons beforehand. She'd still taken advantage of a situation, and the guilt from that wrongness had... Had what?

Tarryn was talking, saying something with a quizzical expression on her face.

"I'm sorry, I was miles away. What did you say?" *Miles away reliving a kiss that shouldn't have happened.* Her face burned hot from more than the heat radiating from the pot-belly stove.

"I asked if you preferred a dark or medium roast." Tarryn held up two coffee pods.

"Medium, please." She shook herself back to the present and set the box of clips on the bench. "These clips will hold the banner over the street. The banner's still in my car, plus there's a box of yard signs for anyone who wants them. While you're out and about, you can offer them."

"Got it." Tarryn busied herself with her pod coffee machine. "Did you sort out the portaloos?" She swung around to face Allie and raised an eyebrow.

"Not yet," Allie admitted. Sophie had called to say her original supplier was trying to assist. "Hopefully tomorrow." Guilt crawled in her chest. The error was Sophie's—understandably so—and it very definitely wasn't Tarryn's fault. "I owe you an apology."

"You do, yes. I didn't enjoy being treated like an idiot in front of my friends."

"I'm sorry." How much should she say? The truth would make her—Sophie and her business—look incompetent. But Tarryn deserved some explanation. She bit her lip. "Soph—I— drafted an email to you with the second to-do list, but there was a typo in your address, and you wouldn't have received it."

"I see." Tarryn looked down at the coffee dripping into the mug. "So, rather than accept you could *possibly* be wrong, it was easier to blame me? I live in this town, Sophie. I rely on odd jobs like this to supplement my art. It's not helpful to have my proficiency questioned in such a public way."

"You're right. I'm—"

"Sorry?" Tarryn arched an eyebrow. "That's great between you and me. But when it next comes up at a planning meeting, it would be good if you acknowledged it wasn't my fault."

Allie smoothed her damp palms down the front of her jeans.

Tarryn's gaze followed the movement, licking down the front of Allie's thighs.

"I will."

Tarryn gave a short nod. "Good." She pushed the mug and the milk carton toward Allie and put a fresh pod in the machine. "You know, Sophie, sometimes I can't figure you out."

Allie's pulse kicked up a notch. "What do you mean?"

"You've got such great ideas, but other things... It's like you don't know how to cope. Phyll said your business was just kicking off, but you were very experienced. Even so, I wonder at times."

Allie licked her dry lips. "You said it. My business is new, and this is my biggest contract to date. I've managed bigger before, but not when it was all on my head. I just…want everything to be perfect." She gripped her mug tightly, willing Tarryn to accept the explanation.

"I guess." Tarryn's gaze didn't stray from her face. "Don't fuck this up, Sophie. My town is relying on you."

"I won't." And she wouldn't. At least, she hoped not. It wasn't only Quandong relying on her. Her twin stood to lose everything if she messed up.

Tarryn sipped her coffee, and Allie counted her heartbeat in her ears. After ten, she said, "So you and Phyll are counting the votes tomorrow."

"We are. I'm fairly sure Garrett and Will have it." Her lips tightened. "It better not be you and me. No offence, but I don't want to walk down any aisle with anyone, not even a pretend one."

"And certainly not with me." Allie huffed out a breath. "I get it. You're not my choice either."

Tarryn laughed. "I know. Your choice would be…let me guess…" She tapped a finger on her lips.

Allie tried not to look at her finger tapping on those full and curvaceous lips.

"Another femme, like you. Sweet, very girly. You'd both wear white dresses and carry matching bouquets."

"Wrong, actually." The words slipped out before she realised her mistake. Now Tarryn would ask what her type was, and that wasn't something she could answer truthfully.

"Then what is your type?"

An image of the woman who'd kissed her leaped into her mind. Ronnie, that was her name, short for Veronica. Tall, statuesque, blonde. Her jeans had hugged her curvy thighs lovingly, and her T-shirt had skimmed the top of those jeans, brief enough Allie had seen a strip of pale stomach and a belly ring.

Allie shrugged. "It's more about the whole person for me."

"The last woman you kissed, then. Or person. I shouldn't presume."

Allie strangled a nervous laugh. The last four people she'd kissed had all been male. But in the here and now, she was Sophie. And Sophie was firmly the L in LGBTQI+. If she talked about a male partner, it might make it harder for Sophie should she return to Quandong in the future. "Ronnie, short for Veronica. Amazon type. More sporty than femme."

"Relationship?"

"No. Just a kiss in the corridor of a dark nightclub."

"Good kiss?"

The memory made her lips curve into a smile. "The best." With a jolt, she realised it was true. As kisses went, it was at the top of the heap. She took a sip of coffee. But that didn't mean much. Relationships, sexuality, partners were all more than a kiss in a dark place. For a moment, she stared at Tarryn. What would she be like to kiss in a shadowy corner?

"Then that's another reason to hope we don't get picked as the fake couple." Tarryn's voice hummed with a smokiness that had been absent a minute ago. "Your eyes have darkened with the memory. The kiss must have been a scorcher. If we had to kiss as part of the ceremony, I couldn't compete."

"Right. But Will and Garrett will have it." Allie's gaze rested on Tarryn's lips. A low buzz started in her mind. What if she *had* to kiss Tarryn, if she had to find out if her lips were as soft as they looked. What if she had to hold her hand and smile and gaze into her eyes. If she had to pretend she was marrying a woman. *Oh my God.* It would be torture. Torture of the exquisite kind.

Tarryn stared at her with an inscrutable expression. "Earth to Sophie. You look quite horrified. Don't worry. It won't happen."

Allie forced a smile. Tarryn thought she looked horrified? *If only she knew.*

She took another mouthful of coffee to allow time for her whirling thoughts to subside.

"I met Ally and Elly," she said. "They're adorable. The grey one let me pet her."

"That's Elly. She's nicer natured than Ally, and better with strangers."

"I'm trying not to draw a comparison with my sister Allie," Allie smiled to show she was joking. "Elly was gorgeous. So soft."

"They'll both be shorn in another month or so when the weather gets warmer, so they're at their softest now. You can pet them again before you go."

Was that a hint? Allie drained the last mouthful of coffee and stood. "I need to leave. I'm meeting Phyll. She sent me a list of possible inclusions for the parade. Some are good. Others are impossible. And it's probably too late to include most of them anyway. You did well getting four dogs in wedding costumes."

"You underestimate Phyll. She'll ring up every person in Quandong who isn't already doing something in the parade and press them into it. That's why she gets to organise most things: because whether you like her methods or not, she gets things done."

"Still, she's treading on toes."

"That's Aunt Phyll."

"Is she your aunt on your mother's side or your father's?" Tarryn hadn't mentioned her parents—indeed, why would she—but she presumed they didn't live in Quandong. If so, Allie was sure she would have met them during the planning.

"She's my dad's sister. Mama is French, and she emigrated over here about forty years ago. She met my dad in a Sydney boarding house. They married and settled here because Aunt Phyll lived here and offered to let them rent a house she had. I was born in the local hospital."

"So you've always lived here?"

"No. Mama didn't like small-town living. She moved to Darwin, taking me with her. She's since moved back to Sydney. Dad stayed here. He's dead now, but he left me this land. I returned when I was seventeen." A brief smile. "Reckon I'll stay."

"It's a good place. I've never lived outside of a city, but I'd like to one day."

Tarryn touched Allie's hand. The touch held the warm comfort of a sheepskin glove. "If you want to, you'll make it happen."

For a moment, Allie sat there, staring at Tarryn's tan hand on her paler one. There were many things she could make happen—if she wanted to.

"I thought we could print some headshots of our most anti-gay politicians. Ones who constantly try to undermine gay rights," Phyll said. "Then we'll have people marching in the parade with a huge cardboard cut-out of the faces over their own. We'll sell those powder bombs they use for the colour runs, and people can bomb the politicians' faces, turning them into rainbows."

Allie's mouth hung open for a moment. "That's a great idea, Phyll. But I'm not sure we can organise it in time. We'll need the cut-outs, source enough paint bombs to sell, and find volunteers who don't mind dressing up and having their clothes ruined."

"The powder washes out," Phyll said. "The school will do the printing for us, and even if we only have two or three of our most hated pollies, it will be enough. I can get the volunteers. Can you get the powder bombs?"

"If you can do the rest, I'll make sure we can. I'll get Tarryn on to it."

"Tarryn's a good girl." Phyll shot her a censorious glance. "Didn't deserve to be chewed out last time."

Allie fidgeted. "You're right. I've apologised. It wasn't her fault—it was mine. The email didn't go through."

Phyll gave a short nod. "Glad you apologised. Right thing to do."

"You'll be seeing her tomorrow," Allie said. "For the vote counting. You can check how she is then."

"Don't need to. You strike me as a genuine person, Sophie. One of the reasons we hired you. How are you getting on with my niece?"

"Fine." Allie pushed aside the thoughts of Tarryn's lips from the morning. "She's very efficient."

"I didn't mean that." Phyll's brows lowered. "If you both are voted as the fake couple, you'll need to look the part, y'know. All cosy-like."

"I doubt it'll be us. People will realise it's impractical with the last minute organising we'll both have to do."

"And people know I could do it blindfolded with one hand behind my back," Phyll shot back. "She's single, you know."

Allie sighed. "And so are you."

Phyll huffed a laugh. "Maybe not for much longer. Got my eye on a chicken farmer up the valley. You and Tarryn, though. Could be a match."

Allie's left eye started to twitch. How could Phyll possibly think that? She held up her hands. "Please don't go there. We're working together, that's all. And I'll be back in Sydney soon. Let's not complicate things." She took a deep breath, willing her nervous twitch away. It just flickered faster. "Now, I want to talk about the on-the-day running of things. Please don't take this wrong, Phyll, but I think you might be spreading yourself a bit thin. You're the point of contact for the wedding fair, and now you're very involved with the parade as well. If Tarryn and I were to be voted as the fake couple, there's no way you could also take that on."

Phyll hmphed. "Someone's got to do it. Kirra was organising the parade, but she's on the lead float as well, so someone needs to corral the participants, get them ready to go in the staging area, that sort of thing."

"Tarryn can do it."

"I don't think so." Phyll's chin jutted forward in a gesture that reminded Allie of Tarryn. "The wedding fair will mainly be organised the day before—that's the main fair day. And the wedding attire catwalk finishes before the parade starts."

"Still. There's not much time between the two. I think it best if Tarryn organises the staging area for the parade."

"Okay." Phyll capitulated with surprising ease. "Unless, of course"—her beady eyes nailed Allie—"Tarryn is half of the fake couple. If that's the case, I'll do the staging area. My assistant can handle the finish of the catwalk."

"I'm still concerned you're taking on too much." Allie laid a hand on Phyll's arm. "Why not let your assistant take over the catwalk anyway? It will give her a chance to come into her own."

Phyll's jaw pushed up. "I suppose she could manage. And if you and Tarryn are voted in, she'll have to."

"I'm sure it won't be us." Allie's pulse beat an erratic tattoo. Phyll seemed so sure. She wouldn't rig the vote, would she? But no. Tarryn was the second counter. Phyll would never get away with it.

"But it might be. That's settled, then. Now, I've arranged for the Irish dancers in the parade to do a quick turn on the catwalk. They'll dance in some of the younger, trendier clothes."

"That sounds fine," Allie said faintly. It seemed there was no besting Phyll.

Chapter 12

TARRYN BLEW A KISS TO Ally and Elly, snug in their stalls, and went out to her truck. After Sophie had left, she'd returned to finish welding the final few feathers on her emu, but her mind wasn't on it. The feathers drooped as if the emu were moulting.

Instead, she'd taken the yard signs to people she thought might display them. That had gone well until, when returning home, she'd found a couple of them pulled out and thrown onto the road. Obviously, not everyone in Quandong supported Gay Bells.

She'd made a point of talking to as many people as she could, reminding them to vote for the fake couple. And she'd been cheerleading for Garrett and Will and how they'd be fantastic and exuberant representatives for same-sex marriage.

"Not as pretty as a couple of lasses," one person said. Tarryn rolled her eyes at the old-fashioned sexism but offered a smile nonetheless. And, worryingly, another person said, "I thought you and the event woman from Sydney would be perfect. You've got a lot of support." Tarryn had tried to close that down but didn't know how convincing she'd been.

For a moment, irritation beat a tattoo in her head. Why the hell did people think she and Sophie would be good? They'd be *terrible*. Sophie as stiff as a soldier on parade; herself awkward and uncomfortable.

She pulled open the door of the fridge to figure what she could rustle up for dinner.

The morning had been strange, with Sophie in her space, cooing over the alpacas, apologising for her mistake, and talking about the last woman she'd kissed. There'd been a strange, unsettling sort of intimacy about the conversation, as if they were dancing around the elephant in the room, as if they were sizing each other up for something. Tarryn snorted. It could only be for the fake wedding, if, against all odds, she and Sophie were voted as the couple. But Sophie had looked at Tarryn's lips. Not just a glance; her look lingered. As if she were imagining kissing them.

In your dreams, Sophie.

Or in Tarryn's.

Kissing Sophie would be no hardship at all. Tarryn could all too easily imagine what her slender body would feel like in her arms. Like a sapling, like a wand, something pliable that would not break. Sophie had a fierce, strong core to her. And Tarryn was sure she would kiss like fire, with passion, with delight.

It was a pity she wouldn't find out.

Thoughts of kissing Sophie had driven her from contemplation of the contents of her fridge out to her car. Tonight was burger night at The Hollowman, and a thick, home-made burger with bacon and beetroot and chunky chips was just what she needed. Add in a couple of schooners of beer and someone to chat with who wasn't a tousle-haired event planner and her day would end well. Maybe she'd find an interesting woman to flirt with. A buzz rumbled through her lower body at the thought.

The carpark at The Hollowman was half empty. Tarryn entered through the back door and went up to the counter. Seth, the barman, served her beer, and she meandered her way to her usual seat at the counter.

A slim shape caught her eye. The woman had her back to Tarryn and was deep in conversation with Jason. The woman flicked back her hair and with a jolt, Tarryn realised it was Sophie.

Hell's bells and buckets of blood. Was there no escaping her? If she wasn't at Tarryn's home, she was in her head or she had to listen to others talk about her.

Jason caught her eye and nodded at her over Sophie's shoulder. He said something to Sophie, and she whipped around, meeting Tarryn's eyes with a smile.

Tarryn nodded back, then turned to face the bar. Maybe it was a work meeting. Maybe, Sophie had made another local friend.

Or, maybe, it was a date. Sophie had said it was more about the whole package, after all. A date to admire Jason's trading cards. Well, it kept him happy.

If it was work, Sophie hadn't mentioned it to her, so there was obviously no expectation she join them. Besides, she'd done her hours for the day. For the week, too, if she were honest, despite there still being two days left.

She sipped her schooner and discreetly checked out the rest of the patrons. No one she particularly wanted to talk to—no one who wouldn't want to discuss the festival or tease her about the fake couple for the wedding. And no available-looking women to catch her eye.

Sophie placed her hand on Jason's arm and laughed at something he said. Another tick in the date column.

Damn.

Tarryn pulled out her phone and browsed Facebook while she sipped her beer.

She was three-quarters of the way down the glass when someone hitched themselves onto the stool next to her.

"Hi," Sophie said. "I'm glad you're getting some downtime." She tilted her head at Tarryn's near-empty glass. "Care to join me for another one? Jason was showing me his Babe Ruth and Seiya Suzuki trading cards."

So it was some mutual interest bonding. The knot of tension in her stomach tightened. Strange. Why did she care if Sophie had a date? Pondering that kept her silent for long enough that Sophie said, "No worries if it's too much like work. I was going to have a glass of wine before I head home, but I can sit elsewhere."

She found her voice. "I don't want to interrupt your date."

A frown wrinkled on Sophie's forehead. "Date? Oh, you mean Jason. I'd be a bit miffed if all my date did was discuss trading cards and work." Sophie slid off the stool. "No worries, Tarryn, I don't want to interrupt your quiet time."

She jerked her thoughts back. "No, it's fine. Sorry, I was miles away for a moment." She put her phone down. "Too much fascinating clickbait. Please, sit."

Sophie sat more fully on the stool. "Same again?" She gestured at the glass.

"Thanks."

Sophie ordered from Seth, who returned with another schooner, a glass of white wine, and two menus. "If you're ordering food, kitchen's closing in twenty. Cookie's leaving early."

"Thanks." Tarryn pulled a menu across. "I don't know why I'm looking—I know what I want." She slanted a glance at Sophie. "Are you eating too?"

Sophie worried her lower lip with her teeth. "I've got some leftovers in the fridge."

Tarryn couldn't look away from her pink lip caught between even white teeth. "Burgers are five bucks off tonight. And they're good. I bet your leftovers are pasta and a jar of sauce with grated cheese. This is much better."

One corner of Sophie's mouth lifted. "Have you been looking in my fridge?"

"Lucky guess." She nodded at Seth, who returned. "The pork burger, please, with bacon, extra beetroot, and a side of BBQ sauce."

"You'd sold me until you said 'beetroot.'" Sophie scanned the menu. "Please, can I have a lamb burger with tzatziki but without the garlic sauce?"

Seth trotted off to place their orders.

"It's un-Australian not to have beetroot on your burger."

"It's also un-Australian not to have a fried egg with it, but you didn't order one."

"True. Guess I just like beetroot." Tarryn pulled a drink coaster closer and centred her glass on it. "The lamb burger's great too. Good call on no garlic sauce, though. Everyone you talk to tomorrow will thank you."

"It's that pungent, huh?"

"It is." Tarryn watched Sophie's lips form a smile. "You can tell who's planning on kissing someone by who asks for no garlic sauce."

Sophie turned so her posture mirrored Tarryn's. Their feet alternated on the rungs of their stools like interlocking pieces of a puzzle. "Is that so? What about people who are just polite enough not to stink of garlic in their meetings tomorrow?"

"True. And I didn't think you'd kiss Phyll anyway."

"I don't think she'd appreciate it." Sophie shifted her own glass to the middle of the coaster and appeared mesmerised by the straw-coloured wine. "I don't want to talk about work, but I do want to check you're okay after our chat this morning. I said to Phyll the mistake was mine when she raised it."

A shaft of warmth shot through Tarryn's chest. "Thanks. That was decent of you."

Sophie shrugged. "It was the right thing to do. So, is there anything else you want raise before we bury the subject?"

"No. I'm good."

Sophie gave a quick nod and took a sip of wine. "I loved meeting Ally and Elly this morning. Well, Elly, anyway. I'm not sure Ally took to me."

"Don't take it personally. She's standoffish with most new people. Elly's a little flirt."

Sophie laughed. "My sister Allie is the little flirt in our family."

"What does Allie do?"

Sophie looked down into her glass. "She's an accountant. Although she's not working at the moment."

"Taking a break?"

She pressed her lips together. "You could call it that. Bad situation at work. She…had to leave." She turned her glass around and took a gulp of wine.

Uh oh. Obviously a difficult subject. When Sophie set the glass down, Tarryn touched the back of her hand impulsively. "I'm sure she'll find a new position soon. Accountants are in demand, right? After all, who can navigate the tax system alone? I know I can't. Maybe Allie should do my taxes."

"Maybe. You wouldn't even have to come to Sydney. Many clients are remote now."

"Maybe I'll do that."

"I'll arrange a discount." Sophie shot her a sideways glance that sent Tarryn's insides fluttering. Any other time, any other woman who'd said those words in that low, teasing tone, and she'd pick up the flirtation. But with Sophie, she just wasn't sure.

"So, what will happen to your metal emu when she's finished?" Sophie asked. Her voice was back to its normal pitch. "Is it a commissioned work?"

"Not this one. But if I can come to a deal with the Council, I'm hoping it will go in Silver Creek Park."

"Really?" Sophie's smile lit up her face. "I thought this morning when I saw it how perfect it would be there. But what do you mean by a deal? Surely, they just pay the asking price?"

"In an ideal world, but this is a big piece, and the hours of work mean a steep cost. More than the council wants to pay. I'll get paid, yes, but not the value of the piece. But it'll be good exposure."

A tiny frown creased Sophie's forehead. "Surely you can get more exposure on social media? I doubt the council would offer an accountant half their fee for the exposure of doing their tax returns."

"I get most of my commissions via social media," Tarryn said. "But you're right. Somehow, it's okay to negotiate with creatives as their work is considered a passion project. Something they'd do anyway. Well, I would, but that doesn't mean I shouldn't be paid for it. Aren't we all supposed to love our jobs these days and have good work-life balance?"

"We are," Sophie murmured. "In an ideal world, everyone should be treated with respect and earn a living wage. Doesn't always happen, though."

"So we take what part of that perfect world we can get. And for me, that means I get to do what I love, hopefully have one of my sculptures on display in the town where I live and hopefully get paid enough to at least cover my costs."

"It's still not right, though." A wrinkle appeared between Sophie's eyes.

"If I had a dollar for every supposed 'influencer' who asks for a piece for free and says I'll get paid in 'exposure,' I'd be rich. At least with this, I'm giving back to the town."

"You're a good person, Tarryn. And good people get more beer." She caught Seth's eye.

He brought them refills and then returned with their food.

Tarryn's mouth watered. "Thank you. Every time, I come here, I swear I'm just going to move in upstairs and eat here every night."

"And leave Ally and Elly alone?" Sophie laughed. "I don't think so. They'd miss you."

"At least someone would." Tarryn took a chip and dunked it in her sauce. "Mm, good." She gave Seth a thumb's up.

Sophie eyed her plate. "This looks amazing. Although I'm kind of regretting not getting the garlic sauce now, and Phyll be damned."

"Next time."

Sophie ate tidily but with gusto, wiping her mouth after every few bites. Guess she was the fastidious type. For a second, Tarryn's mind sprang into overdrive. Was Sophie the careful type in other ways? Did she not like getting messy, sweaty, or dirty? She hadn't been fazed by the dust and muddle at Tarryn's place this morning, or by Elly-paca nibbling her hair. And now Sophie was licking the salt from her fingers. It was the most sensual thing Tarryn had seen in a while. Sophie's pink lips closing around her finger and sucking, then repeating the gesture with every other finger in turn. She finished with a swipe of her tongue over her index finger.

Tarryn's burger had been suspended between her mouth and the plate for the last few moments. She set it down with care, but the beetroot fell out anyway, landing on her shirt. Thank goodness Sophie didn't appear to have noticed her sudden fixation with her lips and tongue and fingers and… Tarryn's mind fizzed to white. When had she been obsessed with *anything* Sophie did, anyway?

"That's going to stain." Sophie pointed at the piece of beetroot still resting on Tarryn's chest, bleeding pink into her pale-yellow T-shirt.

She flicked it off. "I am a pro at beetroot stains. This isn't the first time. I'll soak it when I get home." Even if it meant she was now sitting there like a messy toddler. She should just tip her bowl of chips over her head and be done with it. Wasn't that what most two-year-olds did?

"At least put soda water on it," Sophie said.

Tarryn shrugged. "Then I'll be sitting here in a wet T-shirt, and it's not that kind of bar."

Sophie's gaze dropped from Tarryn's face in a leisurely perusal from her throat to her breasts.

Tarryn's breath caught in her throat. Sophie was honest-to-God checking out her breasts. But then Sophie said, "There's still a bit of beetroot on the left side. I'd flick it off for you, but that would be harassment given where it is."

Oh! Heat crawled up Tarryn's neck, and not for the first time she gave thanks her olive skin made her embarrassment less obvious. She squinted at her chest and removed the beetroot. "Thanks." An imp of mischief made her add, "But it wouldn't have been harassment if you'd done it."

Sophie tilted her head. "Wouldn't it? I'm sort of your boss. Even in a social setting, there are boundaries. I've just finished a work meeting. That's the sort of thing that gets HR departments in a tizzy, when—"

She'd heard enough of Sophie talking like a corporate drone, rabbiting on about bosses and workers as if Tarryn had no autonomy, no freedom.

Sophie wasn't her boss, not really, and, like it or not, they were having drinks and dinner together— not as boss and employee but as two people who sort of got along together, and maybe, just maybe, were sort of attracted to each other.

Maybe.

And maybe it was time she found out for sure.

She leaned forward and pressed her mouth against Sophie's, stopping the flow of words that came straight from an employee handbook, with her lips. Her mouth rested on Sophie's, and the heat and the softness of Sophie's lips made her head spin with their perfection, how well they fit with hers.

How much she wanted to deepen the kiss, take it further, and, yes, be glad Sophie hadn't had garlic sauce with her burger.

Sophie's lips parted slightly. Maybe it was a soundless *oh!* Of surprise? Or maybe it was an invitation, or maybe it was a gasp of annoyance.

Reason thumped into Tarryn's brain like a brick through a window. Kissing Sophie—even this half, not-quite-completed kiss—was not one of her better ideas. It was right up there with skinny dipping with her best male friend in high school who turned out to be not so immune to her as she—or he—had thought. She should pull back, make a joke about it, get out of this situation with some grace and a modicum of dignity. It had got her out of the sticky situation with her high-school mate back then, and maybe it would work now.

The trouble was, she didn't want to pull back, and couldn't think of a joke to save her life. Nothing to make this anything other than it was, which was a kiss she had initiated because, yes, she wanted to stop Sophie sounding so stuffy and corporate, but mainly because she'd wanted to know what her lips tasted like.

Tarryn's breath puffed on those lips now. And Sophie was still immobile. Was she stunned by the move? Was she in brain freeze? Was she frozen with something else, some mental fog that stopped her from pushing Tarryn away with a firm "no" even though that was what she wanted to do?

Tarryn wouldn't go where she wasn't wanted. If she'd read Sophie's mixed signals wrong, then the only thing left to do was apologise.

Another heartbeat.

Tarryn eased back, lifting her lips gently from Sophie's mouth, and sat back on her stool, her gaze searching Sophie's face for a hint of reaction.

Sophie swallowed. "That was…" Her words ended in a dried-up husk of breath. "That was unexpected."

Unexpected wasn't necessarily unwelcome. Or was it?

"Should I apologise?"

Sophie lifted a shoulder. "There's no need. But maybe you shouldn't do it again."

"Maybe?" She was pushing it. The drumbeat of her pulse jumping and juddering told her this was a risky move. "Or not in a public place? Or not while we're working together?" She licked her lips and saw Sophie's gaze follow the movement. "Or not at all?"

Sophie slid from the stool. "We're working together, Tarryn. This isn't a problem, though, unless we make it one."

"It's not a problem with me." Far from it. If all problems were as soft and delicious as Sophie's lips, then the world would be an easier place.

Sophie glanced around the bar before her look fixed in one direction.

Tarryn looked around as well. Seth polished a glass, staring intently down at his towel. Jason was talking with a customer in the corner. Had either of them noticed? Had the bar been this quiet…before? Tarryn followed the direction of Sophie's stare.

Kirra stood with one foot on the bar rail, watching them with a knowing smile. So, not so unnoticed, then. Kirra raised her glass to them and turned back to face the counter.

"It's getting late," Sophie said. Her gaze slid away from Kirra's rangy form back to Tarryn's face. "I'll see you tomorrow."

"Okay," Tarryn said through stiff lips. "And this?"

"I think it best if we forget about it. No drama, Tarryn."

She gathered her purse and left with a wave at Jason.

Shit. Tarryn expelled a big sigh and picked up a chip. Sophie hadn't even finished her meal, although her wine glass stood empty. Way to wreck a pleasant evening.

A noise at her side made her look up.

"Not so smooth tonight, girlfriend." Kirra's eyes radiated sympathy. Or was it amusement? In her turmoil, Tarryn wasn't entirely sure.

"I fucked up, didn't I?"

Kirra pursed her lips. "We all do what we have to do. I think it was the stealth bomber approach. Sophie strikes me as one who needs a bit more of a gentle easing in. More definite signals."

"Did I read her wrong?"

Kirra shrugged. "Only you can answer that. Maybe you did. Or maybe you didn't, and it was the public setting she didn't appreciate."

"She said I didn't need to apologise, but I think I do." Tarryn pressed the heels of her hands into her eyes. "Shit."

"So, tomorrow, apologise for being out of line and then drop the subject. I know an uncomfortable woman when I see one. Although…I'm not sure of the reason. But I do know I was right to promote you two for the fake couple. You are hot together. Seems like a lot of people agree too."

"You're campaigning for us to be the couple? Kirra, please don't."

"Campaigning is too strong a word. I'm just chatting with people in the café. Don't worry too much." She caught Seth's eye. "Another beer, girlfriend?"

"Yeah, thanks. Although I'll have to walk home."

"A cool night-time walk will straighten your head. Or you can crash at my place, if you prefer."

"I'll walk. But thanks."

Seth picked up her empty glasses. "Has Sophie left? She must have been in a hurry—she didn't pay for her meal."

Oh great. If Tarryn needed any more confirmation Sophie had been freaked by her kiss, she had just received it. "She had to leave unexpectedly. I'm paying her tab."

"No worries." Seth went off and returned with the drinks.

Kirra clinked glasses with her. "Here's to tomorrow being a better day."

Tarryn chuckled ruefully. "Nothing like starting from the bottom."

Chapter 13

ALLIE FLOPPED ON THE COUCH and stared out the window. It was only eight o'clock. In Sydney, she'd consider going out for the evening. When she had worked at Kirkland & Partners, she often would only be getting home at this time, but she'd still often go out. A drink with friends. Dinner with Leila, if she could get away for the evening—or around at her house if she couldn't. And of course, she often went out with Sophie, or they just hung out together at Sophie's house, chatting, eating takeaway, a enjoying a bottle of wine. It was just the two of them, looking out for each other, as they had done ever since they were fourteen and their parents had divorced.

It felt strange to be home this early after an evening out.

Yeah, but there's a reason for that.

Until Tarryn's unexpected kiss, she'd been enjoying the evening.

Once he'd stopped talking about trading cards, she'd enjoyed her conversation with Jason. He was friendly, fun, and attractive with an expressive, interesting face. In another time, another place, she'd have flirted with him, open to possibilities. But she couldn't do that here. Whether he responded or not, it would make things difficult for Sophie in the future.

And then Tarryn had happened and blown all thoughts of Jason clear out of her head like a nuclear explosion.

A bar, a friend, a glass of wine, a burger. It had the promise of a relaxed evening, of winding conversation, of getting to know an interesting person better. Sure, there'd been an edge of something that pushed past friendship. Allie curled her legs underneath her. Was this always the way when two women were out together? When one was definitely gay and the other was pretending to be? Or when one was definitely gay and the other was maybe a little bit gay and a lot bit straight?

Allie uncurled and went to get a glass of water. It was a cool evening, almost too cold to sit outside, but maybe the chill would clear her head. Not from the wine—she'd only had two glasses—but from the thoughts rocketing around her mind, beating off the inside of her skull, demanding to fly free. She slid open the door and went to sit outside.

She touched her lips. Tarryn had pressed her lips there, just holding the place, her mouth on Allie's. There's been no demand, no pushing forward, just a quiet offer she hadn't accepted.

But she'd wanted to.

And then, of course, Tarryn had withdrawn because what else was she to do? No decent person would push where they weren't wanted. But in those heartbeats when Tarryn's lips had rested on hers, Allie had lit up within, come alive in a way she hadn't for a long time. A flame had twisted in her belly—it was there now, tamped but still ready to flare. Maybe the spark had always been there, waiting for another woman's kiss like a fairy-tale princess. Maybe one long-ago kiss had buried a seed that was now starting to sprout.

She took a long drink of water and licked her lips. Tarryn's kiss. As kisses went, it was so gentle, so nonpresumptive that if she wanted to, she could brush it aside.

But she couldn't.

Allie's chest tightened as the truth beat its wings against her ribs. She'd wanted Tarryn to deepen the kiss. She'd been so close to placing her palms on the sides of Tarryn's head and urging her closer. She'd wanted the movement of lips meshing, mouths opening, tongues touching.

Instead, she'd frozen with that realisation. Then, afterwards, as she'd looked around the bar, looking anywhere except at Tarryn, she'd seen Kirra and the knowledge in her eyes. Oh, no doubt Kirra hadn't figured out Allie was a fraud. It was simply the knowledge that here were two women who wanted to take things further and for whatever reason...hadn't.

Allie leaned forward and stared down at the street. The streetlight on the corner spilled a pool of light into the darkness. Opposite, in the lit shopfront, mannequins posed in bright, rainbow clothes in honour of the festival. And a tall, solitary figure, hands pushed deep into the pockets of her fleece, strode along the street. Even in the low light, she could see tight, iron-grey curls.

Allie shrank into the shadow of the building.

As Tarryn drew level with Kirra's Kafé, she slowed and glanced up at the apartment above.

Allie's breath quickened, chest rising and falling in shallow pants as she remained still, as if any movement would draw Tarryn's gaze to her like a magnet. There was no way Tarryn could see her. It was too dark, too shadowy. For a moment, Tarryn remained staring up at the apartment, where a light burned in the living area. No doubt she could see it was empty, but she'd probably assume Allie was in the bedroom.

After a minute, Tarryn hunched her shoulders and continued on.

Allie's breath left her chest in a whoosh even as a hollow disappointment took its place.

Once she was sure Tarryn was gone, she stood and went back to the living room. She picked up her phone and pressed Sophie's number.

"Hey, best sister. How's things going up there? Fought any fires lately?"

Only the one in my heart.

"Nothing new. Just seeing how you're going with the portaloos?"

"Good news. The original company can supply. I'd say I charmed them into it, but the reality is they had a cancellation. And the stage, too, is sorted. It's a bit smaller than originally requested, but it should be big enough for what you need."

"That's great," Allie murmured. Portaloo problems had been sucked from her head in the last hour and replaced with Tarryn's kiss.

"So, have they found the fake couple yet?"

"Vote count is tomorrow night." And what, if after everything, the winners were her and Tarryn? Awkward, what. "There's a movement to try to vote Tarryn and myself as the couple. I've said it's not a great idea—we'll be needed on the ground and can't be swanning around in posh frocks. It's not what they're paying us for, after all."

"If that's what they want, then that's what they get," Sophie said.

Wait. What? Oh no. "I'm hoping a local couple, Garrett and Will, will win."

"Or not."

Wait, was that amusement in Sophie's voice? "This isn't funny, Soph. How can I possibly do this *and* organise a festival? I barely know what I'm doing as it is."

"You've done great so far, and the festival was always going to be organised at ground level by each of the committees. Your role is purely as overseer. So if you get voted in, well, I think it would be great if you did it. Think of the publicity for my business. An event planner is very much a background role, normally. But if publicity said the fake couple were Tarryn Harris and Sophie Lane of Sydney firm, Events Done Right, it would be awesome."

"I hadn't thought of that." Allie nibbled her lower lip.

"If you really don't want to do it, Al, well, of course I won't ask you to. You've done so much for me already." Sophie's voice had softened, taken on a concerned tone.

Allie closed her eyes. "Okay. If they draw us, I'll do it. But Tarryn isn't keen on this at all."

Sophie laughed. "If they vote you in, they've got the ultimate fake couple: a wedding hater and a straight woman."

Allie was silent as words beat in her throat. "And another thing. Tarryn kissed me this evening."

"And?" Sophie asked softly.

"And nothing. It was no grand passion. Just a closed-mouth press of lips."

"And?"

"And then she withdrew and asked if she should apologise. I said there was no need."

"And?"

"And what?" Allie passed a hand through her disordered hair.

"What did you feel? This is me, Al, you don't have to pretend, whatever the answer is."

"I liked it," she said in a small voice.

"That's good, isn't it?" Sophie said. "Someone you've connected with."

"I don't know. We seem to disagree as much as anything."

"There's no law saying you have to agree with a friend or a partner all the time. Look at me and Bree."

"I'm not sure Bree is a good example here."

"You're changing the subject. Okay, I'll run with it, but Allie…don't just blank out that kiss."

"Like I did the last time?" The knowledge settled in her chest. She hadn't let herself think about the last kiss after it happened. And now, maybe, she knew why. *Not so straight after all.*

"Yes. Like last time."

Allie bit her lip. She needed to think about this herself first before she talked about it more with Sophie. Which she would. Once she'd got it figured out for herself, tucked into orderly columns. And what would the heading be? *Bisexual? Pansexual? Straight with a bit of queer?* Or no label, just Allie and how she was. She shook her head. Later. She'd think about it later.

"Is Bree still helping you out?" she asked.

A hitch of breath came over the phone. "She is. In fact…she's moved in with me for a couple of weeks."

Words jumped into Allie's throat: snarky, pointed words about previous hurt and heartbreak and did Sophie really want to go there again, but she bit them back.

"I know what you're thinking," Sophie said. "And, yes, I'm careful. I'm guarding my heart this time. But she's different. Considerate, kind. And she's doing a lot for me."

"Are you sleeping with her?" Was there a script for these difficult conversations? If there was, she was probably doing it all wrong.

"I can barely move, I'm in fairly constant pain, and if someone touches my leg wrong, I scream. What do you think?"

"I'm sorry. That was a stupid question. And nosy."

"If you can't ask me, Al, well, no one can. At least I know she's not moved in for the earth-shaking sex."

Allie sighed. "I've never had earth-shaking sex. Good sex, yes, really great sex, definitely, but nothing that left me splayed out on the bed with my body turned to boneless mush and my mind singing. Not romance-novel sex. Have you?"

"I have, yeah. With Bree. I hope one day to experience that again with someone."

Envy and longing shot through her like an arrow. Would she ever have that? Her last boyfriend had been romantic, considerate, great in bed…but

somehow fell short of earth-shaking. She shook her head slightly and concentrated on Sophie. "With Bree?"

"I don't know." Sophie's sigh drifted down the line. "I can't say yet."

"I hope I get that too. One day."

"Maybe you've been looking in the wrong places."

Allie fell silent. The wrong places? Or with the wrong people? Maybe
she needed to open her mind to what her body was telling her. If a tentative
closed-mouth kiss could have her lit from within, surely it was time to think
about that.

Chapter 14

THE HOLLOWMAN WAS PACKED. TARRYN pushed her way to her usual seat at the bar to find Phyll already there, the three ballot boxes in front of her.

"I saved you a seat," Phyll boomed.

Jason approached and set a cocktail glass in front of her. "Tonight's house special: the Fake Marriage. It's a mix of things that shouldn't go together but actually do. It's got gin, rum, ginger beer—"

"It sounds lethal."

"One per person."

Tarryn looked around the crowded bar. It looked like half the town had turned out for the vote count. Garrett and Will were talking earnestly in a corner, Kirra and some of the sistergirls were chatting with the high school couple who'd volunteered. They were sweet and earnest. Tarryn hoped they'd win.

"Is Sophie here?" she asked. Her heart thumped against her ribs. She hadn't seen Sophie since the evening before and she wasn't sure if she was avoiding her. She'd had a nervous, churning feeling in her insides all day at the thought.

"Somewhere," Phyll said. "Which is good if you and she win."

"We won't win," Tarryn said firmly. "Garrett and Will have it."

"Don't be too sure." Phyll winked. "I voted for you and Sophie."

"Not helpful, Aunt Phyll."

"I can see the pair of you dressed in white—"

"Never!"

"—riding in an open-top Rolls Royce—"

"And where would we get one of those? The fake couple will ride on the back of the feedstore's ute!"

"—throwing rose petals at the crowd."

"I hate to burst your bubble, Aunt Phyll, but that's about three steps too far. But Will and Garrett will look adorable in white dresses."

Phyll tapped the voting boxes. "Let's see who wins."

Tarryn glanced around. Where was Sophie? She wanted to make the first meeting happen so she could stop stressing, wondering if Sophie was going to freeze her out. And then she was there. Tarryn sensed her standing just behind her shoulder before she saw her. Maybe it was a flick of her mussed blonde hair, maybe it was her scent—something indefinable that definitely wasn't perfume, but was uniquely Sophie, more than just scented bodywash and shampoo. Tarryn's fingers twitched on the Fake Marriage cocktail, and she took a sip to hide her flushed face.

"Hi." Sophie pushed her hands into the front pockets of her jeans and hunched her shoulders. "How are you both?"

"Good," said Phyll. "Ready to count."

Sophie waved at a couple of sheets of butcher's paper pinned up behind the bar. "That is Jason's idea. As well as the cocktail." She made a face. "If you two read out the votes, he'll tally them on the sheets. I talked him out of putting up betting odds."

"I'd say Will and Garrett were at short odds," Tarryn said.

Sophie scrunched her nose. It was endearing. As if she wasn't cute enough already. "You might be surprised. If you believe the betting, it's closer than you might think." She pressed some folded notes into Tarryn's hand. "Thank you for settling my tab last night. If it was more than this, please let me know."

"There's no need." Tarryn scanned her face. Was she okay, or just a good pretender?

Sophie gave a small smile, then turned away to watch Jason as he climbed onto a chair in front of the bar.

"Good people of Quandong," he said. "Welcome to the counting of the vote. Please come and get your free cocktail if you haven't already." He rattled a cocktail shaker full of what sounded like ball bearings. "Let the vote count begin!"

Tarryn sat on the vacant stool next to Phyll. "Let's start with the box from Kirra's Kafé."

Phyll nodded, unlocked the box, and drew out the first slip. "Will and Garrett." She pushed the slip across for Tarryn to read.

A wolf whistle as Jason wrote their names at the top of the butcher's paper and added one tick.

Tarryn plunged her hand into the box. Paper rustled around her fingers. How many votes were in here? It seemed like a lot. She drew one and unfolded it. "Casey and Kai." The high school couple. They bobbed their heads in unison, acknowledging the cheers.

Phyll nodded as she read the vote, then drew another slip. "Will and Garrett again."

The next two votes went to Euli and Bernice, the sistergirls.

The knot in Tarryn's guts loosened. As she'd thought, people were choosing locals they knew would enjoy doing it rather than an out-of-towner and the local who hated weddings. She managed a smile as she drew another slip. *Hell's bells and buckets of blood.* There was no way she couldn't read it, not with everyone staring at her. "Tarryn and Sophie."

More cheers, and Jason wrote their names on the paper with a flourish.

When she dared look at Sophie, her face was frozen in a polite smile, even as Kirra squeezed her arm and whispered something in her ear.

By the time the votes from the first box were counted, Tarryn and Sophie were leading Will and Garrett by one vote. She daren't look at Sophie, but she was sure her face would be as frozen in horror as her own. She forced a smile and applauded along with everyone else as Phyll read out the interim totals.

"Here's to the next box changing things," she muttered under her breath.

The press of bodies surrounding her and Phyll grew closer as people tried to see each vote. By the time the second box was completed, Tarryn and Sophie were five votes ahead.

Tarryn's armpits oozed sweat, and a buzz of nerves juddered in her throat. This was not supposed to happen. She shot a glance at Sophie and found her leaning against the bar away from the knot of people surrounding her and Phyll, sipping a glass of wine.

The third box took the longest to count. Not because there were more votes but because the whooping and cheers after each vote was read out went on longer each time. Garrett and Will had their arms around each other and were cheering the loudest. The sistergirls had already conceded the race and were asking if they could allocate their preferences.

Phyll shot them a steely glance. "This isn't the general election; it doesn't work like that."

The vote was neck and neck between Tarryn and Sophie and Will and Garrett when Phyll tipped the box up, emptying the final three votes onto the counter.

A buzz of panic pushed into Tarryn's throat. "I concede to Will and Garrett. I withdraw."

"You can't!" It seemed everyone in the room shouted the words.

Will winked. "We'll see this through."

The next vote was for Sophie and Tarryn.

Jason put the tick on the board amid whoops and cheers louder than the AFL grand final in extra time.

The second vote went to Will and Garrett.

Relief thundered through Tarryn's blood. *Just one more.* One more and this crazy idea could be put to bed. She met Sophie's eyes over the heads of the people sitting next to her. Sophie had a deer in headlights look, and her fingers clenched the stem of her wineglass.

"Last vote," shouted Phyll. "Winner takes all!"

"What if it's for Casey and Kai?" someone shouted. "We'll have a tie."

"We'll meet that if it happens." Phyll unfolded the slip and peeked. "Oh my."

"What does it say?" Jason asked. "C'mon Phyll. Don't hold back."

This is so not good. Tarryn's breath rasped in her throat, and she seriously considered just walking out, pushing through the crowd, and driving home as if the hounds of hell were after her. That would surely show her feelings on this.

But she'd promised.

Phyll unfolded the slip and threw it on the counter. "Tarryn and Sophie."

Oh fucking fuck it. It was the only word to properly to express her thoughts. Tarryn slapped both hands on her head. *I can't do this. Not the dress, not the fake vows. And the kiss? What about the kiss?*

She searched for Sophie in the crowd, but she wasn't where she'd been a moment ago. Had she left? Then she appeared next to Phyll.

"Quandong has spoken." Sophie winked at Garrett and Will. "Sorry, guys. Close but no cigar. The women have it."

"And to think we both voted for you," Will said. "Imagine if we hadn't."

"But you did. Well fought. If I was having persons of honour, I would pick you two."

Garrett kissed her cheek. "Congratulations on your big day."

Sophie laughed, then came across to Tarryn. "Congratulations to you, future fake wife."

How come she was so perky about this? Previously, Sophie had been nearly as horrified as she was. She frowned. What had changed? Nothing she could see.

Nothing except they'd kissed.

Something sweet hummed in Tarryn's blood. Was that it? Was Sophie looking forward to a replay of the kiss after the wedding ceremony? Was it a way of keeping to whatever rules and limits she'd set herself about not kissing employees, not mixing business with pleasure, not kissing *Tarryn?* Well, there was one way to find out.

"Congratulations, my dear fake fiancé." She leaned forward and set her lips to Sophie's, lingering just long enough to absorb her silent *oh.* Tarryn smiled against Sophie's lips and withdrew. No need to give the packed bar a total show. That was enough to show she'd play her part.

Sophie's cheeks were that adorable shade of pink once more. Tarryn had never known anyone to blush as much as Sophie. It was rather cute. Tarryn squeezed her hand. "Okay?" she murmured.

"Okay." One side of Sophie's mouth quirked up. "We can do this."

"Sophie, Tarryn, wait up." Running feet slapped the pavement as Allie made her way to The Hollowman with Tarryn to discuss more details of the afterparty with Jason.

Kirra puffed up to them and thrust a piece of paper at Allie. "I'm beyond ropeable. I'm so livid, I could spit blood in their eyes. Take a look."

Allie scanned the printed email. "One Union for Christ want to have a float in the parade. They're a"—she glanced at the footer of their email—"fundamentalist religious group who believe marriage is between one man and one woman."

"They're bigoted hatemongers," Kirra snarled.

Tarryn nodded. "They support conversion therapy."

"Because being gay is a 'lifestyle choice.'" Kirra held out her hand for the email. "I'm turning them down, of course. They better hope I've had my happy pills when I do, otherwise they're going to get a blast."

"Maybe we shouldn't turn them down," Allie said slowly. "They'll parade, and they'll get booed. Maybe that would be a bigger statement than not letting them take part."

Tarryn's eyes widened. "Booed? These people don't *care*. They just want to be out there, visible, invading our spaces. This group is one of the worst."

"We're not accepting them, Sophie, and that's final." Kirra narrowed her eyes. "If we give them even a toehold, they'll be back. In our spaces—our *safe* spaces—in our faces. This festival is a happy, celebratory event. Having One Union for Christ on a fucking truck handing out leaflets and lollipops will make it anything but happy. Do you know how many safe spaces there are for queer people in regional areas, particularly queer Aboriginal people? For the sistergirls? Not fucking many. Quandong is one, and while I can't keep everyone out who threatens us, I can *fucking try*."

Tarryn nodded and slipped an arm around Kirra's waist. "We're welcoming, yes, but there are limits. And the One Fucking Union is a non-negotiable limit." She frowned. "Why are you even advocating for their inclusion? You must know what they're like. Have they never handed you a leaflet, got in your face to tell you you're going to Hell—as if that's a threat. If there is a Hell, well, all my friends will be there based on what *they* say."

Allie's stomach churned. This was her biggest mistake yet. Of course she'd heard of One Union, but, of course, she'd never had any first-hand knowledge of what they were like. Sophie may have mentioned them, but she tended to laugh off the haters.

She hadn't known, and while she considered herself an ally to the rainbow family, she couldn't know what it was like. Not completely. Seeing Kirra wild-eyed and shaking. Seeing Tarryn so cold, like an unsheathed knife, brought it home. While she was part of their community as an ally, she wasn't enmeshed in it as Kirra and Tarryn were. As Sophie was. She didn't know how it felt to be on the receiving end of such hate—not for being who she was.

"I'm sorry," she said in a low voice. "Of course we'll refuse them. Do you want me to do it?"

"No." Kirra's shoulders drooped. "I'll do it. Maybe even politely. But I'll be firm and say there is no place for them here."

"Have you not come up against them, Sophie?" Tarryn asked. There was still a wrinkle between her eyes.

"No, not directly. Maybe it's because I live in Sydney. Maybe it's because I"—she swallowed—"often pass as straight. Maybe it's because there are so many safe spaces for us in the city. It's not as…intense as it is here." She put a hand on Kirra's arm. "Are you okay?"

Kirra covered it with her other hand. "I will be. Thanks."

"And you, Tarryn?"

"I'm fine. I just don't give people like them any headspace. Although it's hard to keep them out sometimes, and not safe to ignore their existence completely."

Allie bit her lip. An uncomfortable feeling wound its way up her chest to sit in her throat. *Fraud.* She was a fraud, and however well-meaning her and Sophie's deception was, it was still wrong.

But what could she do now? When the festival was only days away? When Sophie was depending on her?

Nothing.

She had to see this through.

Later that evening, Allie sat on the couch flicking through the brochures of the wedding hire shops that had offered to dress the fake wedding couple. White, lace, more white, sweetheart necklines, and swooping low backs. While she'd always thought she'd wear a white dress if she got married, she wasn't comfortable wearing one for the fake wedding. And what if she dropped something on it? Or someone spilled red wine? They would be mingling with the crowd at the afterparty—wearing white would be a disaster. Surely the shop would want their dress back in a wearable state.

She shuffled the definite no-go brochures to one side and picked up the remaining four. Maybe this one. The front showed two brides, one in a dazzling white tux, the other in a leaf-green dress and a crown of jasmine on her head. Both brides wore matching red hi-top sneakers. That might work, if Tarryn could be persuaded. They were meeting tomorrow with Phyll and Jason to go over the final arrangements for the parade and ceremony. She'd suggest it then.

Her mobile rang, and she glanced at the screen then answered.

"Hey, Leila, how's things in the evil corporate?"

"Evil," Leila said with a sigh. "My great new assistant left—she's got a job with a start-up—and hasn't been replaced. I haven't set foot outside the office at lunchtime since you and I had lunch, and I'm working sixty-hour weeks. Life's just peachy, let me tell you."

"Poor you. Maybe it's time to look for another job? One where you're appreciated."

"And where I can see Hammie for longer than five minutes before he has to go to bed."

"That too. So Hammie isn't going by Muhammad yet?"

"He's trying. Old habits die hard. Lewis is better at it than me. After all, he's the one feeding Hammie and getting him ready for bed these days. But I didn't call you to whinge. I called to see how you are, and also to let you know something interesting happened today."

"I'm fine, Leila, thank you for asking. I'm helping Sophie with her business. It's…interesting. Maybe I'll have a new career at the end of this."

"Maybe. It's got to be better than the last one. Now, the news. We've just lost another major client. There are a lot of closed-door meetings and worried looking people in corner offices. Nothing official's been said—we're not supposed to know, of course—but the rumour is someone screwed up the client's Business Activity Statements. Sound familiar?"

"It does." Allie's heart picked up speed. Maybe they'd find out who did it, maybe they'd clear her name. *Right. More likely…* "Which client? Are they going to pin that on me as well?"

"I shouldn't tell you as you're not an employee anymore, but it's Richard Martin. His waste disposal business is under investigation by the Australian Tax Office, and he came storming into the office to see your old boss."

"I never worked on that file," Allie said slowly. "Craig kept that one close."

"Interesting," Leila said. Her voice hummed with satisfaction. "So who's going to get the blame for this?"

"They'll still blame me." Acid burned Allie's gut. "I'm the perfect scapegoat. They won't let a partner take the blame—Craig will get off. He'll tell the client it was a junior accountant who has already left the firm. Then he'll take Richard out for a boozy lunch, and they'll pat each other on the back and say how hard it is to get decent staff these days."

"Until the next time," Leila said. "I wonder how many clients he tried this on? And why?"

"It lowers their tax bill, and the client thinks Kirkland is wonderful—until the ATO comes knocking."

"When are you back in Sydney?" Leila asked.

"Nearly two weeks," Allie said. "Lunch when I'm back?"

"You bet. Maybe I'll have new and exciting news for you—like a new job, or Craig getting fired, or me finally seeing Hammie at breakfast *and* dinner on the same day."

"That last one would be a great start. Send him and Lewis my love."

"I will. I have to go. Bye, Allie. I'm already looking forward to seeing you."

"You too. Look out for yourself at work."

"I will." Leila's voice was grim. "Don't worry."

Allie ended the call and sat back amid the scattered brochures with a sigh. She had no doubt Craig would blame her for Richard Martin's mess. She tightened her lips. What could she do to avoid that? So where did that leave her? She could call Richard Martin and proclaim her innocence—but why would he believe her word against that of a partner? She could call the Australian Tax Office as a whistle-blower and report Kirkland for their practices. But she didn't have proof—only what had happened to her, and Leila's story about Richard Martin. That wasn't enough to go on. She pressed the heels of her palms to her eyes. She had to do something. The question was what.

She got up from the couch, poured herself a glass of water, and considered her scanty groceries. For a second, the memory of the burger at The Hollowman tempted her. But that burger would forever be entwined with the memory of Tarryn's lips on hers. As they had been again today.

Allie pressed a finger to her own lips, remembering. Imagining where the kiss might have gone from there.

With a frustrated grunt, she closed the cupboard door. She'd get take-away from Thai Dreams. She'd be less likely to run into Tarryn or have to talk with Jason about the festival.

Chapter 15

"I voted for you and the event planner woman."

Tarryn turned away from the feedstore counter where she was ordering hay for the alpacas and forced a smile at the person who'd spoken. Since the vote, it seemed half the town had said the same. "Thanks." She swung back to face the feedstore's owner.

"The hay will be delivered Tuesday," Larry said.

Tarryn nodded, grateful to escape more wedding chat. "That's great. Thanks." She handed over her credit card and once the transaction was complete, fled the store. If she hurried, she wouldn't be late for the planning session.

Sophie's car was already outside The Hollowman when she pushed open the back door and entered the bar.

"Here's our second blushing bride." Phyll's voice boomed out.

Tarryn winced but covered it quickly.

As well as Sophie, Phyll, and Jason, a grey-haired older woman dressed in motorcycle leathers sat by the counter stirring a black coffee as thick as tar.

"George." The woman stood and shook Tarryn's hand in a firm grip. "It's my real name. My mother was an Enid Blyton fan."

"Tarryn." She nodded and smiled, easing her hand from the woman's clasp.

"George is the celebrant for your wedding," Phyll said.

A curl of irritation spiked. "Fake wedding."

George shot her a half-smile. "It's all the same as far as I'm concerned. The only difference will be the ceremony won't be legally binding. Do you have vows or anything you want to use?"

"No," Tarryn and Sophie said simultaneously.

At least they were in agreement over something.

George blinked. "Then we'll go with the standard wording. Are you happy just to use first names?"

"That's fine by me," Sophie said.

Tarryn nodded.

"Gotcha. I'll give a short introduction about marriage—we want this to feel real, to make the punters get the weepy-in-love factor, then go straight to the do-you-take-this-woman part. Are you having rings?"

"No rings," Tarryn said.

"Then you'll kiss—are you going to kiss?" George looked from Tarryn to Sophie and back again.

Tarryn glanced at Sophie. Her gaze was downcast, but there was a slight smile on her lips.

"We'll kiss," Sophie said. "It's got to look real, right? Are you okay with that, Tarryn?"

Sophie wanted to kiss her again. Her heart thumped erratically at the thought.

"Sure." Tarryn slanted a glance at Sophie.

A connection, sweet and fine, leaped into life between them. Sophie's gaze had her trapped, and she couldn't look away. She didn't want to look away. Her fingers twitched with the need to reach out, take Sophie's hand, and stroke her thumb over the soft-looking skin on the inside of her wrist. Another kiss? Hell, yeah.

"We'll run through the entire ceremony," George said. "That's why I'm here."

Tarryn's blood thrummed. She'd get that kiss sooner than she thought. And another after that. And then, well, that was up to them.

Jason indicated the room where the chairs and tables were pushed back to make an open space. "We're ready."

Sophie slanted a gaze at Phyll. "When was this arranged? I wasn't aware we were doing this now."

Phyll harrumphed. "Thought one of you would make an excuse and bail. Best not to give you the opportunity."

"I'm a professional. Tarryn lives here. We both want this to work." Sophie's cool gaze sliced into Phyll, who had the grace to look embarrassed.

"Phyll and I are the audience," Jason said. "George, you stand by the bar. Sophie and Tarryn…you'll enter one from each side of the stage and come to stand in front of George."

Tarryn stuck her hands in her pockets and sauntered off to the other side of the pretend stage. Thoughts of the practice kiss had her lit, but right now, self-consciousness and unease were winning. Was she expected to glide delicately with sparkling eyes and a lovestruck expression? *Good luck with that.*

George stood in front of the bar, a sturdy figure in her black biker gear. She extended a hand to each of them.

"Tarryn and Sophie."

Tarryn arranged her face into what she hoped was a loving smile and strode across to George. A quick glance at Sophie showed her walking in a slow and stately fashion, her tiny steps almost soundless on the wooden floor. Her gaze was fixed on Tarryn, and she wore a soft smile.

She reached George and placed her hand in hers.

"Stop." Phyll shook her head. "Sophie, you were lovely. Tarryn dear, can you at least try to look like you want to be there? You're marrying the love of your life. Aim to reach George at the same time as Sophie, and then you both place your hands in hers."

Okay, she could do this. Tarryn turned on her heel and went back to the side of the stage.

George extended her hands with a flourish. "Tarryn and Sophie."

With a quick glance at Sophie, Tarryn tried to match her slow pace, but it turned into an ungainly sort of shuffle, as she stared at her feet trying to minimise their natural stride. At least they both reached George at the same time and placed their hands in hers.

"Friends, we are gathered here today to witness the marriage of Tarryn and Sophie." George drew them closer and placed Sophie's hand in Tarryn's.

The touch of her skin was almost a physical shock. Soft, warm, and trembling ever so slightly, as if with the nerves of a real marriage.

"Better," Phyll said, "but Tarryn, you looked like you were walking to your doom. Can you at least smile?"

"I am smiling," said Tarryn through gritted teeth.

"You're grimacing," Jason said. "Probably with concentration, but it isn't a happy look."

"Third time's a charm," George said in a bracing tone.

Tarryn shuffled back to the side, trying not to let her irritation show. There were a hundred things she could be doing right now—even her overdue dental visit would be preferable.

With a practiced smile, George again extended her hands. "Tarryn and Sophie."

Small steps, head up, smile. You're going to see Sophie. Smile. Somehow, she made it to George at the same time as Sophie, and she placed her hand in George's.

"Friends, we are gathered here today to witness the marriage of Tarryn and Sophie." George stepped back and joined Tarryn's hand with Sophie's.

The electric buzz of Sophie's touch was even more intense than last time. Sophie was staring at her as if Tarryn was her heart and soul, her eternal love. *How does she do it?* Tarryn gazed back, pushing down the uncomfortable nature of the pretend wedding and channeling her attraction to Sophie.

George was saying something about the joining of two hearts and two women in a bond of love and matrimony. The words washed over her, and she stayed focussed on Sophie, on her intense grey eyes, the soft pink flush on her cheeks, her full smiling lips and narrow chin. Her blonde hair was messy, as if she'd washed it this morning and then finger-combed it. It fell in artful disarray to just below her ears.

Perfect.

The word drifted into Tarryn's mind, and she tightened her fingers on Sophie's. How long until she could kiss her? She kept the smile until her cheeks ached.

"Oh, that won't do at all." Phyll marched up to them. "Sophie and Tarryn, move a little further apart. You're blocking George. Keep holding hands, though. Both hands. Face each other, side-on to the audience. We don't want to see your backs. And Tarryn, I know you're trying, dear, but you look like a cow waiting to be milked. More emotion in your face, please."

"I'm a metalworker not an Oscar winner," Tarryn snapped.

"Noted. But can you try a bit harder? Please?" Phyll asked.

"We'll continue from here," George said.

Sophie shuffled around until she was side-on to the audience and took Tarryn's other hand in hers. "You're doing great," she whispered. "It will get easier."

"When?" Tarryn blew out a breath.

"When we kiss." Sophie arched an eyebrow, and her eyes sparkled with mischief.

An explosion of heat soared up into Tarryn's chest. Oh yes. It would all be worthwhile then. She stifled a laugh. Unless Phyll wanted to stage-manage their kiss as well. She could imagine her getting up close, nudging them into place.

"Wait and see." Tarryn wiggled her eyebrows at Sophie and winked.

Phyll sighed. "You shouldn't be talking. You're supposed to be listening to George's words on the importance of marriage."

"They're figuring out how best to make it work," George said. "Isn't that right, girls?"

She'd overlook the "girls" seeing as how George had saved them from another of Phyll's lectures. And to George, all butch swagger in her leathers, they probably were just girls.

"Now the important part," George said. "Do you, Sophie, take this woman, Tarryn, to be—do you have a preference as to the term? Wife? Partner? Spouse?"

Tarryn shrugged. "Whatever."

"Go with wife," Phyll said. "It's more traditional."

"Your wedded wife," George continued.

"I do," Sophie said. Her hands shook in Tarryn's.

"And do you, Tarryn, take this woman, Sophie, to be your wedded wife?"

Tarryn opened her mouth to say the words, but they stuck in her throat. Fake or not, the words were everything she'd always objected to. Possession, ownership, an outdated institution where women were subservient to men— even if it was now two women getting married. She tried again, but the words still wouldn't come. They wedged in her throat, her breath caught behind them.

George regarded her calmly. "Let's move on. Tarryn obviously knows the words." She cleared her throat. "I now pronounce you wed. You may kiss."

Sophie took the first step, sliding her palms from Tarryn's hands up her forearms to where her sweatshirt bunched below her elbows. She turned her hands and gripped Tarryn's elbows, tugging her closer.

Tarryn's body lit from within as Sophie pressed against her so their upper bodies touched.

"Pretend," she whispered before her lips touched down lightly on Tarryn's.

There was magic in the air, fizzing around them like a corona. Lips touching, bodies pressing, and then the tip of Sophie's tongue swiped across Tarryn's lips. Just once. Just lightly. Just a touch that should have done nothing but did *everything*. Tarryn's breath hitched in her throat, then she wrapped one arm around Sophie's waist while the other trailed up her arm to push into her hair. Her mouth opened on a soundless sigh, and then, in a brief mesh of tongues and lips, the kiss took wings.

"I think they've got that part sorted." George's amused voice broke through the haze in Tarryn's mind.

Sophie stiffened in her arms and shifted away, just a tiny amount, but enough for Tarryn to regain her senses. She'd just kissed Sophie—properly kissed Sophie—with Phyll and Jason looking on. She kept her eyes locked on Sophie, unwilling to find out what was on Phyll's face. When she finally dared to look, Phyll met her gaze with a small nod. Jason busied himself stacking beer coasters on the table in front of him.

Well, that had gone well. She wasn't sure if the silence was approval, surprise, or a wish they'd get this rehearsal over with.

Sophie stepped away. "So, what happens next?"

"That's the scripted part over," George said. "You can hold hands, wave to the crowd, throw your bouquets, jump off the stage and go crowd-surfing. Or lead the way into the afterparty. Whatever you think best. In a real wedding, you'd have to sign certificates and such."

"It's not real," Tarryn said. Her voice croaked. "So I think we could just go and start the party."

"First dance?" Jason said. "I suggest you throw your bouquets, then when the DJ starts, you'll have your first dance. On stage would be good so everyone can see you."

"I can't dance," Tarryn said. Her tongue cleaved to the roof of her mouth. Dancing? No one had said anything about that. Were they supposed to waltz or something?

"Then I suggest just a romantic slow dance, and you can sway together. I'm sure even you can manage that. How about something by Norah Jones?" Jason asked.

"How about 'Get Me Outta Here' by G Flip?" Tarryn shot back.

Phyll tutted. "Please be serious."

"I am." Tarryn looked across at Sophie. "No offence. It's just the whole wedding thing."

"None taken," Sophie said. She came close again and put her hand on Tarryn's arm. "If this is upsetting you, it's not too late to bail. I'm sure Will and Garrett would step up." Her eyes searched Tarryn's face. "I get you're not enjoying this, but if it's more, please say."

"No. It's okay. I promised." Tarryn took a deep breath and stared at Sophie's slim fingers on her arm. "Besides, maybe it's the only way I'll get to kiss you."

Sophie drew a shuddering breath. "Just park that one for now." Stepping away again, she said, "How about 'Fade Into You' by Mazzy Star? It's slow, got beautiful vocals, and it's a tune to just drift along to. I think we could manage that." She arched an eyebrow in question.

"Yeah," Tarryn said softly. "Yeah."

Jason fiddled with his phone, and then the haunting vocals of Hope Sandoval came tinnily from the speaker.

Sophie held out a hand. "Dance with me? We should practice this too."

"Sure." Tarryn's pulse hammered an erratic beat as she put her hand in Sophie's. They slid into a loose embrace, Sophie's hands linked around Tarryn's waist. Tarryn mirrored the position, and for a moment they gazed at each other before Sophie's feet started a slow shuffling glide.

"Move," she whispered in Tarryn's ear.

Over Sophie's shoulder, she saw Phyll and Jason sitting together at one of the tables, staring at them. Phyll's normally rigid face seemed soft, almost approving.

Tarryn closed her eyes rather than look at Phyll and let her hand drift up Sophie's back to brush her hair with the back of her hand. "It's so soft."

"Conditioner." Sophie hummed in amusement. "Relax, Tarryn. You're wound tighter than a roll of fencing wire."

"I'm surprised you know about fencing wire."

"You'd be surprised at what I know—and don't know."

Tarryn was silent, letting Sophie's breath wash over her, allowing the seductive ethereal song to carry her away. Why was she so tense around Sophie like this? Kirra's description of her as the queen of tourist seduction was half-joking, but Tarryn was no stranger to connecting with women passing through town. She was smooth and easy when she sensed her attention was welcomed. But Sophie and her beguiling mixture of sass and innocence had her confused. She was used to leading…but now, Sophie was the one soothing her nerves.

Their bodies found a fit and a rhythm. Their hips pressed together, close enough that Tarryn imagined she could feel the heat, the burn of Sophie's core. Impossible surely, they were both wearing jeans, but all the same… She turned her head and pressed her nose to Sophie's hair. It smelled of something floral, exactly as she'd imagined her hair would smell.

Her stomach muscles tensed. When had she ever imagined the scent of Sophie's hair? She hadn't even thought of it until just then, but it felt right. Sophie threw her off balance, made her normal world wobble on its training wheels.

The song ended on a sigh, and for another couple of seconds, they remained in their loose embrace.

George cleared her throat. "You nailed that part."

Tarryn moved back, suddenly wanting space between them. "Thanks. It's probably the easiest bit."

"For you, maybe." George indicated her motorbike boots. "Try dancing in these."

"How did we do?" Sophie's voice held a tight, artificial gaiety. "Think we'll be okay?"

"Not too bad," Jason said. "Tarryn needs to relax a bit more during the ceremony, that's all."

"You try relaxing when you're doing everything you always swore you wouldn't—even if it's pretend. It would be like you giving the keynote speech at a teetotallers' convention."

Jason laughed. "Not the greatest fit for a pub owner."

Phyll consulted her notes. "Have you decided on the wedding hire place?"

"I like Uptown Funk," Sophie said. "They're bright and not too traditional. But Tarryn and I haven't had a chance to talk it over yet."

"Would they suit you?" Phyll swivelled to Tarryn.

She shrugged. "I haven't looked, but they sound okay."

"Can you both manage to go tomorrow?" Phyll asked. "You'll have to go to Byron Bay."

They both nodded.

"I'll pick you up," Sophie said. "Will nine work?"

Tarryn nodded. What else could she do?

Chapter 16

ALLIE GRIPPED THE STEERING WHEEL as she drove toward Tarryn's place the next morning. Her eyes scratched with tiredness after her sleepless night. Her mind had been full of Tarryn: her low voice, her smooth skin, her dark eyes, and, most of all, the feel of her lips. She'd tossed restlessly in bed, then got up and made herself a mug of a herbal tea she'd found in the cupboard. It had tasted of grass and not much else and hadn't helped her sleep, but it had been something to do.

The events of the day had unwound again in her head. She thought she'd done okay at the rehearsal. Standing in front of George, holding Tarryn's hand. The dance. The kiss. *The kiss.* Allie set her fingers to her lips, reliving it. Tarryn had kissed her as if she meant it. And Allie had been there all the way, falling into Tarryn and her lips and the feel of her under her hands.

If anything, it had been Tarryn who was uncomfortable at the rehearsal. Was it just the whole wedding thing? Or was it Allie?

And that was the question, one she'd have to find an answer to when next she saw Tarryn.

Which was now. Or the now that started in five minutes. Allie swung the car into Tarryn's potholed driveway and wiggled her fingers at the alpacas staring at her over the fence. Surely, on the drive to Byron she could find out what was bothering Tarryn and hopefully reassure her.

Tarryn must have heard the car, as she was waiting outside her shouse. She jumped into the passenger seat and set her bag on the back seat. "Hi." A small smile.

Good. If Tarryn was smiling, things couldn't be too bad.

"Hi yourself." She tapped her fingers on the wheel. "I'm going to stop for coffee and a brekky wrap from Kirra as we head out. I rang through the order before I left—Kirra said you ate the same, so I got you one as well."

Tarryn's white teeth flashed. "Thanks. I've had a piece of toast, but a brekky wrap will be good."

Allie pulled up outside Kirra's Kafé. "They're paid for. Would you mind collecting them?"

Tarryn was back in a minute and set the coffees in the cupholders as Allie pulled away. "I'll wait until you're on the main road before giving you the wrap." She waved at the local policeman with a speed gun hiding behind a bush.

"Good idea."

Tarryn unwrapped her wrap and took a huge bite.

Allie tried to concentrate on the road and not on how Tarryn wiped a speck of barbecue sauce from her mouth with her little finger. *Concentrate!*

"These are so good. Soft wrap, double bacon, free-range egg, crispy potato. And Kirra has to deal with idiots who complain they're not as cheap as that big chain we all know on the highway. There's no comparison."

Allie turned onto the main road, and once she was up to speed held out her hand. "I agree. But maybe I need to check again. Just in case Kirra's cooking has slipped."

Tarryn handed over the wrap. "No chance of that."

Even after driving it for a couple of weeks, Sophie's SUV still felt unfamiliar. It was too big, too lumbering, and it swayed alarmingly on corners, but on the highway, it felt safe enough. She bit into the wrap. "Just as good as I remember."

Tarryn finished hers and chased it with a sip of coffee. She balled the wrapper into a tight shape, squashing it between finger and thumb. "Can I ask you something?"

She gripped the steering wheel and flicked Tarryn a glance. "Sure. Is everything okay?" Was Tarryn about to say she was uncomfortable with Allie's kisses? It was a workplace situation after all, and she may have felt pressured. Coldness seeped into her chest. *Please, not that.* Not with Sophie's business on the line.

"I'm sure you don't need another complaint from me about this whole fake wedding thing." Tarryn sighed. "So I won't give you one. I just have an awkward question I shouldn't ask, but I'm not the sort of person who can wait and see. I need to know."

Allie fixed her stare on the road ahead, and her grip tightened on the steering wheel enough that her knuckles went white. Not good for vehicle control. She made a conscious effort to relax. As long as Tarryn didn't start talking about workplace coercion, she could get through this. And she had wanted to find out Tarryn's problem. She just hadn't expected her to raise it in the first fifteen minutes. "What do you need to know?"

"The kiss. I'm wondering…" She rested her arm on the sill and turned to face Allie. "That is… I don't know where I stand with you. We were getting along, then you got all salty about organisation, and then you kissed the hell out of me to the stars and back. I remember you said it's been a while since you kissed anyone, and I know we were acting in a way, pretending for the fake wedding, but… Hell, Sophie. That kiss was dynamite. To me, it seemed…real. As if you wanted to take things further. And if you were anyone else, I'd be upping my seduction game, but I don't want to step out of line here. I don't give a rat's arse you're supposedly my boss. You're not really, not in any lasting way, and you'll be back in Sydney in a few days. So did I read this right?"

Allie dragged a slow breath through her open mouth. The simple answer was yes, Tarryn had read her right, and they should forget going to look at wedding clothes and instead do a U-turn back to Quandong and find somewhere private with a bed.

Her mind fizzed. Was that what she wanted? The answer settled into her head like soft spring rain: yes, it was. But that didn't mean she would act on it. Flings weren't her thing, and that's all it would be with Tarryn. This time next week, she'd be back in Sydney, caring for Sophie, trying to pick up the pieces of her professional life and find herself a new job. She didn't need any distractions, not even Tarryn-shaped ones. Even if she did have gorgeous skin that made Allie's fingers itch to touch, even if her metal-grey curls were a striking frame for her expressive, handsome face. No. There was only one answer she could give.

She flashed Tarryn a quick smile and returned her stare to the road. "It was acting. Trying to make it look real. After all, we want people to believe in the romance of love. A stilted peck on the lips wouldn't give that impression. We want them to sigh and melt inside and wish they, too, could have part of the romance we're portraying." She flexed her fingers on the wheel. "Sure, I enjoyed the kiss—who wouldn't? You're a great kisser. But I'm not up for a fling, Tarryn."

Tarryn was silent for a moment. "Pity. We could have had a lot of fun together in the last few days."

"Maybe. But it's not what I'm looking for. Let's keep the kisses for the festival." She looked across in time to see Tarryn's lips twitch into a smile.

"I'll look forward to it."

Allie let the silence stand for a moment, then said, "And while we're checking in on each other, I wanted to ask if you're okay too. You didn't seem too comfortable at the rehearsal yesterday."

"I wasn't." Tarryn lifted a shoulder. "But I'll get through it. I've committed, Sophie, and once I've done that, I don't go back on my word. I hope I'll be better on the day."

Allie nodded. "We'll get through this together."

Tarryn eyed the dresses the wedding hire assistant was showing them. Sure, they were lovely, if that's what you wanted. Sure, they were everything most brides would dream of: everything from elegant gowns to sexy skin-revealing sheaths to fun and flirty. But although Sophie was oohing and aahing, Tarryn's request to see something with pants, a tux or a suit, had so far been ignored.

Sophie picked up a couple of the fun-and-flirty dresses. "I'm going to try these. Have you seen anything you like?"

"Not yet. I think I'll look at the male side."

"I'm sorry," the assistant said. "I know you asked for something with pants—like we have in our brochure—but we've had a run on those clothes, and there's very little left in stock. People are definitely moving away from traditional."

Tarryn went over to the other side of the store and started browsing the racks of suits. She pulled out an aubergine-coloured one and held it up. Too drab? She set it to one side and kept browsing.

The assistant hovered. "We have white suits."

Tarryn stifled a gasp of horror. She'd look like a drug lord. "Sophie's looking at colours—it would be better if I stayed away from white as well."

"Fair enough." The assistant tapped her collarbone as she thought. "Your girlfriend's trying on pink hues. Do you want to match?"

"That might be hard." She suppressed a shudder at the thought of matchy-matchy outfits and she and Sophie looking as sickeningly cute as the Bobbsey twins. "We thought of matching shoes—red hi-tops or something, but I don't think we need anything past that."

"How about silver-grey?" At Tarryn's nod, the assistant darted off, returning a minute later with a silver-grey pants suit. The narrow leg pants and boxy jacket had a subtle shimmer under the lights. "There's a tiny rip in the back of the pants." The assistant gave a quick grin. "The last hirer wasn't exactly the size twelve she claimed to be. It's awaiting repair, hence it's not on the rack. See what you think. I reckon we could patch the tear easily enough."

Tarryn tilted her head and considered the suit. It was elegantly androgynous, classy without being trashy. With a white shirt, red sneakers, and some sort of rainbow tie or scarf, it would also be fun. "It's good. Let me try it on." She took the clothes and hung them over her forearm.

A curtain rustled, and Sophie stepped out. She smoothed her palms down the front of her thighs and lifted her chin. "What do you think?"

The dress was simple: a low V neckline that showed a hint of breast, cap sleeves, and a fitted bodice. The skirt flared and fell to just above Sophie's knee, showing a hint of toned thigh. The dress bled from the palest of pinks at the neckline down to a deep red at the hem. It was eye-catching, it was fun, it was definitely flirty...and best of all, Sophie looked amazing in it. Tarryn's eyes drifted from her pale arms over the tops of her breasts, down past the indent of her waist to where the skirt ended in a froth of material.

"Wow." A low burn started in Tarryn's belly. Sophie was lovely in a girl-next-door, cute sort of way normally. Barefoot and dressed in an unconventional wedding dress, she was stunning.

"Do you like it?" Sophie asked. Her voice had a breathy, uncertain quality it didn't normally hold.

"I do."

Sophie's lips twitched. "That sounds like a wedding vow. I'll take it as a sign. So, then, if you can find something you like that complements this, we're home and hosed. Is that what you're considering?" Her gaze fixed on the suit hanging on Tarryn's arm.

"Yes. I was just about to try it on."

"Don't let me stop you. Unless you need a hand?" She winked.

"I'll be fine." Tarryn went into the cubicle Sophie had vacated. She hung the suit on the hook, and, for a moment, she sat, her palms pressed to her cheeks. Sophie had turned her heart upside down, and she struggled for composure. How strange that such a baffling woman could do that. Tarryn took a deep breath. It was just a reaction to seeing her look so gorgeous in such a fun dress, that was all. She'd be fine in a minute.

When her breathing had returned to normal, she stripped her pants, leaving her T-shirt, and donned the silver-grey suit. The pants fit well, clinging to her hips and upper thighs, then falling to the floor in a tapered style. She twisted around to see the rear in the mirror. Yes, a good fit all right. The small tear the assistant had mentioned was barely noticeable. She tugged at the jacket. It didn't sit right; her shoulders were too wide. Maybe she could get away with just the white shirt.

She left the changing room and, for a second, enjoyed the sight of Sophie in front of the full-length mirror, checking her rear view. *Oh yes. Nice.*

The assistant hummed. "That jacket is no good on you." She scurried off.

Sophie turned and her gaze raked Tarryn from head to toe. "I agree about the jacket, but the rest. Wow, the rest is gorgeous." She came over and hooked her arm through Tarryn's and turned them both to face the mirror. "We look good together."

"We do."

Their gazes collided in the mirror. Tarryn studied how their bodies fit together, Sophie shorter than her, her pale skin looking almost ethereal against the soft pink of the upper part of the dress. And herself… The silver-grey looked good against the darker grey of her hair, and the slight shimmer of her suit set off her olive skin. For a moment, she wished she could stand there for longer, her arm through Sophie's, their bodies touching hip to hip, arm to arm. She glanced at Sophie's face. Her lips were parted, and she wore a wistful expression, as if she were far away. Dreaming about a real wedding in her future, maybe?

Sophie's gaze slid away. "It looks like we've found our outfits."

The assistant returned, a rose-pink waistcoat in her hands. "Try this." She thrust it at Tarryn.

It fitted perfectly, and the hue matched a shade in Sophie's dress.

"It looks like we're done." Sophie cleared her throat and smiled at the assistant. "Can we take them now?"

"If you can wait a few minutes, I'll fix that tear in the pants. Pass them out to me when you change."

Tarryn nodded and headed for the cubicle at the exact same time as Sophie.

"You first." Sophie brushed the hair from her eyes.

Tarryn changed back into her jeans and handed the pants to the assistant.

Outside the cubicle, she sat on a cream-coloured bench and tried to regroup her thoughts. Her pulse pounded, her palms oozed sweat, and her guts were twisting themselves into nervous knots. She knew the reason: Sophie. Adorable, beautiful Sophie dressed in an ethereal wedding dress of silk. Sophie, who, despite what she'd said earlier, looked at Tarryn as if she wanted to kiss her.

How was she going to get through the next couple of days without making a fool of herself?

Chapter 17

"The first day of the Gay Bells Festival went fine. Honestly, would I lie to you?" Allie propped her back against the headboard and rested the phone on her knee. "There are a lot of visitors in town, all the accommodation is fully booked. The first day of the wedding fair was very busy, and the local food showcase dinner is at capacity."

"No disasters?" Sophie asked. "Not that I'm expecting them—you've done a great job, Al. But something always goes wrong. Something breaks, someone crucial doesn't show. My money's on Kirra throwing a hissy fit at Phyll's bossiness and storming out."

"All's peaceful—so far. Phyll is too busy with the wedding fair to pester Kirra, and Kirra's caught up with the minutiae of the parade. Many of the entrants are coming to her with requests for positioning."

"What, they all want to be up front?"

Allie laughed. "Mostly it's who they don't want to be next to. The Irish dancers have to be ahead of the rainbow dogs so they don't step in dog poop. The real estate crowd can't be anywhere near the float from the hardware store as the business owners are enemies—the real estate owner's grandmother ran off with the hardware store's grandfather in about 1940, and they still don't speak."

Sophie snorted. "Still? That takes commitment in a small town."

"Kirra's handling it like a pro, but she's come up the last three nights to guzzle wine and vent."

"So, no real drama today, then." Sophie sighed. "That's amazing."

"Don't get too complacent. Tomorrow will be the real test." Nerves leaped in Allie's insides like Irish dancers avoiding dog poop.

"What are you most worried about?"

"The parade. Tarryn and I will have to get ready for the fake wedding, and that leaves the final parade organisation to Kirra—who's on a float herself—and Phyll, who'll have just come from the wedding catwalk. It's cutting it fine. Garrett and Will have offered to help as much as they can, but they're busy too."

"I'm not too worried about that. The town people voted you and Tarryn as the fake couple. They knew it would be difficult, but they did it anyway. They must think you can do it."

"I'll strike hoping you're okay with it off my angst list, then. That leaves quite a few things to worry about. Thirty-two at last count."

"What's the top one?"

Allie adjusted her position and repositioned the phone when it fell onto the quilt. "Honestly? 'Marrying' Tarryn. I keep telling myself it's just a job, just acting, no worse than playing a von Trapp kid in the *Sound of Music* in the school play. But I was more relaxed before my dental surgery."

"Is Tarryn the problem? Is she still giving you grief about how marriage doesn't belong in queer communities?"

"She seems accepting of her role now. She wants the town to do well from this festival. No, I'm…" How to explain that Tarryn was stirring all sorts of things in her that were best left alone? How to find the words to say that, for her, marriage was a bit more serious than prancing around in a pretty frock.

"Has she kissed you again?" Sophie's voice hummed low in her ear.

"Yes. And I kissed her."

"Is that's what worrying you?"

"Partly. I like her kisses. A lot, if I'm honest, but of course it can't go anywhere."

"Because she's a woman?"

"No!" Allie's voice was louder than she would have liked. "I've accepted I'm…well, I don't know what I am, but I'm not straight. Because she lives here, and I live in Sydney, and even if we both lived in the same place, I don't know if I want more. I certainly don't know if she does."

"Does it have to go anywhere?" Sophie asked. "Can't you just have a great fling with a hot woman? You can do your soul-searching back in Sydney."

"It's the deception. She thinks I'm you—a lesbian event planner. It would feel very wrong to go into even a fling with that lie between us."

"I get it. You're such an honest person—that's why the whole Kirkland thing is such a bitch. Al, if it gets to that point with Tarryn and you want to own up to who you really are, then do so. Don't hold back on my account. By then, the festival will be over, and hopefully it'll be a success, so with luck, no one will hold it against us."

"It's easier to just walk away." Allie picked up her phone and turned the speaker off. "Tarryn could be angry at being deceived. Phyll could be ropeable. The committee would rightly be pissed off they didn't get who they paid for. It's not just a warm, breathing body—it's your experience they hired. Not me, your mouthpiece."

"They're getting my experience, just filtered through you." Sophie's sigh gusted over the line. "I'd be happiest if you leave there without it ever coming to light. But I don't want your happiness to be the casualty. I trust you, Al. You do what you have to do."

"Even if it blows your reputation out the water? I can't do that to you, Sophie. Especially not for what would be one night, maybe a couple of nights at most."

"I should never have done this, should I?" Sophie's quiet admission sent a ripple through her. "No matter how I thought I was saving my business, it was wrong to send you in pretending to be me. I should have been upfront, told Phyll and the others what had happened and that I was sending you in my place."

Allie was silent. Now, in hindsight, that was exactly what Sophie should have done. But had she, there was every chance she'd have lost the contract, and then, like a row of dominoes, her business would have fallen, and then her house when she couldn't meet repayments. On top of her major health issues, that would have been the final straw.

"You did what you had to." She spoke in a low voice as if someone might overhear her words, although there was no one who could. "And I think I've done okay. Phyll's happy. I haven't heard anyone complain. Let's just leave it alone. I'll be home in three or four days. And apart from the wedding, I'll try to stay away from Tarryn in a kissing sense. After all, won't I be back in Australia's gayest city soon? If I want to see where this new self-knowledge takes me, well, Sydney's the place to find out."

"Okay."

Allie could picture her twin in her bed, her leg on pillows, biting her lip and twisting the sheet between her fingers. "It's a plan, then."

It was the only thing to do at this point. But why did it make her feel so uneasy?

Allie watched the first models parade down the wedding attire catwalk. A woman wearing a traditional lace and satin white gown with a full-length veil was followed by a man wearing a pale-blue suit, the pants rolled up to mid-calf to reveal bare feet. Then two older women dressed in floaty boho tie-dye sauntered out hand in hand, waving to the crowd, followed by two teenagers in identical skinny-leg hot-pink suits. Allie recognised Casey and Kai, the high school kids.

Her walkie-talkie beeped, and she took a few paces away before answering.

"Have you got a moment to bring over a cart of food from the kitchen?" Ziggy's harried voice asked. "We've sold out of many items."

"No worries. I'll go now." Allie hurried over to the Council's commercial kitchen which was being used by several of the slow food vendors. The second day was going well so far. Food was selling fast, the wedding fair was jammed with people, and yet more folks were browsing the more general market stalls lining the main street.

Allie's nerves twanged like a badly tuned guitar. The parade would be starting in two hours, and soon she'd have to go over to the community hall to get ready for her role. And then she'd have to wave and smile and pretend to be in love with Tarryn. Whoever thought this was a good idea should be made to star in next year's festival. She delivered the food to Ziggy and then headed for the hall to check on preparations for the fake wedding.

Tarryn jogged up to her. "Hey, Sophie, do we have any more of the colour bombs? They've sold out."

"I think there's a couple more boxes in the hall, but that's all." She snuck a sideways glance at Tarryn. She appeared cool and calm, speaking into her handset. "I'm going there now, if you want to come along, I can show you where they are."

Together, they walked to the hall and collected the colour bombs.

"How are you feeling?" Tarryn asked as they walked over to deliver them. "Nervous?"

"I'm supposed to be asking you that. I'm fine. It's just a job to me." And that was a big, whopping lie if ever there was one. If her nerves got any worse, she'd have to go to The Hollowman for a shot of tequila. Or three.

"That's good." Tarryn shot her a grin. "Another few hours and all this will be over. We can relax and enjoy the afterparty."

"You're okay with this? You're not going to spring a terrible surprise on us by making a speech about the unnecessary nature of marriage?"

"No. I wouldn't do that to the town. We've invested a lot of money in this festival. We've invested a lot of money in *you* and your expertise. I wouldn't sabotage Quandong. I still live here and would have to face my friends in the morning."

How to pour on the guilt. Quandong had paid a lot for Sophie's services, and what had they got: Allie blundering her way through. The guilt knifed her in the stomach once more. "That's good to know. I'd hate for you to be a no-show at the altar."

Tarryn reached to squeeze Allie's hand. "I wouldn't do that to you." Her walkie-talkie chirped again, and she lifted it to her mouth. "I'm on my way." She cocked her head and stared at Allie. "Want the truth?"

The intensity of Tarryn's gaze nailed her feet to the pavement. "Of course."

"I'm scared shitless about this." She fiddled with the leather thong at her throat. "This whole acting a part thing. Pretending to be in love and getting married… You know it's everything I've never wanted." She gave a weak smile. "The only thing keeping me going is the thought of the kiss at the end of the ceremony. I know we can do that, and I'm focussing on it. I know you don't want to make it real, Sophie, but know I'll be pretending you're someone I've met in a bar and you're attracted to me. I'm sorry. That's probably not what you want to hear, but it's going to get me through this. I hope."

A drumbeat thundered in Allie's mind. The kiss. Yes, the kiss would be the highlight of the day. Hell, of the week, the month, even. And if pretence got them through it, and in a way that looked realistic, well, that's what both of them would do. "I'll be doing the same." She lifted a shoulder. "If it works, that's a good thing."

Tarryn's tight expression eased fractionally. "Most of the time, though, I can't help wishing I'd stuffed the ballot boxes with votes for Garrett and Will."

Allie reached for Tarryn's hand, linking their fingers together. "We'll get through this, okay?"

"Yeah. But hell's holy arseholes, I hope you're not expecting me to stay sober and on duty afterwards. I'll need all the help I can get."

Allie laughed. "I was seriously considering slipping over to The Hollowman for a couple of shots. And I don't do shots."

Tarryn's radio crackled again. "How long are you going to be, Tarryn? I have a line for the colour bombs."

"Sorry." Her eyes didn't leave Allie's face. "I'm thirty seconds away." She increased her pace to the stall, leaving Allie to follow.

Allie blew out a breath. Soon, this day would be over. She couldn't wait.

Chapter 18

THE CARPARK AT THE END of the street was crammed with trucks, tractors, cars, dogs, horses, and people. The marching band was tuning up in one corner, and the wail of bagpipes rent the air like a banshee. Small children in rainbow dresses ran around shrieking to beat the bagpipes, and the Irish dancers adjusted the volume of their music from loud to deafening.

Allie dodged around the group of people with dustbins over their heads plastered with pictures of homophobic politicians. She hoped they had decent eye holes in the bins and safety goggles underneath. Her pink dress fluttered around her, and she adjusted the waistband once more as she went up to the wedding float directly behind the Bundjalung Nation's float. She caught a glimpse of Kirra and the sistergirls and brotherboys already up there.

Allie reached her truck. It might only be the feedstore's ute, but it was detailed to a gleaming white, and the sides of the tray were festooned with artificial white and pink roses. Fake grass covered the ute's tray. On the top, there was a rope enclosure and a banner proclaiming *You're invited to Tarryn and Sophie's wedding*.

Tarryn reached a hand and helped her up. She was wearing the silver-grey pants and pink waistcoat with a blinding white linen shirt. A lesbian flag enamel pin adorned her waistcoat, and her red hi-tops looked new. "Welcome aboard. Kirra says we're to remain in the roped area—so we don't stray too close to the edge apparently—and wave and smile. Dance a bit when we hear music." She side-eyed Allie. "She said kissing wouldn't hurt either."

"Right." Damn her fair skin. She just knew a flush was creeping up her neck to rival the brightest pink of her dress. "We'll do our best."

Tarryn hadn't let go of her hand. It still clasped hers, her fingers wrapped around Allie's. Her thumb made a slow pass over the inside of her wrist. Surely, her fingers would feel how her pulse pounded, beating at a rate that would surely be off the charts. Her stomach churned, and an empty feeling of nausea rolled over her. She'd been too busy—and too on edge—to think about eating. She stared down at her red Vans until the feeling passed.

Will came up to the truck with a basket. "Here, these are for you throw to the crowd." The basket contained multicoloured lollies with *LOVE* written on them. "Try not to eat them all."

Tarryn stuck her tongue out at him and unwrapped a lolly. "Try to stop me."

Allie grabbed one as well. Maybe it would ease the nerves doing the bump and grind in her stomach. Tarryn seemed strangely relaxed, especially given she'd been so tense earlier. "You seem like you're doing good now. Or have you been in the drag queens' weed stash?"

"How do you know about that?" Tarryn's eyes crinkled. "I've only had a few puffs, plus a couple of shots of tequila. I'm at the happy, euphoric stage of everything. I just hope it lasts long enough to get me through the ceremony and out the other side."

"I wish I'd had your forethought." Allie's foot jiggled, and she clenched her hands together.

"Here." Tarryn reached inside a cluster of artificial roses and withdrew a small bottle. "Have a swig of this, courtesy of Jason."

The tequila burned enough to make Allie's eyes water. "Drinking at work. I should give both of us a written warning."

"I think we're off the hook for this."

There was a lurch and a rumble of diesel motor as the truck started and edged forward into position.

Phyll stood with a megaphone at the entrance to the car park. "Gymnastics club, you're behind the wedding float, then the vintage cars."

"I guess it's too late to back out now." Allie grabbed for the rope as the truck lurched.

Tarryn took her hand. "Way too late. Besides, Will and Garrett won't fit these clothes."

"Bundjalung float, move forward to the street for the Welcome to Country," Phyll yelled.

Allie listened as an elder gave the Welcome to Country, welcoming visitors to the Bundjalung Nation. Once he stepped back, the Bundjalung float inched forward, and musicians started playing didgeridoos accompanied by clapsticks. She caught a glimpse of Kirra and the sistergirls and brotherboys dancing on the long flatbed of the truck.

"We're off!" Tarryn grinned. She flung a handful of lollies to some kids who were jumping up and down at the side of the street.

"Irish dancers next," yelled Phyll.

Where had all these people come from? They were two or three deep along both sides of the street, and this was only the start of the parade route. How many were there at the end, in front of the wedding stage?

Music poured out from the Bundjalung float, and Allie grabbed Tarryn's hand. "Let's dance!"

She jigged and stamped, her hands on Tarryn's shoulders, gripping tight, and she focussed on Tarryn's face so as not to get dizzy. She concentrated on her eyes: warm, dark, steady. If she kept staring at Tarryn's eyes, she could get through this.

For another few seconds, their gazes connected, then Tarryn released her to throw another handful of lollies.

Allie slung an arm around Tarryn's waist, unwilling to let the contact go, and waved to the crowds. Tarryn was close enough that the heat radiating from her body could have warmed her on a winter's night. Without stopping to think, she moved in front and put her arms around Tarryn's neck, leaning in to kiss her.

She'd meant it as a stage kiss, something quick and sweet, a peck and a smile, but the minute her lips touched Tarryn's, she was lost. Her mouth parted on a soundless O, and there was a corresponding hitch in Tarryn's breath. Then Tarryn's arms went around her shoulders, and she was kissing her like a black-and-white movie hero, bending her back so Allie had to clutch at Tarryn's waist for balance. Tarryn's tongue swept around Allie's lips, and it was impossible not to react, not to open them, not to allow her in. Allie's pulse thundered in her head, her mind a fizzing white-hot burn of passion.

And then Tarryn was gone, leaving Allie with weak knees and a head full of desire, spinning her out of time and place until all she wanted to do was keep kissing Tarryn for the rest of her life and into the next.

She clutched the rope and heaved a breath, returning to the float, the crowds, the festival. She waved and tried a smile. Next to her, Tarryn flung more lollies and then, linking arms with Allie, swung her in an impromptu Irish jig. She seemed unaffected by the kiss, her eyes shining, as if this were the biggest and most welcome party of her life. But then, Tarryn kissed women all the time—why would she be affected? She wasn't the one pretending to be someone she wasn't.

Allie longed for another swig from the hidden tequila, but how could she do that when all eyes were on her? Instead, she linked her arm through Tarryn's and kept on smiling and waving as if she was on a royal tour of the Commonwealth.

By the time the truck reached The Hollowman, the crowds were thicker, the music louder, and Allie had the start of a headache. Their truck stopped beside the stage while the rest of the parade continued past to the finish point. Allie stood close to Tarryn and smiled, applauded, and shouted encouragement to the rest of the parade.

When the final float had passed, they looked at each other. Allie's heart thumped a nervous rhythm. She'd never thought of the transition moment, when they had to get from the float to the stage where George already waited in front of a low table bedecked with flowers.

Jason stepped forward and walked up to the stage. "Good people, thank you for attending the wedding of Quandong's most beloved couple, Tarryn and Sophie." He went on to talk about how this wasn't a real wedding but was staged to show the love and joy that could be shared and then invited everyone to stay and watch the ceremony before the music and afterparty started. "We'll have a few minutes' break for you to grab a cocktail, if you wish, or find your position for the ceremony."

"I guess that's our cue." Allie smiled. "Do you think one of those cocktails will come our way?"

At that moment, there was a whistle from the side of the truck, and Seth stood there, two glasses of bubbles in his hands. "Thought you might enjoy these." He handed them over and disappeared back to the bar.

"He's a mind reader," Tarryn said. She clinked her glass with Allie's. "We're nearly done."

"We are." Allie's nerves settled to a gentle simmer. This *was* fun. Everyone seemed to be enjoying it, and, honestly, who would give a second thought to the women pretending to get married? They were actors on a stage. It wasn't as if she were really marrying Tarryn. Allie swallowed hard. No. She was here in borrowed finery, drinking what tasted like very expensive champagne, and she was with Tarryn, who had sworn never to marry anyone. She stretched her mouth into a smile. She was being paid for this—well, Sophie was—and she was being paid to put on a show of smiles and looks of love.

She wrapped her free arm around Tarryn's waist again, and together they watched the milling crowds laughing and drinking cocktails.

"Okay?" She squeezed Tarryn's waist.

"Yeah. It's going well. The festival, that is. I'll still be glad when the next thirty minutes are over."

"Me too." Allie leaned over and pecked Tarryn on the cheek.

"That's not a kiss. What we did earlier was."

She laughed, and the jitterbugs were back in her stomach. "Save it until the 'I do.'"

"The 'I do.'" Some of the light went out of Tarryn's eyes. "Right."

Chapter 19

ALLIE LOOKED OVER TO WHERE George was on stage, her head through the curtain that separated her from DJ Strokes, obviously having a chat with him. She didn't seem to have nerves—to her it was a job. As it should be for her and Tarryn as well.

Jason was gesticulating from the door of The Hollowman. He was either asking them to get off the truck and get ready, or else giving someone directions to Byron Bay. Taking the hint, Allie and Tarryn got down from the truck. Before they parted, one to each side of the stage, Allie squeezed Tarryn's hand. "It'll be okay. Just a few more minutes."

Tarryn flashed her a wide-eyed look. Her cocky stance—hips pushed forward, hands in the pockets of her pants—didn't fool Allie: Tarryn was nervous.

With a nod and wink, Jason returned to the stage and picked up the microphone. George straightened her bow tie and tugged her dark suit into place over her sturdy frame.

"Welcome, everyone, to Tarryn and Sophie's wedding," Jason said. "Conducting the ceremony is George Patterson from Your Wedding, Your Way, for anyone who wants their wedding done exactly how they want it. Over to you, George."

Allie stamped on her nerves as George gave an introductory speech about marriage. The tequila roiled like acid in her stomach. How had she ever been talked into doing this?

George wrapped up her speech and extended her hands to each side of the stage. "Tarryn and Sophie."

Allie swallowed hard and fixed on a smile. She tried to think of someone who would put a romantic, sensual smile on her face. Who? She summoned her usual celebrity fantasies. But Chris Hemsworth and the male singer from a Sydney band faded from her mind. She concentrated, summoning all the romantic and sexual feelings she could muster. Tarryn's high cheekbones and serious face slid into place. Allie tried to push it aside—after all, it was obvious she would think about Tarryn right now. But try as she might, she couldn't do it. Tarryn filled her thoughts utterly and completely.

"Tarryn and Sophie," George repeated.

It would have to do. Summoning the smile again and clutching the bouquet of native flora Phyll had shoved into her hand, Sophie took the slow and careful walk toward George. A swift glance to her right and—thank God—Tarryn was there too. Her steps were jerky, and she looked more like she was part of a funeral procession than a wedding, but she was in place.

Allie placed her free hand in George's outstretched one. George gave a reassuring squeeze as she encouraged them to come closer and then nudged them until they were side-on to the audience.

"Friends, we are gathered here today to witness the marriage of Tarryn and Sophie." She drew them closer and placed Allie's hand in Tarryn's.

Shivers coursed down Allie's spine as she listened to George's opening words. *This feels so real.* As if she were really about to marry the love of her life. A wave of emotion swamped her, clinging to her skin.

Allie lifted her stare from their clasped hands to Tarryn's face. Her expression had a fixed, stunned look, and her hand shook slightly in Allie's grasp. Dimly, Allie was aware George was coming to the end of her part and now they were expected to participate.

"Now say after me," George said. "Do you, Sophie, take this woman, Tarryn, to be your wedded wife?"

Her heart thundered. She could do this. It wasn't real. She was playing a part. Allie drew on her fantasies, her dreams of a real wedding day, and channelled it all into her smile. "I do."

The crowd cheered, and Allie looked out at them with a huge grin. That wasn't so bad.

"And do you, Tarryn, take this woman, Sophie, to be your wedded wife?"

Tarryn licked her lips once, a quick flick of her tongue that nonetheless sent a coil of heat into Allie's chest. She knew what that tongue could do. She knew how Tarryn kissed.

Tarryn's lips parted, but no sound emerged. Allie had seen plenty of deer-in-headlights looks from her accounting clients—generally when caught out on a dodgy tax deduction—but Tarryn's was the frozen, immobile look of pure panic and shock.

George shuffled her feet. "And do you, Tarryn, take this woman, Sophie, to be your wedded wife?"

Tarryn swallowed, and her fingers trembled in Allie's clasp. "I..." Her gaze flickered around as if searching for the way out. "I can't do this..."

Allie hoped it was quiet enough that the mics wouldn't pick it up and broadcast it to the crowd.

"Come on, love," a woman in the audience shouted. "If you don't want to marry Sophie, I will!"

A ripple of laughter rolled through the crowd.

"Help me, Sophie," Tarryn whispered.

The shake in Tarryn's voice chilled Allie to her core. The underarms of Tarryn's linen shirt oozed like a swamp, and a bead of sweat rolled down the side of her face. The day was warm, but Allie doubted Tarryn's clammy hands were due to the sunshine—it was panic. Pure panic.

She gripped Tarryn's hands and smiled in what she hoped was a reassuring way.

"Please, Sophie," Tarryn whispered. "Do something."

Allie kept the smile on her face, although it felt more like a rictus. "You can do this. It's just two words. They don't mean anything here."

Tarryn swallowed hard, and her hands shook despite Allie's tight clasp. Her gaze darted around the crowd before returning to Allie's face. Her olive skin had an ashen tinge, as if all the blood had drained to her feet. She swayed slightly.

Allie moved her thumb across the inside of Tarryn's wrist. "Two words. Two tiny one-syllable words. You're not really marrying me: this is for Gay Bells. For Quandong. For your town and your people. It's okay, Tarryn. You've got this."

Still Tarryn hesitated. Another bead of sweat rolled down her forehead.

Allie flung a nervous glance at George. Her smile appeared as fixed as Allie's own, and her eyebrows were lowering toward her nose. White noise buzzed in Allie's mind. What could she do to break Tarryn's frozen state? She dared not look at the crowd shifting restlessly in front of the stage or at Phyll, Jason, and Kirra in the wings.

Tarryn's hands jerked in Allie's grasp. Was she about to bolt? Turn tail and flee the stage, leaving her and George alone? Would Phyll stomp onto stage and take Tarryn's place? Allie stifled a nervous giggle, which died when she again looked at Tarryn's face.

Tarryn appeared locked in her own head, a prison of her own convictions. Allie hesitated. Would it be wrong to coerce Tarryn into doing this? But she'd agreed. She was doing this for Quandong.

Allie had to try something. She took a deep breath and tugged Tarryn closer, wrapping an arm around her neck. Her other hand, still clutching the bouquet, settled on Tarryn's waist.

"You can do this," she whispered. Her breath puffed on Tarryn's face.

Allie kissed her, slow and gentle. Her heart pounded. Her mind flashed with memories of the kiss they'd shared at the rehearsal, how she'd fallen into the moment, how sensual and hot it had been. How she'd wanted so much for it to continue.

She lifted her arms and wrapped them around Tarryn's neck, pulled her closer, and breathed in the scent of her—the smell of cedar, fresh sweat, and sunshine. For a moment, she thought Tarryn was not going to respond. Her body was as unbending as steel, her lips were cool and immobile, and her heart galloped an erratic beat against Sophie's chest.

She softened her own lips, let her tongue flick at Tarryn's full lower lip, until finally—finally—Tarryn's mouth relaxed under her own. It was a gradual opening, like a bud in springtime, a tentative unfurling.

Tarryn's neck muscles lost their rigidity, and her hands rose from their fixed position at her sides to wrap around Allie's waist.

"Can you say the words now?" Allie whispered.

"Yes." It was barely audible, but it was there.

Allie drew back and rested her palm on Tarryn's cheek. Somewhere in the hazy distance, she was aware of the crowd and of George sporting a shit-eating grin from ear to ear.

George cleared her throat. "Tarryn? Do you take this woman, Sophie, to be your wedded wife?"

Tarryn took a breath, then another. Her chin lifted. "I do."

Allie barely noticed the cheers from the crowd in front of the stage. Her gaze locked with Tarryn's relieved stare, and she didn't miss the way her shoulders dropped as the tension left her.

"I now pronounce you wed," George said with a faint air of relief. "You may kiss."

Relief thrummed through Allie like a hive of bees. Surely, the worst part for Tarryn was over. She caught Tarryn's growing smile as that realisation hit her as well, as if her paralysing dread had lifted away like petals in a breeze. Somewhere there were real petals—Kirra and Phyll throwing them from the sides of the stage.

Tarryn lifted her face to the sky and laughed, her body regaining its usual looseness.

"I'm glad you've found something to laugh about," Allie said. "Do we kiss again, or do we count the impromptu one before your vow?" Her focus on getting Tarryn through this had blotted out her anticipation of their kiss. Now, though…

"We kiss again. Consider it a thank you for saving me from looking like a bad actor who couldn't even remember a two-word script."

"I kissed you last time," Allie said. "It's your turn."

Tarryn lifted a wisp of hair from Allie's face and tucked it behind her ear, where it promptly sprang free again. "I would hate to disappoint you." She smoothed both palms up Allie's neck until she cupped her jaw and then leaned in until her lips hovered over Allie's. "Just one small kiss. That's all."

"That's not fair." Allie's voice was barely more than a whisper. "I kissed you properly."

"Is that what you want?"

"What do you think?"

"Just kiss her already!" A voice in the crowd yelled, and other voices took up the chant. "Kiss her! Kiss her!"

"It looks like we have no choice," Tarryn said.

Allie slid a hand around the back of Tarryn's neck and pulled her closer, and her lips found Tarryn's mouth. One tiny part of her mind remembered that this had been scripted. She had reason to do this, one that meant she didn't need to think about it too deeply.

But she wanted to.

A kiss. Another. A soft slide of mouths over each other, and Allie tilted her head and deepened the contact. Her tongue sought entrance to Tarryn's mouth and then delved inside. Tarryn tasted faintly of tequila, but also of sunshine, heady and fresh.

Fire bloomed in Allie's chest. The rumble of voices from the crowd faded into insignificance. Kirra and Phyll might as well have been on another planet. There was only Tarryn and how she kissed.

Tarryn's body was firm against her own, her strong arms wrapped around Allie's shoulders, holding her close. So very close. Heat trickled down into her belly, and she lifted her mouth to change the angle before returning to explore and taste Tarryn's mouth. The fire inside her burned fiercer, twining through her abdomen in tendrils of desire, lower, down between her legs where her clit pulsed.

She moaned softly, and her hands slid down Tarryn's back to grip her hips. Dimly she heard the opening bars of Mazzy Star's "Fade Into You," and she swayed to the music, close to Tarryn, no room for air between their bodies.

She gathered her closer and pressed a kiss to her cheek, nearly on her mouth. For the length of the song, they moved together, Tarryn's lips in Allie's hair. Somewhere, the audience was singing along. Somewhere, there was a whole world outside of their embrace, but it wasn't important. There was just her and Tarryn and the gathering intimacy between them. Allie kissed her again, a long, slow, drugging kiss that took and supped and gave and teased.

The music ended on a storm of applause. Slowly, reality returned. How long had they been kissing? She hadn't a clue. Her lips pulsed and tingled with the need to kiss Tarryn again.

Where would this lead? Allie swallowed hard. She knew where it should go, where she wanted it to go. For a second, nerves and doubt flared. Tarryn seduced women often—Garrett had said she attracted women like bees to a honeypot. But herself...she had no experience to draw on. None that counted for them now. She bit her lip. What should she do? What *could* she do?

Even as her confidence shrank, Tarryn's seemed to expand. She waved to the crowd and blew them kisses.

Allie stared around at the crowd and at Jason, waiting beside George. What now? She glanced at the bouquet still clutched in her hand and stepped to the front of the stage. Tarryn followed, and they held their bouquets high before tossing them to the crowd. A sea of hands grabbed for them. A woman caught Tarryn's and held it aloft for a moment before presenting it to the woman next to her with a flourish.

Jason went back to the mic. "Everyone, you've seen the wedding, let us now party!"

He led the way off the stage, the curtain swept back, and DJ Strokes launched into a gay party anthem.

Allie blinked as the anticlimax washed over her. "We should get out the way."

"Do you want to hang around?" Tarryn's fingers brushed the back of Allie's hand. "Or shall we go somewhere quieter."

Allie opened her mouth to answer, but Phyll bustled up to them. "No sneaking off. You have to dance, be available for photos."

Tarryn formed one soundless word: *later*.

Chapter 20

FOR THE NEXT COUPLE OF hours, Tarryn whirled around the dance floor with a succession of people. She posed for countless selfies, received a few glasses of champagne and whispered propositions. From time to time, Sophie flashed into her vision: laughing, dancing, or smiling for photos.

Just as Tarryn was despairing of getting close to her, their gazes locked on the dance floor and they pushed through the crowd to each other.

Sophie grasped her hand. "I missed you." She reached up to kiss Tarryn, but they were interrupted by other people wanting a part of them. A drag queen pulled Tarryn away for a dance, and when she extricated herself, Sophie wasn't to be seen.

Kirra approached and thrust a glass of champagne into her hand. "Girlfriend, you are on fire. You're totally hot in that waistcoat." It hung undone, and Kirra ran her hands up Tarryn's sides. "The shirt shows off your boobage." She leaned closer. "And if you don't get lucky tonight, you can slap my arse and call me Shirley."

The blood pulsed anew in Tarryn's veins, and she gave Kirra an enigmatic smile. "What about you? Jason keeps your glass topped up, and he watches you when you're not looking."

Kirra's smile dropped at one corner. "I don't have a good record with cis men. I'll stick with my queer mob. Besides, Jason's straight."

"Is that what he says?" The memory of Jason talking with Sophie flashed through her mind. Straight, gay, bisexual, pansexual, queer. The label didn't matter as long as a person was honest in their intent.

Kirra shrugged. "I haven't asked, he hasn't offered. I'm not out to get my heart broken." Her gaze turned sharp. "You though…Sophie's going back to Sydney in a couple of days. How will your heart hold up?"

Tarryn scoffed. "When has my heart ever been in danger? Aren't I the queen of tourist seduction?"

"You are. But Sophie's different. And possibly a bit fragile. More so than you, anyway. Be considerate."

Kirra had never before said that to her. But then Kirra seldom knew Tarryn's partners. She flashed her a smile. "I will."

Kirra whirled away. Tarryn made her way out the crowd and down the street where things were quieter. Kirra's Kafé was in darkness, and Sophie's flat above had a single light, probably left on for her return. Her stomach rumbled, and she turned back to where the food trucks were grouped. There were some nachos there with her name on them.

She was in the line for food when Sophie appeared at her side.

"Hey. I thought you were slipping out on me, then I saw you here. Can you grab some for me too? I was too nervous to eat earlier, and all the alcohol is sloshing around on an empty stomach."

"Sure." She ordered two serves with pulled pork.

Sophie took her portion. "Thanks. I don't know about you, but I figure I've done enough. The festival doesn't need us any longer—it's purely party central. What say we sneak off to eat our nachos in peace? You can head back to the party after, if you want."

Tarryn examined her words. Did Sophie expect her to continue partying? Her voice was neutral, her smile polite. But earlier, when they'd kissed, there had been no way Sophie would have let Tarryn leave. Maybe she'd changed her mind. After all, she'd said at the rehearsal she wasn't looking for a fling. Maybe the flirting and kisses were purely for show.

So be it.

"I'd love to eat with you."

"My place?" Sophie's smile tilted. "I mean, Kirra's place."

"Sure."

They walked the couple of hundred metres to Sophie's apartment in silence. Tarryn looked around. Considering Sophie was leaving in a couple of days, the apartment looked much as it had done for the last three weeks:

slightly messy with papers on the dining table, a half-drunk bottle of red wine on the counter, and Sophie's sky-blue sweatshirt slung over a chair.

"Wine or water? They're my only choices."

"Water, please." The champagne she'd drunk was mixing with the tequila, and there was no way she wanted more alcohol.

Sophie grabbed the roll of kitchen towel and a couple of forks. "Are you okay with eating inside? I'd rather not be on display on the balcony for anyone walking past."

"I'd prefer that too." Tarryn waited while Sophie pushed papers aside to clear a space, then sat, her nachos in front of her. She lifted her glass of water. "Here's to a successful festival."

"Yes, it went well. Thank you so much for all your help, Tarryn. I couldn't have done it without you. You were great."

"I think we turned out to be a good team."

"We did—our rocky start smoothed out well. And thank you, too, for stepping up for the fake wedding. I know it's the last thing you wanted to do—"

"You don't say!" Tarryn smirked. "I thought I hid it well."

"As well disguised as a lioness in a cat café."

"Maybe I could open an alpaca café in Quandong." Tarryn dug a corn chip into the pile of beans and followed up with a pass through the sour cream. "Ally and Elly could make my fortune."

"Elly, maybe. I'm not sure Ally would play along."

"She'd learn. Eventually. We all can learn whatever we put our minds to, can't we?"

Sophie's smile flattened, and she stared into her glass of water.

What had she said? Tarryn couldn't think of anything that wasn't compliments and banter, but Sophie definitely looked less at ease than she had a moment ago. "Okay, I guess alpaca café is off the list of career choices. Maybe I could learn to make nachos as good as these instead. Now that would be a sure-fire money spinner."

"It would." Sophie ate a corn chip. "This pulled pork is amazing. Like they slow roasted it for hours rather than buying it ready made from a supermarket freezer."

"I don't know I'd go that far." Tarryn paused. "Why are we talking about nachos?"

"What do you want to talk about?" The purr was back in Sophie's voice. "We can talk about anything now we're married." She tilted her head. "Are you Tarryn Lane or am I Sophie Harris?"

"How about Harris-Lane?"

"It sounds like a street in inner Sydney," Sophie shot back. "How about Lane-Harris?"

"I don't know how same-sex couples sort it out. Do they toss a coin? Is it alphabetical order? The person who proposed gets to go first?"

"If your last name started with A, I'd change my name in a shot," Sophie said. "I always wanted an alliterative name."

What was she missing in the wine-and-tequila fog? "Don't you mean started with S?"

The pinkness crept up Sophie's neck and she glanced down to one side. "Uh, yeah. I don't know what I was thinking there."

Tarryn smiled; she was very adorable when flustered, even if right now, Tarryn didn't understand why. "We could make up a name."

"Harrane."

"Larris." Tarryn shook her head. "If someone had said to me even a month ago I'd be spending Saturday night trying to think of a married name for myself and my fake bride, I'd have laughed them all the way back to the tequila bottle. It's right up there with little girls playing dress up as brides."

"This is a bit surreal. I played brides when I was a kid. I married my best friend countless times when I was five. Then we played house," Sophie said.

"Did you practice kissing too?"

"We were five. Of course we did. Usually in Robyn's treehouse."

It all sounded so simple and happy. A treehouse, a best friend, practice kisses. There was probably a puppy.

"Robyn's puppy always wanted to join us, and we made her be our bridesmaid," Sophie continued. "We hoisted her up to the treehouse in a shopping basket on a rope."

Well, there it was. It was official—the most wholesome thing she'd heard all day.

"What did you do with your best friend?" Sophie asked.

"Ran wild through the bush. Skinny dipped in the waterfall."

"And then picked leeches off each other, I suppose?"

"There was a bit of that. Quandong is a special place, though. I was happy to move back when Dad left me the land." Emotion and alcohol swamped her in a wave, and she blinked back unexpected tears.

Sophie set down her fork and moved around the table to stand behind Tarryn. She wrapped her arms around Tarryn's neck from behind and bent to rest her cheek against her hair. "Are you okay? Please, tell me if you're not."

"I'm okay." She had to push the words past the lump in her throat. Sophie's arms around her shoulders, her face against her hair, felt…good. More than that. It made her feel wanted in a way her one-night stands seldom did. Sophie made her feel cared for. She raised her hands and rested them on Sophie's forearms. "Thank you for asking."

For a few moments, they rocked together. Tarryn exhaled softly, Sophie's body close to hers, the scent of her surrounding them. Her caring. She turned sideways on the chair, and Sophie moved around so they faced each other. Tarryn rested her head on Sophie's breast. The steady thud of her heartbeat sounded in her ears. For a minute, they remained like that, breathing in sync.

Tarryn's moment of self-pity dissipated as if blown away by a breeze. She was aware of Sophie's breast under her ear, her warm arms holding her close. She latched her own arms around Sophie's waist, her fingers stroking gently across her lower back.

Sophie's heartbeat sped up, faster, more erratic. Her arms tightened around Tarryn's shoulders, and one finger slowly moved back and forth on her upper arm.

Tarryn licked her lips. Thoughts of the afternoon came crashing back in a tsunami of emotion. How nervous she'd been, how her stomach had tilted and buzzed, the knowledge that even though it had been fake, no more real than a plastic doll, the thought that she was selling out all she believed in, all she had adamantly sworn she would never do, had overwhelmed her. Anger had flared, to be overwhelmed by a paralysing panic rendering her unable to say a word. Any words. Especially *the* words, the ones she'd sworn she'd never say: *I do.*

And Sophie had got her through it.

"Did you mean it?" she asked. "When you said, 'later'? Have you decided to live for the moment? Can we take this further and see where it leads?"

Sophie shifted her weight, and Tarryn raised her head to look into her eyes. Sophie's gaze seemed fixed on some far point, as if she were having an internal debate with herself.

Tarryn waited, her arms loosely around Sophie's waist, for her answer.

Sophie lifted a shoulder, and her smile lifted with it. "We'll never know if we don't try. If it's one night, well, we better make it memorable."

The fluttery feeling in her belly intensified, spreading outward in a circle of heat. She stood, and Sophie's arms fell away from her shoulders. "Shall we start with a kiss?"

"I can't think of anything better."

Chapter 21

Allie had thought pretending to be an event planner was a stretch. She stifled a nervous giggle. That was nothing on pretending to be a lesbian. It was one thing to admit to herself she was bisexual; it was another to sleep with a woman for the first time when that woman thought she was experienced. The nerves in her stomach fluttered up to her chest, balancing the heat pooled in her abdomen.

But she was in no doubt this was what she wanted. Her breath caught in her throat. Tarryn stood in front of her, and the open lust scrawled across her face made Allie's knees shake. She moved closer, enough that their bodies leaned lightly against each other. She slid her palms up Tarryn's forearms, marvelling at their softness over hard muscle.

She took a breath, doubt creeping in. It wasn't worry she couldn't do this…it was the wrongness of not telling Tarryn the truth. Of not telling her who she really was. *I'm sorry, Sophie.* She took a lungful of air. "I need to tell you something."

"Are you changing your mind?" Tarryn pulled back to stare into her face.

"No! Not at all, but—"

"Then, Sophie, please…don't talk now. We've got to this point. Please, just kiss me. We'll talk later, I promise."

She opened her mouth to insist, to say the words.

"Sophie, whatever it is, if you still want this, then, please, can we talk later? Not now."

At the naked longing scrawled on Tarryn's face, the words jammed in her throat. She swallowed them away and tried again. "I still want this."

Her nipples tingled as she pressed them against Tarryn's breasts, and then she touched her mouth to Tarryn's. Lust exploded in her body in a maelstrom of feelings. She wanted to touch Tarryn all over, feel her skin against her own, slide their legs together, and then, finally, learn the secrets between her thighs. She deepened the kiss, urging Tarryn's mouth open so she could slide her tongue inside and taste her.

Tarryn gripped Allie's hips, pulling her closer.

A deep throb started between her legs, and she straddled Tarryn's thigh, pushing against her.

Tarryn cupped her buttocks, and her tongue duelled with Allie's in a hot, wet, sensual dance.

It was nothing like kissing any of her previous male partners. Some of them had been amazing kissers, but this was not like anything she'd ever experienced. Her mind started cataloguing the kiss, but she shut it down with a snap. This was about the moment, not producing a spreadsheet of the differences. This was about feeling and doing, not studying and learning. As if something like this could be studied for, anyway, like tax laws. Allie pushed the thoughts from her mind and let her mind be subsumed by her body, sliding deeper into the kiss like a dive underwater to where everything was breathless and fresh. A new beginning.

Her breasts tingled, and she eased back from the kiss, not wanting it to end but wanting more. "Shall we go to the bedroom?"

A quick nod, and Tarryn released Allie's buttocks so she could step back. Her knees trembled, her skin alight with want, and she took the few steps to the bedroom. There, she flicked on the bedside light, throwing the room into a warm cocoon of mellow light.

Tarryn stared at her with a serious expression on her face. Was she having second thoughts? Allie stifled a nervous laugh; how ironic if Tarryn was the one to call a halt to this.

"I was just thinking how strange this is, in a way." Tarryn swept out a hand, the gesture encompassing the two of them, the bed, the warmly lit room. "One fake wedding. Is this now our fake honeymoon?"

"As long as I don't have to prompt you this time."

Tarryn's eyes crinkled as she smiled. "Don't worry about that." With a purposeful step, she closed the gap between them and touched Allie's waist over the pink dress. "How does this come off?"

"There's a zip on the other side." Allie closed her eyes briefly as a surge of nerves pushed to the fore. *It's happening. It's really happening.* Then Tarryn's fingers found the zip and lowered it, then slipped inside to smooth Allie's skin from waist to hip, and the nerves vanished in a puff of arousal. She was about to sleep with someone she liked, someone whose smouldering glances made her melt. Impatiently, she pushed the dress from her shoulders and wiggled it from her upper body.

Tarryn withdrew her hand and watched in silence as the dress crumpled around Allie's hips, then fell at her feet in a soft, pink cloud.

Allie tilted her head. "Do I have to undress you too?"

"Do you want to?"

In answer, she stepped away from the dress, moved forward, and undid the buttons of the waistcoat, lingering over each one so her fingers brushed Tarryn's breasts and abdomen. Once gone, she turned her attention to the shirt. The fine white linen was now crumpled from the day, and the buttons slipped easily until it, too, joined the waistcoat on the floor. A flash of guilt surfaced for their treatment of the hire clothes, but she pushed it down. Surely, they weren't the first newly married couple to treat them so carelessly in their rush to remove them.

Her fingers drifted over Tarryn's soft skin to trace the edge of the plain white bra. White made Allie look ghostlike; on Tarryn, it emphasised her strong body. When Allie's exploring fingers reached the waistband of the pants, she hesitated. A quick glance at Tarryn's face, a questioning head tilt to be sure that yes, this really was what she wanted. At Tarryn's nod, Allie fumbled with the button and dragged the zip down with shaking fingers.

"There's something we need to remove first." Tarryn shot her an amused look and shuffled to the bed where she sat and removed the red hi-tops and socks. She tugged off the pants and when she was dressed only in matching white boyshorts, she returned to where Allie still stood, feet glued to the floor.

"While shell-pink undies and red Vans is a great look on you, I think you can do better."

"I chose these undies with care." Allie tossed her a cheeky glance. "I was going to wear black, but they showed through the dress."

"I like the pink. But the shoes have to go."

Allie undid the laces, then toed them off, removing her socks at the same time.

"Better."

When had Tarryn taken the lead in this? Allie summoned her confident face and strutted over to the bed. She rested a hand on her hip. "Any more directions, Ms Harris?"

"You don't need them." She sat on the side of the bed and swung her legs up. "Why don't you join me? That's a suggestion."

Allie wet her lips. She walked to the bed and sank, joining Tarryn until they lay face-to-face. A kiss, that was what she wanted now. She leaned in and kissed Tarryn, putting all her longing and desire into the touch of her lips. Tarryn's hand brushed down Allie's side, from shoulder to her hips. For long moments, they did nothing except kiss and explore, skin to skin, fingers brushing the bands of underwear but not yet removing them. The secrets hidden underneath would be revealed, Allie was sure of that, but there was no hurry.

They had all the time in the world...for tonight at least.

Tarryn rested her fingers on the catch of Allie's bra strap and broke the kiss to ask, "You okay with this?"

"Oh yes." Allie breathed the words over the white noise in her head. The bra was too confining, a barrier she didn't want.

When Tarryn fumbled the catch open, Allie moved back enough that she could draw the bra away. Tarryn urged her onto her back and pressed a kiss to the hollow of her throat.

Allie's heartbeat thundered in her ears, and she pressed her thighs together as if that could assuage the heat building between them. Tarryn's lips travelled slowly, at an infinitesimal crawl, down from her throat to her breastbone. She hovered, her breath moist on Allie's skin, then her lips meandered to Allie's right nipple. When Tarryn covered it with her mouth, her tongue swirling around the tip, Allie arched her back as darts of pleasure radiated out from that point. She rested her hands on Tarryn's tight curls as if she could keep her mouth there, right where she wanted it.

When Tarryn kissed her way to the other nipple, the abandoned one shone wetly in the soft light, puckering in the air.

Allie's fingers clenched on the quilt as the pleasure kept coming. When Tarryn lifted her head, disappointment shot through her, but Tarryn only sat up to remove her own bra. Her breasts were small, her large nipples a rich copper brown, darker than her skin. Allie sat up too, needing to touch them. Her fingers traced a path from Tarryn's throat, down her sternum, then stroked a circle around the edge of her breast. One circle, then another, a smaller one, again and again until finally her fingers touched Tarryn's nipple. It peaked under her fingers. Another circle, this time wider until she repeated the entire movement on the other breast.

Tarryn lay back on the bed, her arms over her head, her gaze locked on Allie's face.

Allie's breath caught in her throat. Tarryn was magnificent; her body laid out for her to appreciate, her eyes dark and hooded, her breasts rising and falling with every breath. The white boyshorts banded her flat stomach and narrow hips. Allie's fingers itched to explore around and underneath.

And she could, she realised. Tarryn's pose invited that.

She straddled Tarryn's hips and touched her breasts again before smoothing a path down over her stomach to the band of her underwear. Slipping a finger underneath, she kept her gaze fixed on Tarryn's face, watching how her pupils widened, darkening her eyes even more.

Her fingers drifted to the sides of the undies. "I think it's time for these to go."

Tarryn lifted her hips, and Allie hooked her fingers into the top of the boyshorts and dragged them down to where she straddled Tarryn's thighs. She swallowed hard, feasting her eyes on the dark, springy curls between her thighs, at odds with the grey hair on her head. Tentatively, she placed her palm over that place.

Tarryn shifted restlessly. "You have me trapped."

Allie flicked her a wicked smile. Her pulse thundered. "I'm taking my time." It was as much for her as for Tarryn. It was all so new, so different. Not strange, but natural. *Why haven't I done this before?* She had no answer, but the main thing was she was doing it now. She pressed down on Tarryn's thighs, her clit throbbing against her damp undies.

Again, she dragged a finger along the top of Tarryn's mound, then down to the apex of her thighs,

Tarryn gasped and tried to part her thighs, blocked by the vice of Allie's legs.

"Harsh and unnecessary cruelty," Tarryn said. She brought her hands forward and caressed Allie's nipples.

That feels so good. So unbelievably good. The pressure in her mind eased, and suddenly it was all so easy. Allie moved off Tarryn's thighs, freeing her. Her fingers dropped lower and into the cleft of Tarryn's parted thighs. "You're so wet." Was that her voice, so smoky and dark, so husky with arousal? She eased the tip of one finger between Tarryn's folds and stroked.

"More," Tarryn said.

Allie swallowed. Was there a rule for this, for how many fingers and what she was supposed to do with them? She took a deep breath and expelled it, forcing herself to relax. She knew what she liked when she masturbated, what she liked with a partner. She would follow Tarryn's cues. She added a second finger and pushed inside. How good it felt to be inside Tarryn, inside her narrow, wet channel. Allie moved gently, loving how Tarryn clenched on her fingers. She withdrew and circled Tarryn's clit, softly, until the push of those hips urged her on and her strokes became surer, defter.

When Tarryn's back arched and her eyes closed, her mouth making a soundless O, wetness coated Allie's fingers, echoed by the moisture between her own legs. A ripple of pride beat in her chest. *I've made Tarryn come.*

She withdrew her fingers and shifted so she could lie next to her. "Okay?"

"Hell, yeah." Tarryn drew her closer so she could kiss her, her tongue softly stroking Allie's lips. "More than okay." She rested her hand on Allie's waist, content, it seemed, to continue kissing her.

Allie shifted restlessly, the drumbeat of arousal still beating in her blood. Should she bring herself off? She didn't want to pressure Tarryn. She lifted her hips and dragged one side of her undies down so she could slip her hand between her legs.

"Impatient." Tarryn's voice held a lilt of amusement. "Do you really think I'd leave you unsatisfied? What do you want? What do you like best?"

What indeed? The answer was known but unknown. The same but different.

"You've shown yourself pretty able so far," she said. "Surprise me."

"These are in the way." Tarryn's fingers tugged at Allie's undies, the remaining barrier between them.

She lifted her hips again so Tarryn could remove them.

"Kneel on the bed," Tarryn said. "I want to see you."

She did so, parting her knees enough that Tarryn could see between her thighs.

Tarryn rose to kiss her again, and one hand drifted down across her breasts, down her belly, to delve between her legs.

At the first touch of her fingers, Allie gasped, the final twinge of nerves evaporated. When Tarryn stroked, her body shuddered into lightness. How did Tarryn know how to touch her? How did she know the pressure, the moves, the angle? There was no need for directions, no "softer, please" or "don't pinch." There was just Tarryn and her talented fingers bringing her ever closer to the edge.

She gripped Tarryn's shoulders, and her eyes trembled shut. Just when she thought she'd reached the point of no return, Tarryn stopped.

"Lie down," she instructed.

Allie did so, and Tarryn swung over onto her stomach, pushing Allie's thighs apart in the same movement. Then her mouth was between Allie's thighs, tongue curling between Allie's folds, circling her clit, as one finger pushed inside.

She clenched her fists on the quilt as quivers ran through her body, centred between her legs. Her stomach muscles tightened, and her inner muscles clenched. And then Tarryn covered her with her mouth and sucked, and Allie exploded into a million pieces. She realised the voice crying out in pleasure was her own.

For a moment, she was boneless on the bed, gulping air.

Tarryn moved up beside her to kiss her again, and she tasted herself for the first time: salty, earthy. Good.

"Okay?" Tarryn asked. She lay on her side and wrapped an arm over Allie's stomach.

"More than okay. You?"

"Oh yeah." Tarryn sighed into Allie's shoulder.

"I guess that's our wedding night," Allie joked.

"The only one I'll ever have."

"Well, I'm glad to have made it good for you."

"You did. You still are." Tarryn pressed a kiss to Allie's upper arm. "And I know how you can make it better."

She raised her head to stare into Tarryn's face. The light in her eyes left her in no doubt as to what she meant. Her hand started to explore again.

"I think I can manage that."

Chapter 22

THE SUNLIGHT FILTERING THROUGH FROM the living room woke Tarryn. For a moment she lay there, getting her bearings. Whose bed was she in? A tourist's motel? Then the events of the night before came back in a heated rush. *Sophie.* She turned her head. Sophie was sleeping curled on her side facing her, one hand under her cheek, her chest rising and falling.

Tarryn considered her options: Leave quietly as she often did after a night with someone, to avoid the awkward morning after? Or wake Sophie with a kiss and see where it led. Warmth settled in her stomach. Even if Sophie hadn't been her friend, her sort of boss, sneaking out wasn't an option. She wanted to end their working relationship on a good note, and stealing away into the morning wasn't the way to do that. She had to own what had happened. It wasn't that she regretted it—anything but. It had been *magnificent.*

She looked at Sophie's lashes on her cheeks, the way her tousled hair snarled on the pillow, her shoulders as pale as the sheets. Sophie was a surprise package, both in her working style and in herself. A rush of tenderness engulfed her, and she reached out a hand to stroke Sophie's hair back from her face but then hesitated. That would wake her, and she wasn't sure she was ready for that yet.

She glanced over to where her wedding suit lay crumpled on the floor. She should at least get up, smooth it out, and put it on a hanger. For a moment, she remembered Sophie's calmness and confidence in getting her through the fake ceremony. Sophie had freed her from the worries and doubts that had surged to the fore and sealed her lips. She shook her head. One fake marriage hadn't changed her views one iota, but that wasn't her concern. No, her life was her shed, her welding tools, Ally and Elly watching her from the end of the barn, and a quiet life in a small town. One night with a beautiful woman hadn't changed that in the past, even though she'd had invitations from tourists to travel with them for a while. Sophie was no different in that respect, even if she were to suggest it.

Sophie's eyes opened, then widened, taking her in.

She smiled. Sophie's bemusement mirrored her own.

"Good morning." Sophie sat up in bed. The quilt fell to her waist.

Tarryn's glance went to her breasts. Yes, still as gorgeous as she remembered.

Sophie licked her lips. "I need water. Want some?" She got out of bed and pulled on a robe from the back of the door. "We didn't drink that much last night, did we?"

"Yes to the water, and I think we had more to drink than we should have."

"My head says you're right. I'll add paracetamol to my morning."

Sophie disappeared into the bathroom and returned with a box of pain-killers which she dropped on the bed, then went out to the kitchen for water.

When she returned, she handed a glass to Tarryn and sat on the edge of the bed while she drank.

"It's been a while since I woke up with someone new. Do I ask if you're okay with this? I don't want to pressure you, but I'd like it if you stayed for breakfast."

The yes hovered on Tarryn's tongue, but she shook her head. "I'd love to, but I can't. Ally and Elly need feeding, and I'd like some different clothes. My jeans and T-shirt must still be in the community hall where we changed."

"I'd forgotten about that." Sophie's eyes widened. "You're welcome to borrow anything of mine, if you think it will fit." She eyed Tarryn's length. "But I'm not sure it will."

"Thanks, but I'll go home to change."

"Okay." Sophie worried the sheet with her fingers. "So we just say 'thanks for a great night and see you around,' then?"

Tarryn huffed a laugh, then sobered at Sophie's expression. "Were you expecting more?"

"No. Well, I expected a kiss, at least, and maybe breakfast. After all, we're not strangers, and we still have today to get through as colleagues.

How about I grab some muffins from Kirra's, and we have coffee? Have you time?"

"Of course. Ally and Elly aren't that demanding."

A quick nod. "Then I'll go now. Feel free to grab a shower, if you want." She leaned in and kissed Tarryn, a quick brush of her mouth. "I'd kiss you properly, but I haven't brushed my teeth."

She shed the robe, slipped into a pair of jeans and a sweatshirt, and disappeared.

Tarryn blew out a breath and lay back. It was true she needed to get moving, and the alpacas would be a bit tetchy about their late breakfast, but there was no immediate reason to rush away. She got out of bed and went to investigate the shower. Once out, she cleaned her teeth with a finger and followed the sounds of the coffee maker to the kitchen.

As well as muffins, there were a couple of pieces of zucchini slice on the table. Sophie added a bottle of hot sauce, then returned with the two coffees. "Good timing."

"Is Kirra busy?"

"Frantic. Every table is occupied with visitors, and there's a line out the door. She let me queue jump."

Tarryn went over and wrapped her arms around Sophie's waist. "Now I get to say a proper good morning." She nuzzled her neck, then moved up for the kiss.

Sophie sighed into her mouth. "Good morning to you too." She broke the kiss. "It's gone eight. I'm not rushing you, but we'll need to eat if you want to get home to change. We've got a debrief meeting at nine before we start the clean-up."

A hollow feeling settled in Tarryn's stomach, and for a moment, she considered saying the alpacas could wait, breakfast could wait. Instead, she would take Sophie's hand and lead her back to bed. But she still had to get proper clothes, so she nodded and sat, reaching for a muffin.

Ten minutes later, after a final kiss, she clattered down the stairs and out to the street.

"Oh, ho! No need to ask where you spent the night." Kirra was lowering the blind outside the café, and she looked Tarryn's wedding clothes up and down, then raised an eyebrow. "You took the fake wedding seriously after all, girlfriend, if it led to a fake wedding night."

Tarryn huffed. "Okay, you've sprung me."

Kirra threw up her hands. "No blame, no shame. Sophie's lovely." She moved closer. "Good night?"

Her smile grew until it felt like her face would split. "The best."

"Good. Make the most of it. Tonight's her last night in town, and I can't extend the booking on the apartment. Although she could always stay at yours, if she can stand the rustic conditions." She winked.

"I think she has to get back to Sydney." Tarryn went to thrust her hands in her pockets, remembering at the last moment the smart pants had only tiny ones. "No worries. It was a great night, but I'm not looking to make our marriage a real one."

"Shame," Kirra said. "Sophie would be great in Quandong."

"I'll see you at nine for the debrief. I gotta change."

"You do that." Kirra winked. "Unless you want everyone to know where you spent the night."

Allie sat at the table, staring at the space where Tarryn had been. Well, that was pretty much that. Her first night with a woman, but she already knew it wouldn't be her last. In her mind, she pictured Sophie's reaction. No doubt there would be an "I knew it!" and a huge grin.

She rose and headed for the shower. Before talking to Sophie, there was a debrief and a day of clean-up to get through. And one more night in Quandong.

As she soaped her body, the image of Tarryn's hands running over her skin engulfed her. *Tarryn.* How could she have ever thought her prickly and difficult? Now, with hindsight, she came across as determined and true to her values. But she'd set those values aside for the sake of her town. If Tarryn lived in Sydney, would they date? An echo of last night's lovemaking unfurled as heat in her belly. She hoped they would. She'd want to—but Tarryn was the self-described queen of the one-night stand. She probably wouldn't go there, even if distance wasn't an issue. Allie bit her lip. So, a fling, then. She was a big girl—she could handle it. And it wasn't as if she'd never had one-night stands before. Previously, though, they had been with strangers, not someone she was friends with.

Not someone she could fall for.

Was falling for.

Had fallen for.

The water streamed over her head. She'd fallen for Tarryn. And that was a dead-end with no hope for a relationship.

But they still had tonight.

Allie surreptitiously looked at her phone. Phyll had been speaking for fifteen minutes. So far, she'd thanked half the committees and helpers, which meant there was probably another fifteen minutes to go.

"And, of course," Phyll said, "we couldn't have done this, all this, the festival, the publicity, the last-minute changes without Sophie Lane. She swooped in to save us when we were floundering at the start, then she dived in again to help us sort out the last-minute hitches. Like the portaloos."

Allie pasted on a smile and hoped she looked amused at Phyll's dragging up of the portaloo issue.

"Seriously, Sophie, we are very grateful to you. And, of course, no thanks to you goes without a mention of your hard-working assistant, our very own Tarryn Harris."

Next to her, Tarryn grinned around the room.

"We all know Tarryn's aversion to weddings—even same-sex ones—and to marriage in general, but she ponied up and stepped in—"

"And got paid," Ziggy said.

"And got paid far less than she's worth and for far fewer hours than she actually worked," Phyll continued. "As you all know, Sophie and Tarryn were our couple for the wedding ceremony, the culmination of the festival, and they played their parts with good grace and amazing enthusiasm."

Curse her pale skin. Allie tried not to flush with embarrassment as the good-natured laughter rippled around the room. Of course everyone had seen her and Tarryn kiss with far more gusto than the part entailed. Her face when she smiled her thanks was as hot as Tarryn's kiss.

"For going above and beyond," Phyll continued, "we all chipped in for a thank you gift." She approached Allie and Tarryn with two envelopes.

"There's no need to thank me," Allie said. "I was only doing what was necessary for the success of the festival. I appreciate the thought, but I'd be happy if you would give mine to Tarryn."

"As you wish," Phyll said. "But you might want to share them anyway." With an exaggerated wink, she handed both envelopes to Tarryn.

"Thank you." Tarryn held the envelopes aloft.

"You have to open them now," Phyll said when it seemed Tarryn was about to pocket them.

"Is it embarrassing?"

"No. Just a helpful gesture. Your friends in Quandong can read the room."

That doesn't sound good. Allie hoped it was something tame like a supermarket gift token, but she had her doubts.

Tarryn ripped open the envelope and pulled out a folded piece of paper. She opened it. "It's an Airbnb voucher. Thank you, everyone. This will be great when I go visit my friend in Mackay."

A few faces looked disappointed. Allie mentally shrugged. They may have hoped the two of them would share the nights, probably halfway between Sydney and Quandong, but it obviously wasn't going to happen. It wasn't practical.

What a shame.

After a pause, Phyll turned to Allie. "Do you want to give the wrap-up?"

Allie leaned forward. "I don't have too much to say. Mainly that you all were the most amazing bunch of people to work with and you made my job so easy. I've already forwarded the advance articles about the festival to Phyll—if someone could keep an eye out for others. Those are the news sources you should target first in your marketing campaign next year. Feedback I received over the two days from festivalgoers was overwhelmingly positive. The only slight niggle was people saying they had to wait too long for their food at the local food dinner. That was mainly due to more people than anticipated attending—vendors and suppliers were caught on the hop; you'll know for next year. I also suggest increasing the number of stalls."

Phyll nodded. "I'll take care of it."

"That's it, then. It's been a wonderful festival, and it's been my pleasure to assist you in making it the success it was. Now we just have to take down and clear up. I'm leaving tomorrow morning if anyone has any last-minute questions for me."

"You all know your clean-up crews," Phyll said. "Let's get to it."

Allie and Tarryn were part of the crew disassembling the stage area where the ceremony had taken place. Allie stared at it for a moment. This was the place she'd kissed Tarryn in front of hundreds, *thousands, hordes,* of people. Talk about a way to come out. There'd been TV cameras at the event. For a moment, she wondered if Sophie had seen it. She frowned. There hadn't been a peep out of Sophie since yesterday afternoon. She'd have to call her.

With so many people helping, the main street was restored to order quite quickly. Allie shed her work gloves and looked around. Most people had headed away. Only Jason and a couple of his regulars were still working around the front of The Hollowman, and Tarryn was talking to the hire crew who had come to pick up their equipment.

She hesitated. Would Tarryn suggest a final night together? Her new-found feelings pulsed in her throat. It was what she wanted, another night with Tarryn before she returned to Sydney to try to figure out her life. Another night to allow her emotions to come to the fore, to accept Tarryn wasn't simply an experimental night in her life but was someone she could care for. Did care for.

Did Tarryn simply see her as another one-night stand? Almost certainly. But that didn't negate Allie's feelings for her. No one should tell her how to feel.

And she could be the one to ask Tarryn to dinner.

Tarryn came over and pulled off her gloves. "That's the stage gone. Are we done here?"

"We are."

"Then I'll be off." Tarryn hesitated. "Sophie, you're returning to Sydney tomorrow?"

Tarryn's stance had the look of a farewell speech. Allie jumped in before she could say more. "I am. I was wondering if you'd like to have dinner tonight. My treat."

Tarryn's smile crinkled her eyes. "Is this purely to thank me for my superb help, my over-the-top willingness, the extra hours I haven't billed?"

"Partly," Allie admitted. "But mainly, I was hoping we could have dinner and that you might like to stay over." Heart pounding, she waited for Tarryn's answer.

Tarryn came closer, enough that Allie could see the shine in her eyes. "I'd like that."

"I'll pick you up. Is six okay? How about we go somewhere in Byron Bay?"

"That sounds good. I'm already looking forward to it." Tarryn closed the gap and rested a hand on Allie's waist. "Especially the part after we come home." She leaned in and kissed Allie, her lips soft and exploring.

Allie melted against her. What did it matter if someone saw them?

She broke the kiss. "Until later."

Chapter 23

ALLIE HAD PICKED A RESTAURANT on the waterfront, the prices matching its glamorous position. Even on a Sunday, it was busy, with most tables already occupied when Allie and Tarryn arrived. The waiter seated them with a view of the bay, brought menus, and explained the specials.

Allie perused the selection, selecting the local seafood catch of the day even as she winced at the price. *Making memories.* If this was to be her last night with Tarryn, she wanted it to be as perfect as she could make it.

When the wine was poured, Allie lifted her glass. "To Quandong."

"To Quandong," Tarryn echoed and tapped her glass with Allie's. After they had drunk, she asked, "Are you looking forward to getting back to Sydney?"

"Not particularly. I've really enjoyed being here, although I need to get back to real life. I need to find—" She shut her mouth with a snap. She'd been about to say she needed to find a new job. Her stomach suddenly dragged as if she'd swallowed a rock. She was in a wonderful restaurant in a glorious seaside town, about to have an expensive meal with a beautiful woman, one she'd come to care for. And it was all a fake. All lies. The mouthful of wine roiled in her stomach.

"Need to find what?" Tarryn cocked her head.

"My next big project."

"I would have thought you'd already have that lined up?"

"Small ones, yes, but nothing the size of the wedding festival."

"How do you find work?" Tarryn asked.

The stone grew to the size of a boulder. Working on the festival hadn't made her feel this much of an impostor. She'd been doing it for Sophie, and her needs were the bigger, the ones that took priority. But this…this was lying to someone she cared for. But she couldn't change now. And tomorrow she'd be gone, and she'd likely never see Tarryn again.

"Can we talk about something else?" She summoned a smile. "I'll be back at work soon enough."

"Sure." Tarryn took a mouthful of wine. "Tell me about your life in Sydney. Where do you live?"

Oh God, this was worse. What had she said before?

"I have an apartment in Darlinghurst. It's nothing special—everything there is so expensive, but it's central, and near friends and my sister."

"Allison? Or do you have another sister?"

"Just the one. She'll be pleased to see me home."

"The accountant?" Tarryn leaned across the table.

"She was. But she recently lost her job, and she's also recovering from a major car accident." Her heart pounded, increasing in speed with every lie she told. *Change the subject. Fast.* "What about you? Any siblings?"

"No, just me and Mama. I should get down to see her sometime soon. She lives in Sydney."

"Maybe we can catch up when you do." Why had she said that? Compounding the lie. She needed to stop this, make the clean break and get on with her life, with finding a new accountancy job, with a life that didn't include the gorgeous woman sitting opposite.

"I'd like that. I might be—"

The waiter appeared bearing their starters, and Tarryn sat back to let him place the plates.

What was she going to say? Maybe she was planning a trip soon. Allie smiled her thanks as the waiter placed her pumpkin gnocchi in front of her.

"Ally and Elly will be pleased to have more of your time," she said once the first mouthful had been taken.

"They will. Ally spat at me yesterday. She normally leaves me alone—knows the hand that feeds."

"I'm sorry I didn't spend more time with them." Allie paused and took a forkful of food. There was the opening, right there, for Tarryn to say she was welcome back to see them. But Tarryn remained silent.

When the waiter cleared their plates, Allie topped up their wine glasses. Her stomach churned, filled with a mixture of rich food and lies. It had all seemed so harmless in the beginning—she'd simply been helping her sister out of a bind. She'd never planned on seeing any of these people again. Certainly, she'd never planned on falling for Tarryn.

"I'm thinking of training the alpacas as pack animals," Tarryn said. "Maybe I could take people on longer guided walks in the rainforest. Elly would be fine, I think, but I'm not sure about Ally. She's a feisty little minx. I'd have to lead her all the time."

"You could trial it with people you know," Allie said. "Maybe Will and Garrett would be into it. Would you camp along the way or stay somewhere?"

"If Will and Garrett were my trial, it would have to include a roof and a big bed. Can you imagine either of them in a leaky tent in the rain?"

"Not easily. You could use your Airbnb vouchers." She wasn't hinting, she really wasn't, but if Tarryn were to say she thought she'd save them for the two of them to use together, then she would probably smile and give up all her plans to agree.

"It seems a bit of a waste. But yeah, I could."

The waiter brought their main courses, and for a few moments, they were silent. Allie flicked a glance at Tarryn. She had her head down, eating steadily. Allie picked a piece of fish from the bones. It was good fish, great really, succulent and cooked to perfection. A shame she wasn't enjoying it as she should.

She put down her knife and fork. "This is a bit awkward, isn't it? Us being here, not really knowing what to say." She sighed. "Maybe we should have left it at last night, said our goodbyes this afternoon, and I'd drive off to Sydney tomorrow, remembering a certain one night with great fondness."

Tarryn, too, put down her cutlery. "Part of me says you're right, but part of me is glad for this extra night." She took a quick breath. "Last night was quite special, Sophie. I don't know why. I'm not a relationship type of person most of the time. Maybe it's because we worked together that I feel closer to you. And maybe, because I knew you'd be returning to Sydney, that allowed me to run with my feelings while I could. But...well, if you lived here, I'd ask you out again. And again after that. Until maybe we went out on so many single dates, we were in a relationship without knowing it." A shoulder lifted. "But you're going back to Sydney, which isn't the end of the earth, but it is a big city, one where I would be stifled. My life is here, and yours is in the city."

Allie's fingers clenched on her wineglass. Tarryn wanted to go out with her. For a moment, she allowed herself a moment to dream of the two of them. In Quandong. Training the alpacas together. Dinner with Will and Garrett. Coffee and sass with Kirra. Maybe helping to organise the next Gay Bells festival.

But then it all came crashing down. She lived in Sydney. And the big one: she was Allie, not Sophie. Allie who was an accountant, who wasn't the lesbian Tarryn thought but a baby-gay in training—not straight, but whichever way you looked at it, she wasn't who she'd said she was.

She was deceptive and deceitful—a liar in so many ways.

She had to shut this down. But she couldn't. Not entirely. There was no way she could let Tarryn believe she didn't want her, not when Tarryn had just opened herself to the possibility of a relationship.

"I would date you too, in a heartbeat. I'd walk the alpacas through the rainforest with you, and I wouldn't complain if Ally spat on my shoulder. But my life isn't in Quandong. And it would seem crazy to move…now."

"We could see how we go. Visit each other. Meet halfway. Use those Airbnb vouchers as everyone intended."

"I don't know, Tarryn." Allie cut a piece of broccoli and raised it to her mouth, then put it down untouched. A few minutes ago, she'd been ready to offer Tarryn the moon and stars if she suggested something like this. But reality had crept in again, along with the renewed knowledge of what her lies would mean to Tarryn. She took a sip of wine to ease her suddenly dry mouth. "It could be the slow death. I'd rather remember one amazing, incredible night than suffer that."

Tarryn's face held the immobility of granite. "What about tonight?"

Allie reached across the table and took Tarryn's hand. "We can have tonight. So we have two amazing, incredible nights to remember. If you want."

"I do." Tarryn tightened her grip. "Strange how I can say those words now but couldn't yesterday."

"Different time, different place. Different headspace."

Tarryn's thumb passed back and forth over Allie's hand. Shivers danced across her skin, and she focussed on Tarryn's lips, on her sensual mouth that had worked such wonders. Suddenly, she didn't want to be here in this overpriced restaurant, eating food she didn't want. "I'm not hungry anymore."

"I'm not hungry for food. Just for you."

"Then let's go home."

The drive home was mostly silent. Tarryn watched the dark land-scape slide past, the winding road through the rainforest leading back to Quandong. Sophie drove carefully, obviously aware of the likelihood of wallabies darting in front of the car. Tarryn rested her hand on Sophie's thigh, feeling the muscles shift as she changed gear, enjoying the warmth under her hand.

At the edge of Quandong, Sophie looked across. "My place?"

Tarryn nodded. Kirra's apartment was more comfortable than her shouse. And, a tiny voice whispered, she'd rather not be reminded of Sophie in her space. They'd agreed a clean break was best, but the niggle inside her said it would take time for Sophie to leave her head.

Strange how it had worked out. The woman who'd seemed a bit difficult at first had become...certainly someone she liked. A friend. More. Tarryn compressed her lips. That was the problem. Despite what she'd told Sophie, she wanted more than friendship. A hollowness echoed inside her, an ache, a space that could only be filled by Sophie—and Sophie was already sliding away, vacating her place in Tarryn's chest. And there was nothing to fill it.

But they had tonight.

Last night had been wonderful. Sure, Sophie had been an enthusiastic and giving lover, but it had been more than that. Their existing relationship had been...not brushed aside, not ignored, but it had deepened. Sex had forged a new connection unlike anything Tarryn had experienced. She'd woken in the morning, and the new curling shoot of tenderness had taken her by surprise. Would it be the same tonight, or would she be able to walk away in the morning, her nights with Sophie already relegated to casual sex, stuffed in a box marked *Fantastic Fling*?

Sophie halted the car outside the apartment. The street was quiet; only a few visitors strolled, probably on their way back from The Hollowman. In silence, they walked up the stairs. Sophie left the light off, allowing only the streetlights to filter in.

"Do you want anything?" she asked. The words *before bed* hung unsaid.

Tarryn licked her dry lips. "Some water would be good."

Sophie handed her a glass of water and watched as she drank it, then refilled the glass from the tap.

"Bed?" Tarryn held out her free hand.

Sophie nodded, and together they walked to the bedroom. The bed was the same inviting space it had been last night. Tarryn had expected a clearer head to have dulled the anticipation, but instead, the thrum of longing was greater, intensified.

Inside the room, she turned to Sophie and drew her close, kissing her with her all the pent-up longing in her heart.

Sophie returned the kiss, wrapping her arms around Tarryn's neck, her tongue seeking entrance to her mouth.

She reached down and cupped Sophie's buttocks, urging her closer and nudging her own thigh between Sophie's.

Their clothes disappeared in a slow, leisurely fashion, piece by piece, with kisses on each newly exposed piece of skin. Sophie spent long minutes exploring Tarryn's breasts, feathering her fingers around their curves, sucking her nipples until Tarryn's clit pulsated with need. And when Sophie pushed her back onto the bed, parted her thighs and settled between, Tarryn's skin lit with flame.

"Can I taste you?" Sophie asked, her voice husky with need.

She could only nod in reply, and then, when Sophie's tongue lapped at her lower lips and then curled around her clit, it was as if the moon and stars had fallen to Earth and landed on Sophie's tongue. She was quicksilver in the dim light, her pale skin ethereal against the white sheets, her tongue dancing in a glorious motion, exactly as Tarryn liked. How did she know the exact thing? How could they be so perfectly compatible in bed?

Tarryn arched into her orgasm, her mind exploding with stars.

Allie lay awake long after Tarryn had fallen asleep. Her gaze traced the strong lines of Tarryn's shoulders and arms and lingered where her breasts were covered by the sheet. This second night together had brought one thing into blinding clarity: this was no experimental one-off. Tarryn was someone she would like to see more of, to let her into her life and see where it led.

But she couldn't. Even though Tarryn had suggested a way forward for them, Allie just couldn't. She closed her eyes and tried to will sleep to come, but her eyes popped open again as if the ceiling was the most fascinating thing she'd seen all day.

What should she do? Her heart told her she needed to confess who she really was—but was there any point, now? She was going home tomorrow. What good would it do except to finish their time together on a sour note? She pressed her lips together. That would probably settle it once and for all; Tarryn would be angry and probably wouldn't want anything more to do with her.

Maybe. Or maybe she'd laugh, and tease, and maybe, just maybe, they could find a way forward.

But then there was Sophie. Outing herself meant exposing Sophie as well, and that put her business on the line. Everything they'd tried hard to avoid. It might mean bad publicity for her, a demand for the return of her fee. It could be disastrous. As if Sophie didn't have enough to deal with in her life right now.

For a moment, she thought about going onto the balcony and calling Sophie, asking her advice. But she already knew what Sophie would say. She'd tell Allie to do what she needed for her own sake, that she'd already done so much to help Sophie's business and should put herself first.

But Sophie was the most important person in her life. How could she do that to her? She wouldn't add to her current difficulties, and for what? For maybe a short-lived long-distance relationship with someone she liked? There were plenty of women who dated women in Sydney. Just because Tarryn was her first, didn't mean she'd be her only. She just had to return to Sydney, sign up for a dating app, and see what happened.

She turned over in bed and closed her eyes again. That was the answer. There was nothing else she could do.

Chapter 24

"WHAT TIME ARE YOU LEAVING?" Tarryn asked as they sat with mugs of coffee on the balcony. "Not that I'm pushing you away. Anything but. I'm just wondering how long we've got." She winked.

Allie clutched her mug harder, enough that the heat of it was uncomfortable on her palms. "Kirra asked if I could be gone by noon so she's time to turn the room around for her next guest. If I head away then, I can get home in one day." She twisted the mug in her hands. "And I should."

Tarryn nodded. "If you want, you can stay with me tonight. Leave early in the morning."

Allie hesitated, the words "yes, please" on her tongue. But she just couldn't, not without explaining who she was. She'd finally got to sleep last night in the early hours, and her mind was dusty with tiredness. She stared at Tarryn, her mind buzzing.

There was no way she could walk away without sharing the truth. She'd always been a straightforward, truthful person. She couldn't change now, even if it angered Tarryn, even—Allie swallowed hard—if it led to repercussions for Sophie. She would have to understand.

"I'd like that." She set down her mug and reached for Tarryn's hand, grasping it like a lifeline. She licked her dry lips. "But I need to tell you something first."

Tarryn tilted her head, her dark eyes soft and warm. "That sounds ominous. Is this what you wanted to say the other night?"

Allie nodded.

"Are you going to elope with Kirra? Are you moving to Nepal to lead Everest base camp treks?"

"Neither of those. Please listen to all I need to tell you before you say anything." She swallowed the lump in her throat along with the thought she was about to destroy everything. "You know I have a sister. What you don't know is that we're twins. Our names are Allison and Sophie." She took a deep breath. "But I'm Allie, short for Allison, and my sister is Sophie. She's the event planner, the person Quandong hired to organise the festival. Sophie was severely injured in a car accident, and she's still struggling. She begged me to come up here and take her place."

Tarryn's forehead wrinkled, and her hand was slack in Allie's grasp. "Why the pretence? Why didn't you just tell us who you are? Sophie was unable to be here, so she sent her replacement."

"It's not that simple." The beginnings of a headache beat at the base of Allie's skull. "Sophie is a one-person business, and her contract with Quandong stated she had to be the person to come here. She asked me to come because if she was forced to pull out of the contract, not only would she be leaving Quandong in the lurch but her business would go under. It's a new business, and she can't work at the moment. She'd have lost her business, and likely her home."

She dared a look at Tarryn. She didn't seem horrified; her flickering expressions hinted at confusion more than anything else. Allie sucked a shallow breath. Maybe it would be all right. But she still had to admit to the big thing.

"You've seen how we are here," Tarryn said. "If Sophie had explained, said she was sending her assistant in her place, in the circumstances, we would almost certainly have agreed."

The headache pounded harder. "She was too afraid to take that risk. The stakes were too high. Also, I'm not her assistant. I'm an accountant, not an event planner. Well, I'm an unemployed accountant at the moment, and that's why I was able to step in."

"Still. You did well. I've talked with Phyll and others—they're all very happy with how you handled things."

"Now they are. Would they have taken a chance before?"

"I don't know," Tarryn admitted. She tugged her hand from Allie's grasp and cupped her mug. "It's not right, Allison. You did a great job, but we were paying for an experienced person."

"Sophie took all my calls and gave advice. She directly worked on everything else—except she wasn't here in person."

"Still. Imagine if you call an ambulance and the person who attends isn't a paramedic but it's okay, their sister is and she's on the phone. It's not the same, of course, but things can go wrong quickly—"

"But they didn't. Issues that came up—like the portaloos—were sorted."

"They were," Tarryn admitted. She folded her arms. "But the fact remains we were paying for an experienced person and got you. And you did a great job, but you—Sophie—should have levelled with us in the start."

"I know that—now," she whispered. "I didn't do it to deceive Quandong—or you. I did it because I love my sister, and she's in so much pain and struggling to even walk. And this was something I could do to make her situation a little better." Allie stared at her hand, resting on the table between them. It was all going west. Tarryn's expression was closed, her voice clipped. *Oh, Sophie, I'm so sorry.* But she had to go on. There was probably no more damage she could do, and she needed to finish. "There's more."

"More?" Tarryn huffed a laugh. "I suppose you're married with a couple of kids."

"No! I wouldn't cheat on anyone. But another reason why I couldn't say who I was is because Sophie said one reason she was hired was because she was a lesbian. That's true. She is." How hard was it to say the next words. "But I'm not. I identified as straight. Now I know I'm not, and I'm very happy accepting that. But Sophie thought Quandong wouldn't allow her straight twin sister in her place instead of someone who's part of the community. I've always been around queer people, I spend a lot of time in queer spaces, but as an ally, not…" She couldn't continue. The blank expression on Tarryn's face surely reflected her anger.

"So you're gay for pay." Her words were cold. "And you led all of us on, talking about your girlfriends, identifying as something you're not. And me…what was I? Some sort of no-strings experimental sex? You'd just had an immersion course in being gay, and now you wanted to try sapphic sex for yourself? Well, fuck you, Allison, I won't be used like that."

"No! Please, Tarryn, that's mostly wrong."

"Mostly? It sounds all wrong to me. You were straight. And while it's not for me to tell you how to identify, it's not looking good."

"I understand how you're feeling. But although I identified as straight, while you're the first woman I've slept with, you're not the first woman I've kissed. I kissed a girl once, and I liked it. A lot."

"You sound like a Katy Perry song. I suppose she wore cherry Chapstick, and you're about to tell me your boyfriend didn't mind." If her voice was anymore biting, it would shred Allie's skin.

"No. I liked it, but I didn't seek out more of the same. Maybe I just needed the right person. Maybe I just needed you." Could her voice be any quieter? She wasn't even sure if Tarryn had heard the last part.

"So I'm the predatory lesbian who's led you from the straight and narrow, and you expect me to be proud? Chuffed? Another notch on the bedpost? I've had other 'straight' women, and they've been wonderful. I'm sure at least a couple of them realised some truths about themselves too. But none of them were as much of a liar as you." She smashed the mug down on the counter and stood. "I'm going, Allison. I'm so very sorry it ended like this, but I'm not sorry I found out exactly what your game was—yours and Sophie's—before I made a fool of myself. For what it's worth, I liked you a lot. And here's your notch on the bedpost—I was going to ask you again to reconsider a long-distance relationship. See if we could have anything together."

"We can still—"

"No!" Tarryn clenched her fist. "You played me for a fool. Worse, you and your sister played my town for idiots. It's going to take a bit to get past all of that. I'm going home."

Allie's heart fractured and splintered into big, hurting pieces. So this was it. Sophie was right all along; she should never have said anything. She should have said a fond farewell, walked away, driven back to Sydney and tried to forget all about Tarryn, about Quandong. Then she'd leave with good memories, happy times, the feeling she'd done something good for the town. Not this. Not this sour taste, this bitter finish to her time here. "Will you tell Phyll? About who I am and why Sophie couldn't be here?"

"What do you think?" Tarryn snapped. "Should I just keep silent and let her think you fart rainbows? That you're the great event planner?"

"I understand." Her misery was complete. Three weeks here and she was leaving Sophie's business in a more perilous state than before she came.

"Do you? I get the impression you'd be happy if I just shut up and didn't say anything." Tarryn's fist clenched on the leather thong at her throat. "Listen, Allison. I'm angry, yes, and I'm angry you've duped Quandong. But you did do a good job, and the festival was a success. But the final straw for me is you duped me about yourself. You weren't honest with me. And you haven't been honest with yourself." Her expression eased a fraction. "For what it's worth, I'm so sorry things ended this way. I hope you're able to be true to yourself going forward."

Allie stared. What could she possibly say in response? She wouldn't beg, wouldn't apologise—again. She nodded once and watched, her heart in pieces around her feet, as Tarryn picked up her things and went to the top of the stairs.

"Goodbye, Allie. Be happy." She turned and clattered down the stairs. Her truck door slammed, and the engine started.

Allie wrapped her arms around her middle as if she could hold in the hurt and turned away from the window. Her fledgling feelings lay rejected on the floor. She couldn't watch Tarryn drive away. Instead, she turned back to the room and set about finishing her packing.

She had to call Sophie.

Three hours out of Quandong, Allie pulled into a service station beside the Pacific Highway and picked up her phone. There was a text message notification. Maybe it was Sophie.

Maybe it was Tarryn, asking her to return.

Allie pushed her phone into her bag and swung out the car. She needed coffee and something to eat if she was to get back to Sydney that night. Whatever the text was, it would read better with coffee.

She found a quiet spot in the food court and settled with a coffee and a sandwich. Her churning stomach wouldn't allow her more. She weighed her phone in her hand. The text had to be from Sophie or from Tarryn, and she didn't know which would be the best option. She took a deep breath and swiped her phone open.

The text was from Sophie.

Hey, I know you've been busy after the festival "debriefing" with your assistant ;) so I haven't bothered you, but I'm dying to know how it all ended up. When will you be back home? Love you. Soph xo. PS You kissing Tarryn was on the news. That's how I know you're busy. That was NOT a duty kiss. PPS I love you.

She set down the phone and picked up the coffee, pushing aside the sandwich. The coffee was lukewarm, but it was still warmer than her. That explained Sophie's silence. She should be glad to hear from her sister—and she was. But the knot of misery tightened her abdominal muscles until the coffee churned alarmingly in her stomach. She couldn't help wishing it had been from Tarryn.

Allie picked up the phone again and shot off a quick text to Sophie saying she'd be back in Sydney in a few hours and she'd catch up with her tomorrow. She put the phone down again and forced herself to unwrap the sandwich and take a bite. Her phone pinged with an incoming text, and she snatched it up.

Looking forward to it. Come for brekky. Early as you can make it. Can't wait to hear how things went.

She sent a thumbs up. Her stomach rebelled again, and she rewrapped the sandwich to take with her.

Her life was in Sydney. Her sister, her friends, hopefully a new job. Maybe someone new to date.

Maybe a woman.

Chapter 25

RETURNING TO HER POKY APARTMENT hadn't helped. Allie had turned on the light and been struck by its dinginess. The low ceilings pressed in on her, and the air had a stale, musty smell. She'd climbed into bed, checked her phone for a final time, then turned it off.

The next morning, she dragged herself out bed to shower and wash her hair and then picked up some pastries from the local coffee shop. But there was nothing she could do about her emotions. Her mind swirled in a grey mist; her heart hung as a deadweight in her chest.

She used her key to let herself into Sophie's place. "Hi," she called.

A head popped out Sophie's bedroom. "Hi, Allie." Bree entered the hallway. "It's been a while."

Of course. Sophie had said Bree was staying for a couple of weeks. She stretched her mouth into the semblance of a smile. "It has. How have you been?"

"I'm doing better now. Things weren't good for a while." She pushed her hair from her black-skinned face. "Maybe we can talk later? Right now, Soph is dying to see you. Now you're here, I'll go and sort out breakfast. You're probably starving—I bet there was hardly anything in your apartment."

"You're right." She held out the bag of pastries. "My contribution."

Bree peeped into the bag. "Ooh, you've been to The Pink Bean. Fantastic. Thanks." She carried on down the hallway to the kitchen.

Allie took a deep breath and went into Sophie's room. Time to face the music.

Sophie was in bed, propped up on pillows, her injured leg resting on top of the covers. Her face had gained some colour since Allie had last seen her, and the shadow of pain around her eyes seemed less.

"Allie! Oh my God, it feels like forever. Give me a proper hug." Sophie held out her arms, and Allie bent to hug her around the shoulders. Sophie's hair smelled fresh, floral, as it always used to before the accident, and she clung tightly for a few long moments before releasing her. "Bree's giving us some time alone, so I want to hear everything: the festival, the people, how it all ended up. And I particularly want to hear about you and Tarryn. I saw you on the news, and, of course, so did a lot of my friends. They've been calling, asking how come I was up in Quandong, because, of course, the news gave my name, not yours."

Allie pulled the bedside chair around so she could face Sophie. "I've a lot to tell you. Not all is good." She pressed her lips together but couldn't entirely stop their tremble. "I hope you're still talking to me when I've finished."

Sophie reached for Allie's hand and linked their fingers together. "You're my sister. My shared heart. Nothing you tell me could change my love for you. *Nothing*. And nothing can be so bad we can't face it together."

Allie dropped her head, unable to look Sophie in the face. She blinked fiercely, willing the tears not to fall, but one tracked its way down her nose to drop on their joined hands. "I hope you still think that when I've finished talking."

"Talk. I love you."

Allie heaved a deep breath and filled her in on the festival and the fake wedding. She looked up at Sophie, blurry through her tears. "I told her who I was, that I was pretending to be you so as to save your business. And I told her I'd always thought I was straight." She stared back down at her hand again, linked with Sophie's. "I admitted I was wrong."

"What happened?"

"She was furious. Angry we'd duped Quandong—they'd paid for an experienced event planner—they paid for *you*. And they got me, who was winging it more than a fried chicken shop. But even more, she accused me of faking being gay. And she was right."

"Not entirely. You thought you were straight; you realised you weren't. She can't blame you for that."

"But still. I was pretending to be you, talking as if I was you. As if I were a lesbian. Gay for pay, she called it."

"You care for her," Sophie said softly. "I can see it in your face."

"I do." Those words again. They seemed to be coming up in her life a lot.

"And it's not just because she's a woman? A new and exciting experience?"

"No!" The knot of unhappiness that was her heart twisted tighter. If only that was all it had been. If it had been novelty, a simple one-night stand, she wouldn't feel like this now. Like she was covered in a grey net of misery.

Sophie nodded slowly. "I'm so sorry, Allie. I wish I'd never sent you there in my place."

Allie shook her head. "Then I wouldn't have discovered this about myself. I wouldn't have—" *Wouldn't have met Tarryn.* And that would have been worse. She closed her eyes, and Tarryn's face flashed into her mind. Not as she last saw it, twisted with hurt and anger, but open and alight with pleasure in her bed. The softness of her skin, the steel of her convictions. Her loyalty to Quandong and the people she cared about. "She's the whole package, Sophie. For me, at least."

"And there's no way back to her?"

"I can't see one. I just have to move on. Rebuild my life in Sydney. Maybe I'll sign up on a dating app."

"To match with men?"

"Men, women, nonbinary. At least being in Quandong opened me to that." Allie hesitated. "There's more. Tarryn said she'd tell Phyll about our deception."

"Were people unhappy about the job you did?"

"No, but all the same, it was misrepresentation. Fraud, maybe."

Sophie nodded. "I should never have sent you alone. At the least, I should have explained I was sending you in my place."

Allie took her hand away and clenched it in her lap. "Tarryn said they would have understood. And I think they would have."

"But we didn't know at the time." Sophie sighed. "What a mess. I'm so sorry, Al, I got you into this. It's up to me to try to fix it."

"I don't think you can. She was so furious. She doesn't want anything to do with me. And once Phyll hears about what happened, I think she'll be livid as well."

"This is what we'll do." Sophie jutted her chin. "I'll get out this damn bed. We'll go and have breakfast because any minute Bree is going to yell it's ready. And I still have to tell you about Bree. Over breakfast, you can tell me all about the festival: what went wrong, how you fixed it. The ideas you came up with, the extra work you did—and I know you put in way more than you had to. Then I'll call Phyll, try to repair the damage. I'll offer a thirty per cent reduction on my fee."

"No!" Allie's gasp strangled in her throat. "You'll make a loss. I know you already cut the price to the bone. If you do it for a third less—"

"It's the right thing to do. I should have done it at the start rather than asking you to go in blind."

"But your business." She spread her hands. "Your house. You won't be able to keep up the mortgage payments. You said—"

"I know what I said." Sophie's lips twisted. "But things will be worse if I don't do this. Worse for my business in the long term, and worse for you now."

"It's too late for me."

"You don't know that." Sophie flung back the bedclothes and used her hands to lift her injured leg to the floor. "Now, find me some clothes. I'm going to get dressed."

Allie lifted her chin. "I'll call Phyll. Quandong came to mean a lot. Maybe she'll listen to me."

Sophie eyed her for a moment. "Are you sure? Because this is my mess to fix."

"Yes. I need to do this."

"Okay, then. But still offer the fee reduction."

"Five minutes!" Bree called down the hall. "Come and get it."

"What did I tell you?"

Allie went to the drawers and pulled out undies and a T-shirt. "These do?" She added the shorts that were hanging over a chair.

"Yeah, thanks."

Allie waited as Sophie struggled to pull on undies and the shorts without knocking her leg. When she was ready, she handed her the crutches. "Are you back with Bree?"

"Sort of. As much as anyone can be when they're restricted like this." Her mouth turned down. "But, yes, we've made up, and she's said she's with me for the long haul. She's being great, Allie. I couldn't do without her."

"She's changed? The Bree I remember was a lot more"—she picked her words carefully—"self-absorbed."

"I think so. And I want to try again. I still love her, Al. I tried to get past her, even before this." She gestured to leg. "I'm just hoping not to get my heart broken—again."

Ain't that the truth. Allie sighed. That was all most people could do. For her, it was already too late. Hopefully, Sophie would find her happiness.

"She lied to me, Will. Straight-out lied about who she was. She's Allison, not Sophie, and she's straight." Tarryn tipped the last of the red wine into her mouth.

Garrett refilled it and shot a glance at his partner.

"She doesn't sound very straight to me. I can't remember your exact words, but 'great sex' was in there, along with 'amazing lover.'" Will rested a hand on hers where it lay on the counter.

"She said she'd kissed a woman before and liked it but didn't do anything else."

"Not everything is a Katy Perry song," Will said.

Tarryn huffed a laugh. "That's what I said. She deceived me. And Quandong. Surely, you're mad?"

Will gripped her hand. "So I'm supposed to be mad because she's the real event planner's twin. The real Sophie couldn't make it—and from what you say, it sounds as if she had very good reason—and Allie stepped in to save both her sister's business *and* our festival. And, apart from a couple of small hiccups, she did an excellent job. She worked long hours, smoothed Phyll's turf wars, came up with some great suggestions, and then played the part of fake bride with good grace. She may not have been as experienced as we thought, but she obviously had her sister on the phone to help her."

"She lied. To me. To us. We became her friends."

"She's still my friend," Garrett said from the kitchen where he was stirring something on the stove. "Friends try to understand."

"I tried. Really, I did. But some things are too big to get past." She took another slurp of wine. "And this is one of them."

"Did you know Allie called Phyll this morning?" Will said.

Tarryn shook her head. "What did she want?"

"To apologise and explain. The real Sophie is still bedridden."

Tarryn set her jaw. "She should have told us beforehand."

"People often don't think clearly in desperate circumstances."

"It was wrong."

"It was," Garrett agreed. "But she's trying to make up for it now. She offered to reduce the fee by a third. Before you say 'so she should,' remember Sophie's bid was the cheapest by a long way. Remember we asked for more involvement, and she didn't charge us more. And Allie worked far more than the contracted hours."

Tarryn was silent, her mind buzzing like a hive of bees.

"Phyll thanked her for the offer but said we were more than happy and would pay the full fee." Garrett pulled plates from the cupboard. "Dinner's ready. I'm not half the cook Will is, but you need something fast to soak up that wine you're guzzling. Say 'yes, Garrett,' and I'll open another bottle. The good stuff."

Tarryn drained her glass. "Yes, Garrett."

Garrett pushed a second bottle over to Will, who opened it.

"So, Quandong is happy. We're happy. Even Phyll is happy—and praise the lord as we all know that doesn't often happen. The only person not happy is you. So there must be more you're not saying." Will pointed a fork at the plate Garrett set in front of her. "Eat. Drink more wine. Think. And then tell us what's actually wrong. Maybe we can help. We're pretty good as agony uncles. Especially after two bottles of wine, including this fine Montepuliciano."

Tarryn's lips twitched spontaneously. She may not have Allie, but she had good friends. Fine friends. Ones who weren't afraid to tell it as it was. She picked up her fork and dug into the plate of pasta Garrett had set in front her. "It's good."

Garrett tutted. "It's pasta and a jar of sauce. You're breaking Will's heart."

"It's filling. But it's not a patch on Will's gourmet, made-from-scratch creations."

Will fanned himself. "Lucky. You were on the edge of being banned from my dinners." He grated Parmesan over his own plate and followed it with pepper and dried chilli.

Garrett poured more wine. "Don't slurp this like the last one. This is better than you deserve in your current mood."

Tarryn laughed. "My mood is improving thanks to you two."

Will ate a forkful of pasta, winced, and added more cheese. "So, what aren't you telling us? You were getting along with Allie—we all saw the kisses. You slept together. You were a happy little Vegemite until she left. Then, you locked yourself away with those antisocial animals of yours—"

"They needed food and love."

"Don't we all," Will continued. "And then you come stomping around here with a face like an alpaca's bumhole, drink a bottle of our wine—"

"Not the good stuff. You've only just opened that."

"There was no point wasting the good stuff on you at first. You inhaled it as if you'd spent a week in the Simpson Desert," Garrett said.

"—and we're yet to get to the heart of the issue."

"There is no heart. I was deceived. I've vented to my best friends. And now I've moved on. No more Allie. No more fake weddings. It's back to the welding, the odd jobs, and dinners with my friends. No more love and romance, just some hot flings with passing travellers. There'll be more of them now, thanks to Gay Bells."

"Do you mean that?" Will pushed his plate aside. "Really, Tarryn? I've never seen you like this. So angry. Defensive."

"Heartbroken," Garrett said.

"Yes, that. This isn't your way. Quandong is accepting of the circumstances and happy with Allie's work. You've slept with straight women before, and you've *never* been like this." Will took a sip of his own wine. "I'm going to take a punt that, this time, your heart's involved and you don't like it. That maybe you wanted more. That you did want more until you thought you'd been made a fool of. Allie didn't do that. You're the fool now for not going after what you really want."

Tarryn ate a forkful of pasta. "I feel like an idiot. I should have known she was lying."

"How? None of the rest of us did," Garrett said.

"Relationships need to be built on trust. How can I trust someone who lied about who she was? Her sexuality."

"Sexuality…well, not everyone pops out of the womb knowing they're gay. Some people take longer. Allie's obviously the latter. She was protecting whom she loves. I doubt she came here with the intention of falling for you. Sometimes these things just happen." Garrett cast Will such a dewy-eyed look, it stole Tarryn's breath.

He was right. She knew, deep down, Allie hadn't intended to fall for her, in whatever way that was. To whatever depth it was.

Maybe I just needed the right person. Maybe I just needed you. Allie's words hammered in Tarryn's mind like a song on repeat. Allie had been open in that. She'd put herself out for her heart to be trampled on. And she didn't have to own up about the deception. She could have kissed Tarryn goodbye and driven off to Sydney, leaving Quandong and Tarryn as blissfully ignorant specks in her rear-view mirror.

But she'd told the truth—knowing it could destroy not only what they might have together but also have immense repercussions on her sister's business. The sister she loved enough to protect in the first place.

Why would Allie blow things apart if she didn't care enough to set things straight?

Tarryn swallowed and stared at her friends. "I've been an idiot, haven't I?"

They nodded in unison.

"Total fuckhead," Will said.

"Understandable," Garrett added. "Your knee-jerk reaction was to protect yourself. But a wise woman would see past that. You have."

"What would a wise woman do now?" Tarryn glanced from one to the other as if the two of them held her future in their hands. "What should I do?"

"Think about it for a day. Be sure anything you do is really what you want, what you can commit to," Will said.

"Sober up," Garrett added. "Make sure it's not the wine making you sentimental. Stay here tonight while you do. Have brekky with us in the morning—Will's cooking, so it will be better than this"—he pushed his plate away—"and we'll come up with a plan of action."

Tarryn nodded. Was this salvageable? Her friends seemed to think so. And did she want it? She'd do as they suggested and sleep on it. No drunken phone calls or texts from her. But they were right. She'd been the worst sort of judgemental fool.

Allie was too much a part of her heart to let her go without a fight.

Tarryn's phone rang loudly, jerking her out of sleep. She stretched. The bed was smaller and softer than her own. Will and Garrett's spare room. Her eyes opened slowly, and she squinted in the light. She needed water, paracetamol, more sleep, a couple of fried eggs, and a pee. Not in that order—a pee was winning. And she needed to answer her phone.

She fumbled for it and managed to answer it before it went to voicemail.

"Are you alive?" Phyll asked.

Tarryn bit back a groan. She should have looked at the screen before answering. "Only just."

"I want to talk about Allie."

Tarryn put the phone on speaker and dropped it face down on the bed, resting her head back on the pillow as Phyll explained that the committee had decided to pay Sophie's full fee.

"Allie thought you had already told me about the twin switch." Phyll's voice held none of the expected censure.

"I was going to," Tarryn mumbled. "But shit happened, and I seem to have got drunk with Will and Garrett."

"Understandable." Phyll's voice held a hum of…surely not approval?

She sorted through the jumbled thoughts in her aching head. "You're not furious I didn't call you the minute I learned?"

Phyll's snort echoed down the line. "I'm glad you gave it some thought. Protecting the woman you love is important."

"What?" Tarryn picked up her phone and looked at the screen. The caller sounded like Phyll, and the screen said it was Phyll. But when had her aunt been this easy-going? *Never* was the answer. "I thought you'd be up in arms and out for blood. Instead, you're positively gooey."

"Love is love." Phyll's smugness came clearly over the line.

"Who said anything about love?"

"I did."

"Great. Who are you in love with?" She was too hungover for this surreal conversation. She just wanted to pee and find the coffee machine.

"Robbo," Phyll said. "And when you're in love, you want everyone else to be. So of *course* you hesitated about dobbing in Allie and her sister. Good on you, Tarryn. There's hope for you yet."

"Robbo?" Maybe she'd fallen into some alternate dimension, one where her grumpy perfectionist aunt was mellow and chill.

"He farms chooks on the Coringlah Road."

"Right." Tarryn had no idea who Phyll was talking about, but right now, it didn't matter. "Phyll, you just woke me up, and I'm busting to pee."

"Go," Phyll said. "And when you've peed and got rid of your hangover, think about calling Allie."

Tarryn ended the call and made a dive for the loo. Phyll was in love and ordering her to call Allie. Could the day get any stranger?

Chapter 26

ALLIE SAT AT HER TINY table in what the rental agent had euphemistically described as "the breakfast nook." She had no idea what to do with her day. Oh, there were heaps of things she should be doing—like making sure Sophie was okay, job hunting, getting groceries, and getting rid of the dust that had accumulated in her three weeks away. Instead, she sat there, staring at a mug of instant black coffee and idly thinking about painting the walls.

Sophie had Bree to look after her. Indeed, Bree had been extremely attentive last night, and it was as if she and Sophie were back at the early stage of their relationship, when they'd been so very in love. After Sophie had gone back to bed, Bree had taken Allie aside and said she realised Allie had no real reason to like her. Sincerity shone from her eyes as she said she was one hundred per cent committed to Sophie and hoped they now had a future. Allie had smiled and said she hoped Bree knew any past dislike was purely because of how much she'd hurt her sister. They'd parted amicably.

Her sister might now have her happy ending, but there would be no such ending for her.

Allie was unloading the banners and equipment she'd taken to Quandong into Sophie's shed when her mobile rang. She snatched it up, heart pounding. How long would it be before she didn't get light-headed with anticipation it would be Tarryn? The screen said Leila. Her shoulders slumped. What had she expected? She likely would never hear from Tarryn again, despite how well the conversation with Phyll had gone. At least Sophie had already received her full fee for the festival.

"I have to be quick." Leila sounded jubilant. "You're going to like this. In a nutshell, the shit has hit the fan at Kirkland and splattered up the walls, covering various people in it from bald heads to polished shoes. Another two companies got audited for their BAS returns by the tax office and had to pay back taxes and a stinking great fine. Your old boss, Craig, is fired. Well… the official line is he 'has left to seek new opportunities,' but that's Kirkland-speak for fired. The word on the street is the tax office is paying *very* close attention to large companies who use us to do their returns."

"Really?" Allie leaned against the wooden shed wall, her mind racing. "I never in a million years thought that would happen. Partners come only from the old boys' network, and they never leave." She thought she'd feel vindicated if this ever happened, the good guys winning out. But there was nothing. No anger, no glee that justice was done. Just a big, flat nothing.

"I know, right? They're worse than mothers-in-law for sticking around. But Craig's gone. His two most senior accountants are also history. Basically, there are a whole heap of clients floating around with no senior person to look after them. All of us drones have been given extra files to work on and strict instructions that any returns have to be checked off by a partner."

"I thought you were going to tell me you had a new job lined up."

"I bloody wish," Leila said. "I'm looking. We've been told we're expected to, 'do what's necessary to service our clients.' I feel like a battery hen."

"Are you able to just leave and hunt for a job? It might show your ethics in leaving once this was known."

"No—we can't afford it with our mortgage. But I have an interview next week with Markovic. I'll have to take a sickie to go. Keep your fingers crossed for me."

"I will. I hope you get it."

"Now, the other thing"—Leila lowered her voice—"is I heard very quietly from my friend in HR they might approach you to see if you'll come back. After all, you worked on many of these accounts, and it's now known you had nothing to do with the fraud."

"Really? After they fired me, refused to give me a reference…*now* they want me back when they're in the shit?" Now she didn't need to analyse her feelings. A white-hot flame burned in her mind, and she swallowed the acid in her throat. *Fuck them.*

"Your voice tells me it's a hard no. Am I right?"

"You're right. I'm sorry, Leila. If I came back, it would make your life easier until Markovic makes the offer—which they will."

"I'd do exactly the same. But now you're primed, you can think about what to say if you get that call. I'm sure you will."

"I'd love to tell them to stuff their crappy job right up their pompous arse, but that will certainly kill any chance they might give me a reference. I'll have to think about it."

"Do. And let me know what happens. Shit! I've just seen the time—I have to gallop. Our lunch hours are down to about twenty minutes, if we're lucky."

"Girlfriend, you need that job. And you haven't even told me about Hammie or Lewis."

"They're both good. Except Hammie is now Muhammad and won't answer to anything else." She sighed. "It had to happen. I just wish I had my cutie-pants sweet-cheeks baby boy for a bit longer. Lewis is fine. He's hoping I get the other job." A pause and the sound of chewing came over the line. "We have to catch up properly soon. I haven't heard about your life, and I want to. Once I'm no longer doing seventy-hour weeks, you must come around and we'll drink wine and eat ourselves stupid. Hammie will sit on your lap and make you read him a story, and Lewis will cook while we catch up."

"That will be great. Take care, Leila."

The line went dead. Allie slipped her phone back into her pocket. So Kirkland were in desperate need of accountants. Desperate enough to want her back. Well, they could eat shit and die before that happened—but maybe there was a way she could turn this to her advantage. Mind humming, she resumed stacking the banners and stands in Sophie's shed.

She had some decisions to make, and maybe Quandong had helped her with a couple of those. Organising the festival had renewed her confidence in her professional abilities—of all sorts. That was what she needed right now.

And, of course, being in Quandong had helped her acknowledge her sexuality, maybe even who she'd love.

No. She wouldn't think about that. That was the path of no return. She didn't love Tarryn. It had been an awakening, an exploration, a joyful positive experience. Until it wasn't. She would remember the good things, not how it ended. And she would remind herself no one fell in love in that short a time. She sighed. It wasn't love, but it could have been. Maybe. If they'd allowed it to develop.

But right now, she was going to take her new-found confidence and flaunt it.

The reception area at Kirkland & Partners was the same black-and-silver décor she remembered. The same curved reception desk with the firm name and logo on the black panel behind the desk. Only the receptionist was new.

Allie gave her a professional smile that gave no hint of her twanging nerves. "Good afternoon. I'm Allison Lane. I'm here to see Ramona in HR."

"Is she expecting you?" The receptionist seemed flustered. No doubt she'd dealt with angry clients and journalists in the last few days.

"I think she might be." Allie nodded and took a seat on the black leather couch where she could see the door to the back office.

The receptionist spoke to someone in muted tones, flicking glances at Allie as she did so.

Allie crossed her legs and brushed an imaginary speck of lint from her wine-coloured jacket.

A few minutes later, the inner door clicked open and a stout, middle-aged woman advanced across the polished tiles. "Ms Lane? I'm Ramona Trayner. How can I help?"

Allie stood and held out her hand. "Thank you for meeting with me, Ms Trayner. Can we talk somewhere more private?"

"Sure." Ramona went across to the receptionist and spoke for a moment before returning with a visitor tag. 'If you could put this on, then follow me."

Two minutes later, Allie was seated in a small office. The sign on the desk proclaimed Ramona to be the HR Manager. She, too, was new.

Ramona studied her curiously. "How can I help you, Ms Lane? May I call you Allison?"

Allie suppressed a smile. Ramona no doubt knew that Allie had been fired and was now on the rehire list and was wondering how best to approach the conversation. "Of course…Ramona." She sat back in her chair, hoping she appeared relaxed. "As I'm sure you're aware, I resigned from

Kirkland & Partners some weeks ago. I'm also sure you know Kirkland are hesitant to give me a reference. In light of recent developments, and the departure of Craig Stockton, I'm here for your assurance that there will be no problem with a favourable response to future reference requests."

Ramona's eyes widened briefly before her face took on a blank mask. "Of course. You can ask prospective employers to contact me directly." She handed over a business card.

"Thank you. I'd also appreciate a written reference be mailed to me."

"I'll see what I can do." Ramona lined up her pens in a neat row on her desk. "Allison, it's very coincidental that you appeared today. I intended on calling you in the next day or two with a job offer. Craig's departure and those of two other accountants has left a gap in the team for a skilled accountant. You are familiar with the accounts they worked on. Kirkland would like to offer you an intermediate role working on those files. We can offer you a substantial raise over your previous position." She named a salary that was higher than any position Allie had applied for.

Allie raised an eyebrow. "This is unexpected. I'll need to give it some thought. Can you send through the full details when you send my written reference? That will allow me to fully consider the position."

"I can do that. And I hope to have your favourable response to our offer."

Allie rose. "If all is as you say, I will seriously consider it. Thank you, Ramona. I'll look forward to receiving the written reference and the job offer." She stood back and waited for Ramona to lead the way back to reception.

Once outside and around the corner, she flung her head back, and as the tension left her body, she laughed out loud. It felt good. It felt better than great. Her newfound confidence in her ability to remain cool and bluff her way through tricky situations had done her well. It had been surprisingly easy.

And she would take great pleasure in declining Kirkland's offer when it came.

Chapter 27

"I NEED YOU TO DO one last thing for the wedding festival." Phyll's voice boomed down the phone line.

"Get fake divorced?" Tarryn asked. "Are we having a gay divorce festival next?"

"Don't be such a cynic, dear. It doesn't suit you. No, I need you to call Allie. She left in such a hurry, I think she took some of our banners. The big ones we'll need for next year. Can you ask her to send them back to us?"

"Really, Aunt Phyll, I don't think I need to do that. Can't you call her?"

"You were Allie's assistant. It's your job. Just let me know when we can expect them."

"Surely a volunteer could do it," Tarryn said. Thoughts of what she'd said to Allie the last time they'd talked left a bitter taste in her mouth, a curdling mix of hurt and anger.

"They could," Phyll agreed. "But I don't want to burn out our volunteers. They all worked so hard."

"And I didn't?"

"You were fantastic, and you know it. We'll pay you for this. I'm not asking you to slave for nothing."

"Okay, I'll do it," she said with a sigh.

"Great. Let me know when we can expect the banners. Oops, another call coming in. Bye." Phyll ended the call.

Tarryn pocketed her phone and went out to feed the alpacas. It seemed she was now a permanent part of the wedding festival, whether she liked it or not. She cut the string on a new bale of hay and tossed a couple of sections to Ally and Elly.

Elly came up to her and blew sweet breath in her face.

Tarryn rubbed her neck, the wool soft under her hand. "I'll take you girls out later. It's been a while, hasn't it?"

Elly blinked, her ridiculously long eyelashes looking so cute that Tarryn pressed a kiss to her nose.

Elly snorted, and Tarryn stepped back with a laugh. "Maybe next year, you two can be in the parade. If we can persuade Ally to be a little more social." The grumpy alpaca was snatching mouthfuls of hay and ignoring the conversation.

Maybe Ally had the right idea: ignore everything she didn't want to deal with.

Tarryn leaned on the gate and watched the alpacas eat. Somewhere along the way, while working on the festival, she'd come to understand it more. Understand why people willingly tied themselves into marriage. It was creeping up all around her. Will and Garrett and their enduring love, even Phyll and her chicken farmer. The many people she'd seen at the festival, hand in hand: queer couples, the occasional triad, a big melting pot of different identities and sexualities, all there to find out how a queer wedding could be. Maybe it was idle curiosity, maybe they had a date set, maybe they wanted a commitment ceremony or simply a big gay day out with a dance party at the end of it. But whatever it was, the warmth and love during the two days had been palpable.

People it seemed, wanted love in their lives. And sometimes, some people wanted marriage. It didn't have to be a copy of heterosexual marriage. It could be whatever and with whomever you wanted.

Tears pricked behind Tarryn's eyes. She been an idiot. A pompous fool, sounding off against marriage. Same-sex marriage was whatever the people marrying wanted it to be. Almost of their own accord, her hands formed the heart symbol. *Love is love.* And, it seemed, she wasn't above that. She wasn't the person outside looking in after all.

And falling for Allie had done that. Getting married to Allie had loosened something in her—even though it had taken Allie to help her through the fake ceremony. But they'd done it. Together.

She dropped her head to her hands where they rested on the gate. Elly came up and nuzzled her hair and puffed breath over her neck. Tarryn raised her head to stare into the alpaca's gentle eyes.

She'd let Allie walk out her life. Worse, she'd been judgemental as fuck, defining Allie's sexuality for her. Allie had said she wasn't straight. Why was it so hard for Tarryn to accept that, especially when she had all the evidence? Anyone who kissed a woman as divinely as Allie did, who made love so fully and completely, was certainly not a zero on the Kinsey scale. Maybe Allie had put a label on her sexuality; maybe she hadn't. It was irrelevant.

The important thing was Allie had been a great part of Tarryn's life, and now she was gone.

Tarryn pressed the heels of her hands to her eyes.

And she still didn't know what to do about it.

She turned and went back to her shouse. She had to get the damn banners back for Phyll—who of course could have contacted Allie herself but had chosen not to. Tarryn set the kettle on to boil. There was no way she could call Allie with her mind churning faster than the Quandong laundromat—but she could call Sophie.

Before she could talk herself out of it, she picked up her phone and scrolled to the landline number she'd called before. The number she now realised was Sophie's. She pressed the call button.

"Events Done Right, this is Bree."

"Good morning, Bree, this is Tarryn Harris from Quandong. Is it possible to speak with Sophie Lane?"

"One moment, please." The call clicked over to chiming hold music.

A minute later, a voice said, "Sophie speaking. How can I help you, Tarryn?"

"I'm sorry to disturb you, but Phyll asked me to give you a call." She outlined the issue with the missing banners.

"We'll find and return them." A pause. "I'm glad you called, Tarryn. I intended to call to thank you for doing such a great job as Allie's assistant during the festival. She's told me how efficient you were and how you did far more than you had to."

Ha! If only she knew how much extra I did do. "No worries. It was just a job to me, but I take pride in doing everything to the best of my ability."

"Was it just a job? Allie said it was more." Sophie's voice softened. "I realise weddings aren't your thing, but Allie said you played the part of fake bride very well. Maybe too well."

Tarryn's nerves twanged like an out-of-tune banjo. Was Sophie about to chew her out for seducing her sister? "I did my best."

"You did. Thank you." Another pause. "You know, it would have been easier to call Allie directly about the banners. She's the one who'll have to send them. I'm still…incapacitated. She'd be pleased to hear from you."

Pleased? What did that mean? Pleased so she could be cold in her words? Pleased so she could gain closure? Pleased…how? "I'm not sure that's a good idea."

"Because you're going to disappoint her again?"

Was she? The empty space since Allie left didn't reek of anger anymore: it was sadness, an incomplete feeling, a hollow shell where her heart used to be. "Sophie, I don't know how much Allie has told you, but I think we both let down the other. It wasn't a one-way thing."

"Maybe not, but…I'm her twin. We're identical in most things: we vote the same, we dress similarly, we like the same foods. But until now, Allie being straight and me being gay was always the thing that stood us apart. Because we're so similar, I used to think one of us would discover our sexuality was different from how we'd always thought. I wasn't sure which one—sexuality can be such a fluid thing. And, too, I wondered if maybe this would always be the thing that set us apart. But if that's what's holding you back from happiness…well, maybe it needn't be."

Tarryn looked down at her feet. First Phyll, now Sophie. Was she that pig-headed she was letting this stand in the way of what she wanted?

Was this it? Was Allie her person?

She'd been silent too long. Sophie cleared her throat. "I'm sorry, I didn't mean to get all preachy on you. I'll pass on to Allie to send the banners back. Thanks for the—"

"Wait." Tarryn's heart thundered in her chest. "I'm coming down to Sydney to visit my mama in a few days anyway. How about I pick the banners up from you?"

"Sure." A ripple of amusement threaded Sophie's voice. "That will work. Can you let me know when you'll be here so Allie can have the banners ready?"

"I'll do that. Thanks, Sophie. I'll see you maybe…Monday, if that will work?"

"That's fine. Thanks for the call, Tarryn. I look forward to meeting you then."

She ended the call. Now she was committed—for better or worse. She snorted. Wasn't that a line out the traditional wedding ceremony? She'd had no intention of visiting Mama—it was the most transparent excuse ever. Sophie was probably calling her sister right now to tell her.

A couple of days to sort out a few things that had been pushed to one side while the festival was on and then she'd leave at dawn on Monday. She'd see Allie. Maybe when they were face-to-face, the right words would come. An apology, a reconciliation, a kinder breakup...she didn't know. Hopefully, she'd figure it out before then.

She picked up the phone again to call Will to ask him to feed the alpacas while she was away.

Chapter 28

Tarryn cursed as the traffic slowed for yet more roadworks on the highway, then came to a halt at the temporary traffic lights. She tapped her fingers on the wheel as the stream of cars, trucks, and caravans rumbled past in the opposite direction. At this rate, she wouldn't get to Sydney before dark—and she wanted to arrive at Sophie's house before five. Not for the first time, she considered turning around and heading home. This was likely to be a wasted trip, a fool's errand. She had no idea where Allie lived, and Sophie was likely not to tell her.

She took a slurp of her coffee and grimaced when she found it cold. If there were no more major hold-ups, she might still get to Sophie's by four. Then, if Allie wouldn't see her, she'd pay an unannounced visit to her mama and drive home tomorrow. She had no clue how this would go. Come to that, she had no idea what to say, or even what she was offering Allie. What she did know was things had ended badly and it was mainly her fault.

Deep inside, in a secret place only now seeing the sunlight, she had accepted she wasn't ready to let Allie go.

Allie scrolled through the food delivery app, trying to decide what to order. Chinese, Japanese, Korean, smoked barbecue, Thai, modern Australian, healthy burgers, Iranian… Sydney's selection was as wide as the Harbour Bridge…and nearly as expensive. In Quandong, it was Thai, pub food, or the prepared meals from Kirra's Kafé. All good choices. She took a sip of wine and rolled it around her mouth.

She flicked past the Thai selections. It reminded her too much of Quandong and the café that had quickly learnt her preferred choices. Sushi maybe. Or Korean. A spicy bulgogi might sear the thoughts of Tarryn from her mind. As she picked up her phone, the security buzzer went. She frowned. She wasn't expecting anyone, and she had no idea who it could be. She put her phone down and went over to the intercom. "Hello."

"Hi Allie, it's Tarryn. Can we talk?"

She released the button in surprise. Tarryn. Here. A wisp of hope uncurled. Tarryn was here and there'd been no anger in her voice, no Antarctic chill. She'd driven for a day to come and talk face-to-face. Surely it wouldn't be to say what they'd had was over. She'd done that very effectively in Quandong. For a moment, she wished hard the intercom had a camera. She could only imagine Tarryn at the front door, shoulders hunched, hands in the pockets of her jeans.

She'd hesitated too long. The intercom buzzed again.

"Please, Allie? I won't take long, if that's what you want. I just want to say…to say I'm sorry, I guess."

So she was sorry. She'd come a long way to clear the air, if that's all it was. Surely a phone call would have done. The tendril of hope grew shoots that curled into her chest. "Sure. I'll buzz you up."

The ninety seconds or so it took Tarryn to find her apartment ticked off as slowly as a week of wet Wednesdays. Allie stood in her kitchen, gripping the counter, mind buzzing through inconsequential things: she had wine in the fridge and fresh milk. She could offer tea, coffee, wine, water. Had Tarryn eaten? Was she going to apologise and leave?

Would Tarryn stay?

Would she let her?

When the knock finally came on her door, Allie uncurled her hands from the counter, took a deep breath, and took the three paces to answer it.

Tarryn stood as she'd imagined: shoulders hunched, hands pushed deep into the front pockets of her jeans. The planes of her face stood out in the dim lighting, and her grey curls shone silver.

Allie stuck her hands into the pockets of her own jeans so she didn't reach out to touch her. "Hi. Come in. I'm not sure why you're here, so I don't know whether to offer you anything."

"A glass of water would be good."

Allie poured one, added a couple of ice cubes, then gestured to the living area. "Sit. If you want."

When Tarryn had sat in the chair, Allie took the couch. She picked up her wine and took another sip, then sat back, crossing her legs, hoping she looked cool and unconcerned.

Tarryn took a gulp of her water, then set it down and leaned forward, elbows on her knees, staring at the floor.

Allie counted her heartbeats. When it got to two hundred, she said, "I know there's a stain on the carpet by your feet, but it's not that fascinating."

"It's the shape of Australia. But Tasmania's missing. Maybe I should drop something to complete the map."

"Please don't. I'll want my security bond back at some point." When Tarryn raised her gaze, Allie said, "Why are you here?"

Tarryn sucked her lower lip. "It's complicated. I told Sophie I was collecting the banners you took. And I might visit my mother."

"Does she know you're here?"

"No," Tarryn admitted.

Allie's lips twitched. "Maybe she's gone on holiday. Somewhere beachy like Byron Bay. She can visit you while she's there. It's possible—it seems not letting others know your plans runs in the family."

"True." Tarryn sat back and picked up her water again. Her chest heaved. "Okay, the truth is I'm here to say I'm sorry."

Allie's heart sank faster than a rowboat in a cyclone. Was that all this was? A quick apology and then Tarryn would call her mother. "The telephone was invented for things like that. Or email."

"I was an arse."

"I'm not arguing."

"I was arrogant and pompous, trying to define your sexuality based on what I knew of you. Which is not something anyone can do for another person, but it was especially bad of me to do that to you, given what we'd shared. That is, while I knew you—or I thought I did—I have no idea how your life was as Allie. I shouldn't have done that, and I'm truly sorry." She twisted her hands together and when she looked Allie in the face, her agonised expression tore a hole in the shell around Allie's heart.

"I've seen Sophie," Tarryn continued. "Talked with her. I went to her place before coming here. And I now understand why you pretended to be her. I had no idea…her suffering." Her face twisted. "She's incredibly stoic for what she's going through."

"She is." The tendrils were now entwining themselves in her chest. She tried to stop their growth; this was, after all, still just an apology.

"I'm making a balls-up of this." Tarryn pressed the bridge of her nose. "It's not for me to offer my approval of your sexuality or your actions. Seeing Sophie's condition for myself shouldn't change anything. It's entitled of me to think my acceptance somehow makes it right. It doesn't. It still makes me an arrogant idiot. One who should have *listened* to you, trusted you, rather than jumping in with my own assumptions. I'm truly sorry, Allie. I was so rude to you. So self-absorbed, I made it all about me."

"There was no reason you should have believed me—except we were friends. And my friends listen to me, or at least don't automatically assume the worst."

"I know. I'm—"

Allie cut her off with a slashing movement of her hand. "Don't say you're sorry again. Apology accepted, for what it's worth. Is that why you came down here? To get my forgiveness?"

"Partly. But partly to see if you think…if you've wondered…if we can…" When she looked up again, her eyes had a distant, troubled look. "If we can make something of what we had."

Allie blew out a breath. A relationship wasn't a cake recipe. And even if she agreed, what would it mean? They had physical distance between them, as well as conflicting long-term goals for relationships—if they even got that far. "I'm not sure what you want. What exactly are you asking for?"

"How can I answer that?" Tarryn spread her hands. "You. Me. We're so different. I'm not offering you a relationship. How can I…now. But I'm asking if you'd like to try."

"With me in Sydney and you in Quandong?"

"I have flexibility. I'm here now, on a Monday. I'm not sure if you've found a job yet—"

"Not in a week," Allie murmured.

"We could meet halfway. Use those Airbnb vouchers we were given. See what we can be."

Allie swallowed. It sounded…tempting. Difficult, yes, but maybe a way forward. But she had to be sure. "And the next time something comes up, something that makes you doubt my truthfulness? What then? I don't want to go through this again. I haven't openly labelled my sexuality—I don't see the need—but if you have a problem dating a bisexual or pansexual woman, then it's best we end this now."

"No! It's not that. My reaction was because you weren't truthful with me, not because you've dated men. Please believe me."

"But what if you think I'm lying to you again? If you jump to conclusions, don't listen—everything you did before—then this is over before we start." Was she the stupid one here, slashing a line across what they might have before anything really began? But she couldn't—she wouldn't—be with someone who didn't trust her on an elemental level. That would eat away at her, the doubt, the insecurity, the worry. Better not to start something than to live through that.

"I trust you, Allie." Tarryn heaved a deep breath. "I'm putting my heart in your hands. If you want it. I've never unreservedly given it before, but I'm handing it to you."

The tendrils of hope unfurled into a sunflower, golden and glowing in her chest. She shuffled forward on the couch and reached a hand to Tarryn. "Are you sure?"

Tarryn stood, and the intensity in her dark eyes made Allie shiver. "I'm sure."

Allie stood, too, and placed a palm on Tarryn's cheek. "Then I'm willing to try. To see how we go."

Tarryn's eyes fluttered closed, then opened again to pin Allie with her gaze. "I'm going to give this my all. Something about you got me in here"— she thumped her chest with a closed fist—"grabbed on and won't let go. Maybe it was the intensity of the fake wedding. But you were in my head before then."

"Even when you were infuriating, you were fascinating." Allie took another step closer. "But right now, I don't want to talk."

Tarryn's breath feathered over her face. A gentle smile, and then they were kissing, and Allie let her kisses speak the words for her.

When they broke apart, Tarryn asked, "What happens now?"

"When you arrived, I was just about to order takeaway. I'd narrowed it down to sushi or Korean. Are you hungry?" At Tarryn's nod, she said, "You choose."

"Sushi." Tarryn came in to kiss her again. Her lips moved softly, then with an assured demand over Allie's. "Then, if we get distracted, we can put it in the fridge."

"Good idea." Allie's lips tingled. Ordering sushi was the last thing she wanted to do right now. She wrapped her arms around Tarryn's waist, pulling her close so their breasts pressed together. Trails of flame licked along Allie's front, from her nipples down, coalescing between her thighs. Her heart swelled with emotion. Tarryn, who avoided entanglements, was seeking that very thing. She kissed her again, her tongue flicking over Tarryn's lips until she opened her mouth and their kiss grew deeper. Her mind spun in joyful circles and she put her heart and soul into the kiss.

"No more lies," she said when the kiss ended. "No more half-truths."

"No," Tarryn agreed. "No more assumptions. Just us and where we can go from here."

"Will you stay tonight?" Allie's heart thundered as she waited for the answer. "This apartment isn't nearly as nice as Kirra's, but my bed is good. And if I ever order, we'll have food."

"I'd love to." Tarryn kissed her again, as if now that they'd reconciled, she couldn't get enough of her.

Allie picked up her phone and ordered. "Delivery in forty minutes."

Tarryn pushed Allie's hair back from her face with both hands and leaned in to kiss her again. "What shall we do in those forty minutes?"

"We talk?" Allie set her phone down. The email notification caught her eye, and she grinned. "I just need to check this. I'm expecting a job offer."

She opened the email, and the Kirkland sender jumped out at her. Sure enough, Ramona had sent through a job offer—and a reference. Allie opened the reference and scanned it. It was on letterhead, and it was…glowing. It mentioned her sound knowledge, integrity, work ethic, and attention to detail and mentioned nothing about her being forced to resign. She sighed in satisfaction, then opened the other attachment. The job offer was even better than Ramona had said. Wait until Leila heard this!

"Did you get the offer?" Tarryn sat beside her.

"Yes, but it's not all it seems." Swiftly, she explained the situation with Kirkland. "So there's no way I want this job. I'm done with the toxic workplace. But the reference means I can now, hopefully, secure another accounting job."

"That's great." Tarryn kissed her cheek, and their hands tangled together again before Allie drew her closer for another, proper, kiss.

"It is. I thought I'd have to try for a career change, but when it comes down to it, I don't want to. Strange as it is to most people, I like being an accountant."

"So you won't be running the wedding festival next year?"

"If Quandong asks, then it will hopefully be Sophie doing it for real. The doctors have given her a guarded successful prognosis long-term."

"Maybe Sophie will hire you as her assistant next year."

"I think that's your role. You aced it this year. But I'd like to help out. Maybe I'll volunteer at the festival. What about you? Will your anti-marriage stance mean you'll stay away?"

Tarryn licked her lips. "No. I'll be there. In fact, the festival, the fake marriage…but mainly you…you've softened me. I see it now. I'm still not sure it's for me, but now I understand why many people want that commitment. Our fake ceremony…I didn't expect the emotion."

"Me neither. In a way, I think it played its part in getting us to this point."

"It did. Totally." Her smile spread slowly over her face like the sunrise. "Now, there's still maybe thirty-five minutes until the food arrives."

"Are you starving?"

"No. Wondering what we can do in that time."

A shudder coursed through Allie's body. "Oh, I have a few ideas." She stood and held out her hand. "I don't believe I've given you a tour of my apartment, have I?"

"No, you haven't. Well, I've seen the living area and the kitchen. What else is there?"

She grasped Tarryn's hand. "This is the bathroom. You look, as if we both go in, we're likely to get stuck. It's not spacious."

"Okay. Bathroom. Great cleaning on the shower screen. It sparkles."

"I do my best." Allie tugged her back to the living area. "Here's the linen cupboard. Towels, sheets, and so on."

"Very neat. I like you've got them colour coordinated."

"That took some work." Allie opened the final door. "This is the bedroom."

Tarryn walked in. "This deserves a closer look." She pressed the mattress. "Good and firm. Nice sheets. The view is lacking." She gestured to the blank wall. "Barely any natural light. Have you had your vitamin D levels checked?"

"No, but I should. My lease is up next month, and I plan on moving to somewhere with at least a proper window." She tugged Tarryn closer again and kissed her, lips moving on hers. A change of angle and then a deeper kiss. "I think you should take a closer inspection of the bed." Her fingers worked the buttons of Tarryn's shirt.

"I should." Tarryn shrugged the shirt from her shoulders and swiftly undressed. Naked, she stood there regarding Allie with an amused smile. "You should do the same. We don't want to keep the delivery driver waiting."

"I'm sure they've seen it all." Allie started undressing, tugging at her clothes, hopping on one foot as she tugged off shoes and jeans in one go. When she, too, was naked, she stopped.

Tarryn stood in front of her. She was glorious, her olive skin touchable like silk. Her breasts with their chestnut nipples stood erect, and the dark curls between her legs drew Allie's look. It had only been a week since they'd done this, but she was as joyful, as anticipatory as if it were the first time all over again. Lust drizzled like melted chocolate down her spine, and her fingertips tingled with the need to touch Tarryn, to circle her breasts, to stroke down between her thighs and relearn the wetness between.

Tarryn's eyes were dark with lust, and she leaned in to kiss Allie, her palms stroking down her arms to cover her breasts.

Allie closed her eyes and let herself be carried away by Tarryn's touch, the fingertips stroking pathways of fire along her body. When Tarryn settled between her parted thighs and licked, Allie's mind spun away into fractured circles until she came in a white light of orgasm. And then she stroked Tarryn, fucking her with her fingers until she, too, came with a shout.

The buzz of the intercom startled Allie out her post-coital haze. "The food!"

She leaped out the bed and buzzed the driver up, then grabbed her robe from the back of the door and her wallet from the counter. She was just about decent when she took the food delivery, ignoring the driver's amused smile at her dishevelled state.

"I wonder where we'll be in a few months' time?" Tarryn asked as they sat at the counter. She wore a T-shirt and undies and nothing else. "Will we be here? In Quandong?"

Her confidence warmed Allie down to her toes. She wiggled them on the rungs of the stool. "Maybe both."

"I hope so." Tarryn took her hand. "I hope we have a future together, Allie. I never would have thought I'd ever say that. But I can see it with you."

She ducked her head as tears of happiness gathered in her eyes, then raised it again so Tarryn could see her wearing her tears proudly on her face. "Me too, Tarryn. Me too."

Epilogue

Two Years Later

WHO'D HAVE THOUGHT SHE'D EVER do a reprise of this? Allie stood in the wings of the main stage at the Gay Bells Festival. She wore the same dress she'd worn two years ago, but this time, it was bought, not rented. Her red Vans were new.

Sophie stood next to her, looking as nervous as she'd ever seen her—including at her own wedding to Bree nearly a year ago.

"Are you sure you've got everything?" Allie asked.

Sophie made a show of patting down her jacket pockets. "Ring, check. Copy of your vows in case you forget them, check. Nerves enough for both of us, check."

She tried to laugh, but it was a tremulous imitation. "Can I have a hug?"

Sophie embraced her, arms closing around her sister's shoulders. "You've got this, Allie. After all, you've already had a rehearsal for the real thing two years ago."

She nodded against her sister's shoulder. They had. But this time, the wedding at the climax of Quandong's festival was a real one.

A huge crowd milled in front of the stage. DJ Strokes was behind the curtain, waiting to launch into the afterparty—one Allie and Tarryn and their friends wouldn't be attending. Instead, they were going to a private family-and-friends reception in the grounds of a local hotel.

And the most important thing of all, on the other side of the stage, was that Tarryn was waiting, wearing the same suit as she'd worn for the fake wedding. Will stood there as her attendant.

Allie closed her eyes as the jitters swelled and she leaned harder into Sophie's hug.

"Okay?" she asked, rubbing her back.

"Yeah. Just need a moment."

It had been a long road to this point. But the highlights shone like beacons over the past two years. She had secured a new job as an accountant in Sydney, in the same firm as Leila. But nine months later, once she could leave Sophie, she'd thrown it in, and made the move to Quandong. There, she'd opened her own one-person accountancy firm, filling a much-needed local gap. Now she had an assistant plus two bookkeepers, and she'd just hired Leila to work remotely from Sydney on a freelance basis.

Allie smiled into Sophie's shoulder. The move had been difficult at first. She'd missed her friends, and Sophie in particular. But the Quandong community already counted her as one of their own, and so it proved easy in the end. They lived in Tarryn's shouse, but over the last year, it had gradually been modified for more space and comfort. They'd added a dog to their family, and Freckles was settling in well, although his arrival had been a bit fraught for Ally and Elly. But the alpacas had adapted and were now so social that Tarryn was doing good business running guided rainforest walks with them. Her metalwork was doing better too—and the emu she'd been making when she and Allie first met now resided in Silver Creek Park, thanks to Allie and Phyll pestering the Council.

The best thing was Sophie was making a good recovery. She still wasn't one hundred per cent, and probably would never be, but she was mostly pain-free and had regained her mobility. Her business was thriving, and the Gay Bells Festival was one of her most valued clients. Bree was still by her side. She was in the roped-off area at the front of the stage, along with their families, Kirra, Garrett, Phyll, and their other friends.

George, the wedding celebrant, strode onto the stage, wearing the same dark suit and bow tie as the last time. The music quietened.

Jason joined George on stage. "Welcome, everyone, to the real wedding of Tarryn and Allison. Conducting the ceremony is George Patterson from Your Wedding, Your Way, for anyone who wants their wedding done exactly how they want it. Over to you, George."

George spoke for a minute about the nature of marriage and the ceremony to come, then extended her hands to each side of the stage. "Tarryn and Allison."

Allie swallowed hard. This was it. When she and Tarryn had cemented their relationship, she'd mentally wiped the idea of ever marrying the woman of her dreams. Because there was no way she'd pressure Tarryn into something she was so adamantly opposed to. But the last years had shown her how people could change, and Tarryn's proposal had cemented that.

They'd been in Silver Creek Park, admiring the placement of Tarryn's emu. "I seem to have more permanency in my life," Tarryn had said. "This emu in the park. A place in this town. You in my life. Will you marry me, Allie?"

Allie had turned to her, sure Tarryn hadn't been serious, but the love and sincerity shining out of her eyes had convinced her it was real. That what she wanted with all her heart would happen.

And now it was happening. She was about to marry the love of her life in a ceremony that combined both of their wishes. Her person. She blinked away happy tears.

Sophie released her and squeezed her hand. "We're on. This is it. You have ten seconds to change your mind."

She huffed a laugh. "No way in hell."

And then she walked slowly onto the stage, Sophie by her side. She didn't see the crowd. She didn't see her loved ones in front of the stage. She barely noticed George, beaming a welcome. She had eyes only for Tarryn, in the silver-grey pants and pink-tinged waistcoat, a bouquet of native flowers in her hands, Will by her side. There was only the love in Tarryn's eyes that she knew was reflected in her own.

She reached George and placed her hand in the woman's outstretched one at the same time as Tarryn did. George gave a reassuring squeeze.

"Friends, we are gathered here today to witness the marriage of Tarryn and Allison." George drew them closer and placed Allie's hand in Tarryn's.

Allie could hardly breathe over the pounding of her heart. This was it. Soon they would be married. She couldn't look away from Tarryn's beautiful face, and as they recited their vows, Tarryn's face shimmered through a veil of tears.

Finally, it came to the moment she was both dreading and anticipating. They hadn't rehearsed this part, but Tarryn's steadiness and certainty about the wedding reassured her.

"Now, say after me," George said. "Do you, Allison, take this woman, Tarryn, to be your lawful wedded wife?"

"I do," Allie said, and her smile stretched across her face as joy thundered in her heart.

The crowd cheered, just as they had the previous time.

George switched her gaze to Tarryn. This was it. The single moment when it would all become real.

Tarryn clutched Allie's hand, her steady gaze on Allie's face.

Any moment now, Tarryn would be her wife. She had no doubt about that. The pounding of her heart became a joyful, anticipatory rhythm.

"And do you, Tarryn, take this woman, Allison, to be your lawful wedded wife?"

Tarryn's gaze on her face didn't waver, nor did her grip on Allie's hand. It was reassuring, but most of all it was steady and loving.

Tarryn raised her chin, and without taking her eyes from her beloved, she said clearly, "I do."

Other Books from Ylva Publishing

www.ylva-publishing.com

The Number 94 Project
Cheyenne Blue

ISBN: 978-3-96324-567-1
Length: 288 pages (100,000 words)

Renovation takes a sexy turn in this light-hearted lesbian romance.

When Jorgie's uncle leaves her an old house in Melbourne, it's a dream come true. Sure, No. 94 is falling apart, and she has to deal with her uncle's eccentric friends. But she'll do it up, sell it, and move on.

What she hasn't counted on is falling for Marta, who's as embedded in Gaylord St as the concrete Jorgie's ripping up.

The Business of Love
Charley Clarke

ISBN: 978-3-96324-752-1
Length: 308 pages (97,000 words)

Driven Mack wants to take over her family company to secure her sister's future. Except the company's CEO must be married and a relationship's the last thing on her mind.

A year of playing Mack's wife will get barista Taylor out of debt. Good thing Mack's too pretentious and arrogant for Taylor to ever fall for her. Right?

Chemistry
Rachael Sommers

ISBN: 978-3-96324-679-1
Length: 276 pages (92,000 words)

Disillusioned Eva never imagined she'd wind up as a high school teacher in her hometown or, worse, suffer the boundless enthusiasm of new colleague, Lily. Their clashing arguments lead to sparks and then the impossible…attraction. But how can two such different people ever work?

An opposites-attract, ice queen lesbian romance about finding the softest of hearts behind the highest walls.

Looking for Trouble
Jess Lea

ISBN: 978-3-96324-522-0
Length: 312 pages (109,000 words)

Nancy hates her housemates from hell, useless job, and always dating women who aren't that into her. She'd love to be a political writer and meet Ms. Right.

Instead, she meets George, a butch, cranky bus driver who's dodging a vengeful ex.

When the warring pair gets caught up in a crazy Melbourne election, they must trust each other and act fast to stay alive.

A quirky lesbian romantic mystery.

About Cheyenne

Cheyenne Blue has been hanging around the lesbian erotica world since 1999 writing short lesbian erotica which has appeared in over 90 anthologies. Her stories got longer and longer and more and more romantic, so she went with the flow and switched to writing romance novels. As well as her romance novels available from Ylva Publishing, she's the editor of *Forbidden Fruit: stories of unwise lesbian desire*, a 2015 finalist for both the Lambda Literary Award and Golden Crown Literary Award, and of *First: Sensual Lesbian Stories of New Beginnings*.

Cheyenne loves writing big-hearted romance often set in rural Australia because that's where she lives. She has a small house on a hill with a big deck and bigger view—perfect for morning coffee, evening wine, and anytime writing.

CONNECT WITH CHEYENNE

Website: www.cheyenneblue.com
Facebook: www.facebook.com/CheyenneBlueAuthor
Instagram: www.instagram.com/cheyenneblueauthor
Twitter: twitter.com/iamcheyenneblue

I Do
© 2023 by Cheyenne Blue

ISBN: 978-3-96324-829-0

Available in e-book and paperback formats.

Published by Ylva Publishing, legal entity of Ylva Verlag, e.Kfr.

Ylva Verlag, e.Kfr.
Owner: Astrid Ohletz
Am Kirschgarten 2
65830 Kriftel
Germany

www.ylva-publishing.com

First edition: 2023

Edited by Genni Gunn and Michelle Aguilar
Cover Design and Print Layout by Streetlight Graphics

Printed in Great Britain
by Amazon

26846655R00128